The Orphan Beach

Flight to Freedom Series
The Glass Bottom Boat-1
The Lighthouse Baby-2
The Orphan Beach-3
The Christmas Cabin-4
Snow Globe Secrets-5

The Orphan Beach

By

Laura Thomas

Dedication:

For Lyndon: To beach walks and palm trees—past, present, and future, always with you…

Acknowledgments

This third book in the "Flight to Freedom" series was originally written whilst editing and publishing *The Glass Bottom Boat* and *The Lighthouse Baby*—three books in a year! I could not have achieved this on my own, and have many phenomenal individuals to thank…

My wonderful publisher, Mountain Brook Ink—my sincere thanks for stepping in and republishing this book to complete the "Flight to Freedom" series! You will never know how grateful I am for this huge undertaking and for putting all the broken pieces back together again… even brighter and better!

My phenomenal editor, Candee Fick—this was the third book originally published within a year! In the frenzy, you kept me focused and able to craft the very best version of this story for our readers. Thanks for being a sweet friend and the most detail-oriented person I know.

My children: Charlotte, Jameson, and Jacob—as I watch you all spread your wings and follow your passions, you inspire me to do the same. I am incredibly proud of you.

My husband, Lyndon—you have been so gracious and patient as we navigated a whirlwind year of writing. Thank you for giving me room to soar and for loving me well. I love you right back.

My Heavenly Father—for giving me life and light and words.

Chapter One

JULIET FARR DROPPED A SINGLE WHITE rose onto the coffin, her entire body numb. Frozen. Not merely because she stood windswept on a rugged bluff overlooking the turbulent Pacific Ocean. She inhaled a ragged breath.

How had life deteriorated beyond recognition in less than a year? Wrenching her eyes from the harsh reality before her, she gazed out over the gray-green expanse of water through a blur of tears. She shivered. Dead inside.

Juliet stepped back and stumbled. A strong hand cupped her elbow from behind. Max. She'd recognize his aftershave anywhere, all musk and forest. His protective touch was another reminder of what she had lost. She pulled away.

Not now.

The bitter late-November wind whipped in from the ocean causing hair to obscure her vision as it flew in her face like a red tornado. She buried her chin in her mother's scarf. It still smelled of lavender.

"Juliet, would you like my coat?"

Her body tensed at the warmth of his whisper in her ear. That deep, rich voice which she had missed more than she cared to admit over the past six months. *Six months.* What was he doing back here? Today of all days. She straightened her shoulders and jutted her chin without turning around.

"No, I'm fine. Totally fine."

Liar.

No way was she fine. Everything would be different now. Colorless.

Time slowed as she clung onto each second of this dreadful day, not wanting the farewell to finish. Gentle murmurs hung on the frigid air. She glanced around. Only a handful of family friends hovered at the graveside now. How long had they even been standing here? Most had paid their respects and left already. Some had even disappeared straight after the church service. How could she leave her mother?

Bella sniffled beside her.

"What now?" Juliet held out her right hand and Bella clutched it in silence. As friends, they had been through more than most. Could Bella sense Juliet's heart fragmenting at this moment? Would she send Max on his way?

Do I even want her to?

Max squeezed Juliet's arm with a feather-light touch and a fire ignited in her belly. Part desire, part distress. She spun around and watched as he paced toward the parking lot, head bent against the elements. Or perhaps bent in shame. His hair was a little shorter than she remembered. It looked good. She closed her eyes for a moment.

"Want me to invite him back to The Lighthouse with us?" Bella's voice was gentle.

"No. I can't deal with him." Juliet turned back around and peered down at the lowered coffin. "Not today. It's hard to breathe, let alone think clearly. Today is about Mom."

"That's understandable. One day at a time."

"I seem to remember giving you the same advice not so long ago." Juliet lifted her eyes to the deepening gray clouds, pregnant with rain. "It was one of Mom's favorite sayings. She always had the best advice, didn't she?"

"The best." Bella's voice cracked. "I can't believe Pippa's gone."

"It feels like my entire life just crumbled. Like I've been abandoned." Juliet sucked in a sob. "Like God doesn't even care."

"Oh, Jules, He cares. More than we can ever imagine. You're hurting—of course, you're hurting. Pippa was your mother, but you know you have me, don't you? You're the sister I never had. There are lots of us who think of you as family, who love you. We're all here for you."

Juliet looked over her shoulder, her long hair swirling around her head. "What about Max?"

He stood next to his car—presumably a rental from the police station—arms folded across his chest and feet planted hip-width apart. His gaze roamed the cliff side area but he was particularly fixated on the graveside gathering. On her. Warmth radiated from her cheeks.

"What's he even doing here all of a sudden and why is he watching me like that?"

"Perhaps he came to pay his respects. I'm sure he's concerned about you."

Juliet shook her head. "After all this time? No. Something's wrong. I know it." A shiver ran down her spine as she angled her body to face him. "I've seen that serious detective look before. It's the one he gets when circumstances are out of his control and trouble's brewing."

She wiped her damp cheeks with chilly fingers and scanned the area. A few hikers made their way toward the trails and her mom's remaining friends headed to the parking lot. The graveyard was almost empty now. All appeared peaceful.

"Maybe he's working on a case."

"Here in Florence?"

Bella grunted. "Stranger things have happened."

"True."

Bella had experienced more than her fair share of drama in their sleepy seaside town.

"I simply don't have the mental capacity to deal with anything else. Especially Max. I'm running on fumes as it is." Juliet squinted. "But now I'm curious."

Bella put an arm around Juliet's shoulders. "Try not to worry. It may be nothing."

"It's something." His body language was on full alert. Juliet sensed her own muscles tense in response.

"Your teeth are chattering—let's get you warm. Adam went ahead to get the jeep started up, and the others will be waiting at The Lighthouse. Do you think you're ready to go?"

Juliet nodded. Only the two of them were left on the clifftop. Surrounded by cold gravestones and the harsh sound of waves crashing behind them, the bleakness of her future hit her with force. She would go back to The Lighthouse for awhile, allow friends to offer comfort, but then she would have to go home alone.

To a new chapter navigating grief and loss and loneliness.

Bella shivered beside her.

"I'm sorry to make you stay this long. You must be freezing, too."

Bella smiled. "I'll stay as long as you need me. I know you don't want to leave." She tucked her chin deeper into her black, woolen scarf.

"But I have to, don't I?"

"At some point, yes, but you can always come back and remember."

Juliet pressed a hand to her heart. She could do this. She would always have her memories...

A familiar ringtone drifted on the wind from the direction of the parking lot, breaking Juliet's moment of peace. Max's phone. She watched as he answered and ran a hand through his hair. He pinched the bridge of his nose as he listened to whoever was on the line. Not a good sign.

He pocketed his phone and strode over to where Adam was parked. They exchanged words and then Max turned on his heel and marched toward her with purpose.

"What on earth?" She felt each heart beat pound in her chest as she watched him. His face was etched with pain and something else... fear? Time slowed again as her feet anchored in place. She couldn't have moved if she wanted to.

"Juliet." Max's raised voice held an edge. "Juliet, we have to leave. Now."

He was warning her about something. What? Why now?

"You were right. Something's wrong." Bella gripped her hand tighter.

Adam left his jeep running and jogged toward the graveside behind Max.

Juliet released Bella's hand and swivelled around. She peered back down at the solitary rose on the coffin.

She wasn't ready.

No.

A moment later, Max lay a hand on her shoulder from behind. "Juliet, I'm sorry, but we need to leave now." His voice was gentle but firm.

"We?" She studied the coffin in the ground.

"I know this is hard and I was hoping not to intrude on your time here today."

"What?" She shrugged his hand away and faced him. "What are you talking about? Why do we need to go? I don't want to leave yet..." She scanned the clifftop. "Is someone here?"

"Please trust me."

Juliet balked. Why should she trust him now?

"I realize you have no reason to trust me as a person, but as a detective, I'm trying to protect you. Let's go. Please." His eyes begged. Was he asking for more than her cooperation? Was he asking for her forgiveness?

Adam grabbed Bella's hand. "We should all leave."

"I'm coming, too." Max surveyed the area. "I promise I'll explain everything when we get to The Lighthouse, if that's okay with you, Juliet?"

She rubbed her eyes. "It seems I don't have much choice, but I'm riding with Bella and Adam." The thought of being alone with him in a vehicle was too much.

Max sighed. "Sure. I'll follow in my car. Now, let's get out of here."

Juliet managed to put one foot in front of the other and kept pace with Max as they followed Bella and Adam.

She turned back once.

Goodbye, Mom.

Chapter Two

A HALF HOUR LATER, JULIET'S MIND was still spinning. Why had Max made an appearance today? What was with the urgent departure from the graveside?

She rubbed her temples as they pulled up outside Bella and Adam's dream house. It had been a subdued drive along the winding coastal road. None of them knew what Max's issue was, and now she had a gathering of grieving friends to navigate.

She craned her neck to see where Max had parked. He was at the end of the driveway but was already walking toward The Lighthouse.

"Adam, would you go and tell Max he has to wait, please?"

He turned off the jeep's ignition and caught her eye in the rear-view mirror. "Sure, if that's what you want."

Juliet pushed her hair behind her ears. "It is."

"You don't want to know why he evacuated the grave site?""Obviously, I want to find out what's going on and why we had to hurry home after his ominous phone call." She blinked sore eyes. "But let's not forget Max wanted nothing to do with me for the past six months. He's been more than willing to give me space up until now—I think he can continue to give me space on the day of my mother's funeral."

"She's right." Bella shrugged. "There are friends waiting inside, and I'm sure Max won't mind as long as he thinks we're safe."

"Okay. I'll go tell him." Adam opened the jeep door and hurried down the sloping driveway.

"Come on, Jules. Let's do this." Bella jumped out of the vehicle and pulled her passenger seat forward so Juliet could get out.

"Thanks." Every limb ached. As the only surviving family member, the funeral details had fallen on her shoulders over the past week. It had been excruciating, and now she battled major fatigue after countless sleepless nights. Juliet grabbed her purse, pulled herself from the back seat and allowed Bella to usher her through the front door of The Lighthouse.

This is going to be awful. It had to be better than the alternative: talking to Max.

Why should she have to be social today? Juliet disliked being the center of attention at the best of times. Hopefully, everyone would say their piece and head on home.

I'm a terrible human being.

She hung her wool peacoat on the iron coat stand by the door, slipped out of her knee-high boots, and made a beeline for the roaring fireplace. Chilled to the bone, she set her purse next to an armchair and thawed out as she stood in front of the flames, grateful for warmth seeping back into her body. Mixed aromas of coffee, cinnamon, and something Thai wafted through the room. When had she last eaten? Her stomach rumbled in response.

Angie, her friend and fellow pediatric nurse, waved from the kitchen island, where she was busy refilling trays of appetizers. She must have come straight here after church to help set up refreshments. A good friend. Especially while Juliet had been absent from work as the cancer had ravaged her sweet mother's body. Six weeks. Where had the time gone?

General hubbub permeated the space as guests wandered around the living area—many had never been inside The Lighthouse before and were mesmerized with the details Adam had included to surprise his bride. The intricate lighthouse features were stunning and the ocean view through the wall of windows at the back of the room still took Juliet's breath away. Although how could people care about things like decor and views when they had just buried someone as precious as her mom?

I want to go home. Home would never feel the same again without her mom's vivacious presence. Besides which, she still had to confront Max and discover what the big mystery was regarding that graveside phone call he received.

Juliet's eyes burned and she took several deep breaths to calm her fury and frustration. *Swallow it down. One thing at a time. Be present.*

For the next twenty minutes, she went through the motions of a grieving daughter as friends from church and Florence General Hospital offered their condolences. Bella brought her a plate of goodies and a mug of peppermint tea—not that she tasted any of it. More conversations, more small talk, more tea.

They mean well. Be grateful. Nod and smile. Don't think about Max.

"You look like you're ready to blow a gasket, pet." Angie placed a hand on her shoulder. Her thick Scottish accent always made Juliet smile. "Why don't you sit down?"

"Oh, I'm good standing. I thought I was plastering on my best 'I'm fine' face. Guess I can't fool you, can I?"

Angie adjusted her glasses on her nose. "So, what's going on? Of course, you're devastated but it seems you're also ready to strangle someone."

Juliet exhaled and tried to relax her features. "I'm frustrated. How can life go on like normal after someone you love dies? I mean, will I ever care about pithy things again?" She watched as people gathered in clusters, chatting and nibbling on puff pastries. "Will I ever be able to make bland small talk? Why do people think I care about Bella's pristine white kitchen or Adam's hexagonal walls? How am I even going to drag my sorry self out of bed to face another day tomorrow?" She ran her fingers through windswept waves of hair in an attempt to smooth out the tangles. If only her emotions could be as easily controlled. "I don't even know who I am anymore. I know I'm not myself."

"You're our Juliet, and we wouldn't trade you for the world. You're always the one who is strong when the rest of us are struggling. You insist it's because of your faith, but you're a feisty lass. May even have a wee bit of redheaded Scottish blood in you." She tugged on Juliet's tresses.

"Who knows? You may not have noticed but I'm sorely lacking in family of any description now." She swallowed the lump in her throat. "Honestly, I'm not feeling strong and I'm not feeling God in this at all." *Why God? Why didn't You heal her this time? I don't understand... and now Max is back on the scene? The timing couldn't be worse.*

"And...?" Juliet sighed. "Then there's Max."

Angie's eyes lit up. "I knew it. I spotted him sneaking into the back of the church." She nodded to a couple of other nurses as they passed by and lowered her voice. "Did he stick around?"

"You could say that." Juliet stepped over to the bay window and peered through the long white sheers. Sure enough, Max stood sentry at the edge of the driveway. *He must be freezing.* She turned back and faced Angie. "I think he's here on a case or something. He whisked us all away from the graveside after he got a phone call. Said we had to leave immediately."

"What?"

"It's weird. He wants to talk with me later and explain but I can't think straight. Especially today." She bit her lip. "Mom would know what to do." *Mom always knew what to do. I've been waiting for six months to have a conversation with this man and still can't find the words.* "What am I supposed to say to him?"

"Love, you don't need to answer to anyone so give yourself a break. You've just lost your ma." She opened her arms, and as if on autopilot, Juliet fell into them.

Angie was the mother-figure to all the nurses and took her role seriously.

I'll be needing her more than ever now that Mom is gone...

Juliet's vision blurred. "I'm sorry. I didn't think I had any more tears to spill."

"It's perfectly natural. Don't try to be brave today. You let yourself have a good old cry." Angie led her to the brown leather armchair where Juliet sank down and buried her face in her hands.

God, why did You have to take Mom? I know these friends are here for me and I'm grateful, but I have no family left now. No one.

How was she so alone in a huge room brimming with people? People who cared for her. She blocked them all out and allowed the minutes to tick by, vaguely aware of Angie rubbing her back.

"Hey." Bella pulled back Juliet's curtain of hair with a tender touch and found her eyes. "Everyone's starting to leave. You have a stack of casseroles on my counter to last you a month. We'll give you a hand taking them back to The Book Nook's apartment whenever you like. Want me to say your goodbyes? They'll totally understand."

Juliet grabbed the armrest and pulled herself upright. She nodded, accepting the fresh tissue from Bella's hand. "Please. I think I've spoken to them all. I'm spent and I don't think I could handle any more kind words."

"Leave it with me." Bella turned to Angie. "Thanks so much for organizing the food and holding the fort for us here. Feel free to stay as long as you like."

"I need to be going, too, lass." She squatted down in front of Juliet. "Why don't you come pay us all a visit next week? The girls on the ward would love to see you and I know there are a couple of patients who miss you something terrible."

Juliet wiped her eyes and managed a wobbly smile. "I will. I promise. It's been weeks and I need to decide when to come back to work. If I come back at all." *Can I even handle being surrounded by sickness and the possibility of death after caring for Mom and watching her slip away from me? Nursing was everything before. It defined me, but now...* She shrugged. "I don't know what to do with my life anymore."

Angie gave her a gentle hug. "Take your time. Get plenty of rest. Call me for anything."

"Thanks, I will." She curled up in the chair like a comfortable cat as Angie retrieved her purse from the kitchen and followed the last of the crowd to the door.

Adam brought a steaming mug of hot chocolate over to her. "Hey, how are you holding up?"

"I'm hanging in there. This looks really good. Thanks." She took the mug and cradled it in both hands.

"Bella asked me to make it for you. Of course, I added marshmallows and whipped cream. Can I get you anything to eat? There's a ton of food in the kitchen. I could grab you some—"

"So, what's up with Max?"

Adam's mouth clamped shut and he stuffed his hands in his pockets.

"It's okay. I'm not going to break. I'm grieving and my life feels like a disaster at the moment, but now that the others are leaving, I have to know why Max is back in Florence. Why he needed us to leave the graveyard in such a hurry."

Bella closed the front door behind the last guest and joined them. "Are you sure you're up to speaking with him now? I could see if he can come back later if you need a nap."

Juliet blew on the contents of her chunky blue mug and allowed the heat to penetrate her fingers. "We haven't spoken in forever and it shook me seeing him today. Last I heard from my nursing friends in Seattle, he's dating someone from radiology. Why take a case here when his life is in Seattle now?"

Dare I hope he came back for me?

Adam shook his head. "I guess there's only one way to get your answers. He didn't seem too concerned earlier about waiting until your guests left but he insisted on standing guard outside." He ran a hand through his dark hair. "I'm sorry this has added to the stress of your day, and I'm sorry he made you leave the graveside before you were ready."

Juliet sighed. "I suppose we should get to the bottom of this case of his. It was ridiculous to think he might have come simply to pay his respects to my mom."

Or to be there for me.

Bella knelt next to the armchair. "He loved Pippa. I'm sure he would have come regardless."

"If so, he could have come *before* Mom died. She stood up for Max until the very end and believed we were meant to be. Instead, she passed on thinking I was heartbroken and worrying I'd be a spinster for the rest of my life and never find love." Juliet chewed a thumbnail. "He had us both fooled."

A buzz sounded from Adam's pocket. He pulled out his phone and studied the screen. "He's asking if you're ready to see him."

Ready? Not even close. Juliet's head pounded. "Sure. Let's see what he has to say."

"Do you want us to give you guys some privacy?" Bella's blue eyes scanned the open space and stopped at the kitchen area. "We could make tea?"

"No. I don't know. Yes. Tea, but be close by? I may lose my cool completely. I have so many questions..." Tears pricked her eyes as she recalled the heartache inflicted by his silence over the past six months. This confrontation had been a long time coming.

Adam hurried over to the front door and pulled it open. "Max. Come on in."

Max shed his coat and hung it on the coat rack. Yes, he looked great. Shorter hair suited him and accentuated the light stubble on his square jaw. When he turned his blue eyes her way, she almost melted.

Almost. Until she remembered the pain he had caused. She flicked her long hair behind her shoulder.

"Max." Her tone was cool. He would know she was faking it, but she had to at least attempt to remain aloof.

"I'll make tea." Bella flitted into the adjoining kitchen, far enough away not to intrude but close enough to bail her friend out in a pinch.

"I'll help." Adam followed.

This was awkward. Why had she agreed to be left alone with him? Slow breaths…

Max strode over and took a seat on the leather sofa, his elbows rested on his knees and hands clasped as if in prayer. "How are you doing?"

She smoothed the fabric of her fitted black dress with one hand and held his gaze. "I'm sad. My mom died."

He flinched. "I'm so, so sorry. I truly am. Pippa was a special woman. She was brave and loving." He glanced up into Juliet's eyes.

"Oh, *please.*" Juliet set her mug on the coffee table and rose to her feet. "You can't waltz in here after half a year when I've heard crickets from you and suddenly tell me how brave and loving my mom was, for goodness sake." She threw her hands in the air. "I am well aware of how amazing she is." It was her turn to flinch. "Was."

He stood and touched her trembling arm.

"I'm sorry, you're right, and I probably shouldn't have come today."

"Then why did you? Why now?" She shook free of his fingers and planted her hands on her hips.

He ran a hand through his short hair and shook his

head. "Can we sit for a minute?" He gestured to her armchair. "Please?"

Juliet flopped down and pulled a striped cushion to her chest. "It's been a long day. Start talking."

He puffed out a breath of air. "Firstly, I came here because I care about you—"

"Did you care about me three months ago? Three weeks ago?"

Max bowed his head. "Yes." His voice dropped. "I never stopped caring..."

Really? A glimmer of hope rose in her chest. *Wait, no. I won't allow myself to be hurt by you again.*

Juliet bit the inside of her cheek. "So, how come I haven't heard a word from you all this time? I don't get it."

"It's complicated. I don't expect you to understand."

"Then help me to understand."

His mouth set in a hard line. "I needed to come back now. There's something you have to know."

"What I need to know is why you left me." Her voice cracked.

"Juliet, there's this case I'm on and—"

"No." She lifted both palms. "I'm sure your case is super important but first, since you're finally here in front of me, I need answers. You *left* me." Tears filled her eyes. How was she supposed to get past the way he hurt her? "You up and left me when I believed we had a future together. No warning. No explanation. You packed up your life and headed back to Seattle. Why? Tell me why and then I'll hear you out."

A muscle twitched in his cheek.

His answering silence was a dagger to her heart.

"Then you don't get to *care* about me." She balled

her fists as she stood. "And you don't get to bother me with some case. You don't get that privilege."

"Please." Max reached out and touched her arm. "I know you're mad but you have to listen. There's a killer somewhere out there and he's targeting—"

She jerked her arm away. "I don't care. I can't take anymore today." Air, she needed air. She raced to the back door before she said something else she might regret.

The door slammed and her eyes adjusted to the dimming light outside. She inhaled the ocean breeze, tasted its tanginess, and allowed the chill to pass through her.

"God, what are You doing?" She bellowed into the silvery mist. "Why are You breaking my heart?"

Chapter Three

M AX RUBBED HIS HANDS DOWN HIS face. So far, their conversation was not going well. Not that he had expected otherwise. He stood and looked over at Bella and Adam in the kitchen. They had frozen in place but he needed to get outside and keep watch over Juliet. *She has no idea of the danger she could be in.*

He cleared his throat. "I'll go get her. It's not safe."

Bella's mouth dropped open. "Seriously?"

Adam put an arm around his wife's shoulders. "It's that bad? What's going on, Max?"

"I'll explain when I get Juliet to come back inside. Which may take some doing." Through the windows, he caught sight of her silhouette pacing the deck and his heart flipped. *My feisty girl.*

Bella plucked a fur throw from the back of the sofa and handed it to him. "In case you're out there for a while."

"Thanks."

He took long strides to the back door and opened it wide. Now Juliet sat on the top step leading down to the beach, her chin resting on her hands. As she gazed out across the darkening ocean, light from inside the kitchen caught coppery tones in her hair. The wind caressed the long strands—it was illuminated, wild, fiery. Much like their passionate kisses back when life was simple and the future full of promise.

He reminded himself to breathe. "Juliet?"

She turned, green eyes vacant. Had his silence dulled their sparkle?

Max shut the door behind him and stepped toward her. She turned back to the view and he followed her gaze. It was a magnificent vista.

The Lighthouse was situated on a small bluff with a skinny strip of empty beach below amidst a smattering of other homes along the shoreline. Yes, he had a decent vantage point from here. They would be safe. For now.

A gust of wind caused him to shiver. He glanced down at her in that fabulous black dress. "You must be freezing." He leaned over and draped the throw around her shoulders.

She said nothing. At least she didn't shrug it off.

"May I sit?"

He took her silence as indifference and lowered himself next to her. She snuggled deeper into the warmth of the fur throw and it was all he could do not to take her into his arms and shelter her from the pain caused by all the loss in her life.

"I'm sorry. Sorry about everything. I don't know what else to say." His words trailed off on the breeze. He didn't want to hurt her heart any more than he already had—and he didn't want to have to share the truth. Not now.

"I trusted you, Max." Her voice was gentle, her temper cooled by the frigid ocean air. "Like I said, I thought we had a future together. Then you were gone. No closure, no real reason. You left me guessing what I had done wrong while I gradually watched my mother fade into a shell of the strong woman I knew and loved."

He ducked his head. He hadn't been there for her through the most agonizing time of her life. What kind of a monster was he?

"Did you think she would be a good distraction for me?"

Ouch. "No. Of course not. I never intended to hurt you. It's hard to believe but it's the truth." He chanced a sideways peek for her reaction. "You were too good for me."

She sprang to her feet like a jack-in-the-box. "What on earth is that supposed to even mean?"

He pulled her back down next to him and looked out over the ocean. It was easier than looking into her sorrowful eyes. "It means you deserve better. When we started talking seriously about the future, I knew I had to give you up."

"But why?" He heard the pain in her voice. "I don't understand, and then the silence—what was that all about? You must have known my crushed pride wouldn't allow me to track you down and beg for answers."

How could he explain without revealing the real reason for leaving her? "I guess I thought a clean break would be easier for us both. I hoped you would heal and move on."

She grunted. "Like you did with Radiology Girl?"

"What?" Was that a spark of jealousy? Didn't she know there would never be anyone else? He turned toward her. "There's no girl of any description. Trust me, there has been no one since I left here. I buried myself in work and haven't had time nor inclination to date anyone, no matter what rumors you've heard."

Juliet spun around to face him. "You know what hurts the most?"

He bit the inside of his cheek. This was going to be bad but she had every right to unload on him. "No."

"The fact that my mom loved you so much."

Tears sprang in his eyes, and he blinked several times. He hadn't deserved the love of Pippa. Especially after he broke her daughter's heart.

"She was convinced we would end up together until her dying day. Literally. She told me over and over that you were the one and I should contact you except I was too stubborn. Her dying wish was for you and me to get back together again." A hollow laugh escaped her lips. "How's that for laying on the guilt trip?"

He had no words. His chest tightened and he shook his head.

"Sucks, doesn't it?"

"Yes. Yes, it does." In keeping his secret and doing what he thought would be best for everyone, he had not only devastated Juliet but he had also disappointed Pippa.

They shifted to face the crashing waves head on. Guilt and shame washed over Max as they sat side-by-side in silence, both grieving.

Eventually, Juliet took his hand. A delicate touch. Her skin was chilled as their fingers intertwined as naturally as they had before. Sparks shot up his arm and into the pit of his stomach. How did she still have this effect on him after all these months? And why did it feel so right?

He glimpsed her profile. Her cute turned-up nose and high cheek bones.

I've missed you more than you can imagine.

He squeezed her hand. "Aren't you still furious with me?"

Juliet blew out a steady stream of air, lifting strands of red hair from around her face. "Yes. You know I am, but I am now acutely aware life is short." She paused. "I'm drained. I have nothing left in reserve to fight with anymore, so I'm done with arguing and even trying to understand you. At least you came to Mom's funeral and I should be grateful for that. I know she was smiling down on us, probably with a glint in her eye."

Max gave a lopsided grin at the thought of Pippa looking on. "So, you forgive me?"

She bit her lip. "No. Not yet. The wound is still too raw and I can't get my mind around your nonexistent reasoning."

He winced. How could he expect her to forgive him when he wouldn't give her the answers she craved?

"I'll shelve it for now and revisit it when I've got some more headspace—and had some decent sleep."

He nodded. "I understand. Thank you." A weight lifted from his shoulders. He might not be forgiven yet, but at least she was communicating with him. Even holding his hand. He glanced down at their clasped fingers and smiled. This was progress. He knew all too well that the wrath of Juliet was something to behold, and he hated being the cause of her fury. Perhaps one day he would tell her the truth as to why he had to break her heart. *God, I don't know what I'm doing but I feel like I'm out of my depth. I ask You to protect both our hearts from any further pain.*

"We should get inside. It's freezing out here." Juliet released his hand and stood.

The sudden emptiness shocked him. Focus. *Remember why you're here.* He surveyed the beach.

"Coming?"

"Yes. I want to talk with all of you about the case. Give me a minute?"

"Sure." She pulled the throw around her shoulders and headed to the door.

Max stood and watched her retreat into the warmth of The Lighthouse. This was a ridiculous idea, coming back when his heart still belonged to Juliet. He thrust his hands in his pockets and leaned against the post.

Lord, You know why I had to come and why I need to stay for a while at least. Help me to do my job and protect Juliet from harm. Guide my steps and give me the right words...

Max straightened his shoulders and headed inside, closing the door behind him with haste to keep the cold air from infiltrating the cozy living room. He hadn't been to The Lighthouse until this evening, and as expected, it was all Adam had proposed it would be. He bit the inside of his cheek. Would Bella and Adam's marriage always remind him of the future he and Juliet had dreamed of having?

Adam's architect design and Bella's artistic touches combined to create something both enchanting and easy. In the unique style and shape of a lighthouse, it felt like a safe haven. Perhaps Juliet would agree to stay here for a while...

Bella stood behind the island in the open plan kitchen and held up a mug. "Tea? Juliet's just freshening up."

"Please."

She passed him a full mug.

"Come take a seat." Adam stood next to the fireplace.

Max walked across the room to the sofa and made himself comfortable. "Thanks. Your home is gorgeous, by the way." He looked from Adam to Bella. "You must be thrilled with the way it turned out."

Bella joined them and slipped an arm around Adam's waist. "Thank you. We love it. This husband of mine is a genius."

Adam grinned. "I built the house but you made it a home."

"Good grief." Juliet plodded past them with a fresh, steaming mug of tea. "You guys are way too sweet. I have to admit, you're a brilliant team." She reclaimed the armchair and set down her mug.

Adam chuckled and sank down on the other end of the sofa with Bella on the sheepskin rug at his feet.

"Here, Bella, come sit next to your husband." Max went to rise.

"No, please sit back down. This is my favorite spot right here. On the rug by the fire."

"It is. Go figure." Adam shrugged.

Max nodded and settled back on the sofa. He took a deep breath. He had to start this conversation.

"I know you're all wondering about what happened earlier at the graveyard. It's important and it's connected to the case I'm working on."

Adam pivoted on the sofa to face him. "What's it all about?"

Max scanned their faces. This could have been their usual Friday night gathering if he hadn't deserted them all earlier that year. His heart sank.

"Okay, first let me say I truly wanted to come to pay my respects today. I get that it's weird after my being gone for so long, but I think Juliet knows now that I'm sincere with my sympathy and my heart aches for her loss." He glanced over at her. She was studying the hardwood floors. "For all of you. I know how close you were to Pippa."

The pain was still raw on their faces.

"So, I would have come today regardless, but as I mentioned, I am also here on assignment."

Bella tilted her head to one side. "It must be something major for them to allow a detective to come all the way to Florence from Seattle for work."

"Yeah, it's a troubling case. My old boss at the station here in Florence forwarded the report to me as he thought I would want to be in the know. He was right. I requested a temporary transfer as soon as I read it."

Max sipped his tea as he considered his words and looked back at Juliet. He didn't want to pile more stress on her day, yet she needed to know how serious this was. "I'm guessing you've been off work for a while. How much contact have you had with your coworkers recently?"

"Other than a few of the nurses attending the funeral today, I haven't seen anyone. I've been totally out of the loop since I took leave to care for mom at home." She sucked in a breath. "Six weeks or so. Why?"

"That's what I thought." Max rubbed his chin as he considered how much information he should share. "I'm not sure what the hospital staff knows yet but it's going to be public knowledge in the next day or so. I wanted to speak with you first."

"What's going to be public knowledge? Something's going on at the hospital?" Juliet sat up straight.

"There's a security issue. It's specific and we are taking precautions in light of past events."

Juliet glared at him. "Would you stop sounding like the detective you are and tell us what's going on in plain English?"

Max pushed the sleeves of his sweater up his arms. How could he say this without causing too much alarm or getting into trouble at work? "The thing is, there have been several incidents with nurses being stalked and then attacked in the past year along the west coast. Now things have escalated."

Adam scowled. "Escalated to what exactly? How bad are we talking here?" He shot Bella a look. They were all too familiar with stalkers.

"It's bad. He physically attacked five women over the course of the past year that we know about—he started slowly with months between each incident. Now they've become more frequent."

"Do you mean sexual assaults?" Adam's forehead furrowed.

"Not as far as we know. He's violent. He beat one victim so severely she was hospitalized for several days… and then I'm afraid to say his latest victim didn't make it. That was a week ago."

"What?" Juliet gasped. "The nurse actually died?"

"Murder." Bella's face paled. "There's a murderer out there who is attacking nurses? That is what you're saying?"

Summed it up. "Yes." *But that's not all…*

Juliet cleared her throat. "Where exactly is this happening?"

"The perpetrator seems to be making his way up the coast. He started in California."

Bella glanced at Juliet. "How close was the last victim?"

Max swallowed hard and took a deep breath. "That's what the call was about today at the graveside. There was another victim reported this morning about fifty miles south of here, so as we suspected, he's getting closer. I needed you to be somewhere safe, Juliet. Definitely not out in the open."

She flared her nostrils. "If there's a serial attacker on the loose, why haven't we heard anything on the news about this?"

"Honestly, the Feds only just linked all these attacks together. They thought it was a bunch of isolated cases because one of the nurses had a boyfriend who was in with the wrong crowd and she believed he had a hit out on her. Another had an abusive ex, that kind of thing. Turns out this assailant was doing his homework and preyed on victims who were already in compromised relationships, so he's managed to lie low."

"But they now know it's the same guy?"

"Yes, they are certain. He has a very specific type he's targeting." He tried not to stare at Juliet's hair as she wound it around her fingers.

"Nurses?" Adam whistled. "There must be thousands on the coast."

"True, but there's a reason why I knew I had to transfer back and be active on this case." His eyes darted toward Juliet.

Here we go.

"He's targeting nurses with red hair."

Her mouth fell open. "Are you kidding me?" She stopped fiddling with her long strands and tucked them behind her ears. "Redheads? Do you know why?"

Max shook his head. "When we figure *that* out, we stand a greater chance of catching him. There's a federal team on the case and I'm spearheading the local investigation here in Florence."

Juliet squirmed in her chair. "Are you here because you think I'm on his hit list?"

"No, not necessarily." Calm. He had to keep everyone calm. "I wasn't sure if you were even planning on going back to work yet, but I couldn't sit up in Seattle knowing there was even a slight possibility of you being in danger."

"Why?" She lifted her chin. "Suddenly you're worried about me?"

He sighed. *I deserve that.* "Yes, okay. I'm worried about you. I want to be close by to make sure this maniac doesn't cause any more trouble. We all want to see him behind bars."

"What do you have on him?" Adam blinked. "Do you have a description or anything to go on?"

How much could he reveal? "Not much at the moment. He's been flying under the radar since we had no idea the incidents were related. Obviously, the homicide drew a lot more attention, which is when the pieces came together. With the victims having other side issues originally presumed to be the cause of the assaults, we are unofficially calling him Red Herring. Red for short."

"Which also encapsulates the hair issue to perfection." Juliet rubbed her eyes.

She was already exhausted, and now he had added even more to her heavy load.

I'm sorry.

Adam's gaze flitted across their wall of windows. "So, we don't know who he is and we don't have a description or anything?"

Max grimaced. This sounded more hopeless by the minute. "No, we are running on minimal details. He fits in, doesn't stand out for being weird, and is comfortable around hospitals. He comes at his victims from behind, so none of them have been able to give us much of a description other than regular height and build. He doesn't speak but two of them saw his black ski mask."

Adam grunted. "That narrows it down then."

"Exactly." Max shoulders sagged. If only he had something encouraging to offer.

Juliet stared into the flames of the fire. Had he given her too much to handle on this day of all days? But her gorgeous red hair was the first thing anyone noticed about her—it reached down to her waist in waves.

"How do you know it wasn't a coincidence?" Bella shifted across the rug and leaned against Juliet's chair. "You say he targets nurses with red hair—could it be chance?"

He pressed his lips together. "No, I'm afraid not. The first nurses didn't realize this until we went back to investigate further." He lowered his voice. "This stays within these walls: the perpetrator cuts a lock of hair from his victims."

Juliet's head snapped up. "Wait. How can they not have noticed?"

"I know it sounds crazy. He threatened them all with a knife from behind. They believed it was attempted robbery at the time—but he was actually cutting strands of their red hair. He didn't steal anything at all."

The flicker of flames from the fireplace filled the silence while the others absorbed the news.

"I think we've heard enough for tonight." Bella reached up and grabbed Juliet's hand. "But what do you want us to do now, Max?"

"I'm sorry to freak you all out but I wanted— needed—you to be extra vigilant."

Juliet groaned. "How? We don't know who the maniac is or what he wants. Or why he killed someone. I can't handle those details today, but I will want to know. You realize that, don't you?" Her gaze was piercing.

"Sure." She was stubborn. She would press him for details as soon as she was ready. "This is information overload. I wish I could have left it until tomorrow, but when I heard he'd struck again and that he's getting closer—I had to tell you."

"What about my friends at the hospital? I'm not the only redhead there."

"I know. By tomorrow morning, the department heads will be updated. Additional security is already being put into motion. I'd rather be safe than sorry."

Juliet nodded. "Good."

"Are you planning on going home tonight?" He visualized the entrance of her building. It was a tight knit neighborhood but she would be alone in the apartment she used to share with Bella.

"Actually, I'm not in the old apartment anymore, in case you weren't aware. I moved back in with Mom above The Book Nook and, yes, I was planning on going back there tonight. It's been a marathon of a day." She looked toward the front door. "The sooner I collapse into my own bed, the better."

Max held his tongue and took a final swig of now cold tea. If he suggested she stay here with Bella and Adam, she would refuse, for sure.

"Why don't you stay here tonight?" Adam scooted to the edge of the sofa. "You know the guest room is yours whenever you need it and I think we'll all sleep better knowing you're here."

Bella nodded. "Please stay. I was hoping you would anyway. You can borrow anything you need from me. You must be ready to drop and I *want* to take care of you. Please?"

God bless Adam and Bella.

Juliet exhaled. "But what about Ebony? Mom's kitty will need feeding—" Her voice caught. "I've been gone all day as it is."

"Let me swing by and feed her." Max stood and placed his empty mug on the coffee table. "I know where everything is if you give me a key."

"We can use my book store key to let ourselves in tomorrow," Bella added.

"Fine, but this is for one night, you guys." Juliet bent over her purse on the floor, delved in, and retrieved her keys. "Give Ebony my love, and tell her I'll be home tomorrow. Make sure you leave a light on for her."

Max smiled at the thought of showering the cat-princess with love. "I promise. Get some rest and please call me if you have any concerns at all?"

"Sure… and Max?" She dropped the keys into the palm of his hand.

"Yes?"

"I can take care of myself. I've gotten used to it."

Chapter Four

KNOCKING. CONSTANT, MUFFLED KNOCKING. JULIET CRACKED one eye open. Was that daylight? She must have fallen into a deep sleep at some point after tossing and turning for much of the night. She rolled onto her back and gazed at the unfamiliar ceiling. Bella's guestroom. Yes, she had collapsed into bed, exhausted after an emotional day saying a final goodbye to her mom.

"Juliet?" Bella's voice. "Are you awake?"

"I am now." Juliet sat up in the middle of the queen-sized bed and regretted the sudden movement. "Ugh. My head." A plethora of tears and the stress of yesterday had taken its toll.

Bella opened the guest bedroom door and walked in carrying a breakfast tray. "Got a headache?"

"That's an understatement." Although the smell of strong coffee was a delight. She glanced at her phone on the bedside table. "Whoa, how can it be after ten already?"

"I'm glad you got some sleep—yesterday was draining. I'm proud of the way you got through it." She set the tray on the bed. Pancakes and strawberries with whipped cream on the side, and a huge mug of coffee.

"Thanks. It feels like a dream now. Or maybe a nightmare." She picked up the mug and took a long swig. "Thanks for all this—I'm starving."

"You didn't eat much yesterday. Want me to get you some painkillers real quick?" Bella stepped back to the doorway.

"Please. Then I should get on home after I've eaten."

"What's the rush? I'm keeping The Book Nook closed for the weekend out of respect for Pippa. Everyone understands and I already put up a sign on the door. If you want a ride, I may get Adam to drive me over there around noon and check on a large book order that came in this week. He can run some errands while I work for a while."

"Sounds good." Juliet smirked. "You must be desperate to get your driver's licence."

"You have no idea. I didn't mind cycling around town before we moved to this place, but now I'm having to rely on Adam to chauffeur me around everywhere." She shrugged. "Anyway, come into town with us later—but you know you can come back and stay here as long as you like. I'm sure Max would keep checking on Ebony."

"Oh, Max." Juliet set the mug back down as she pictured his handsome face, his eyes filled with concern for her safety. Was it just concern? Or did she detect something more? "I still don't know what to think about it all."

"You mean the crazy guy or Max being in town?" Bella leaned against the door jam.

"Both, I guess." Juliet shuddered. "It creeps me out thinking there's someone on the loose who could potentially be on the prowl after me or one of my coworkers."

"I wonder if they all know about it yet. Max said he'd keep us posted."

Juliet speared a strawberry with her fork. "Max isn't great with communication, so don't hold your breath." Tears welled but she forbade them to flow. "If he thinks I'm going to hide out here, he's dead wrong."

Bella scurried back and sank down on the end of the bed. "He's worried about you. I'm worried, too. I know you don't scare easily, but why not stay here a few days? It might all get cleared up by then."

Juliet's shoulders sagged. *I'm so done with the waiting around...* "You're my best friend and I love you to bits, but I'm not putting my life on hold for Max or for this lunatic, or for anything. It's been on hold long enough." Her stomach lurched at the way that sounded. Yet tending to a broken heart for half a year and then having the walls close in while she cared for her mom over the past weeks—it was all too much. She was drowning. "I didn't mean to sound harsh. I would have stopped everything for years if it meant I'd have Mom around longer. It's just I'm feeling claustrophobic and I need to orient myself again. I have some big decisions to make regarding my future..."

"What kind of decisions?"

Skull pulsating, Juliet leaned back against the padded headboard. "So many. Do I stay here in Florence, or is this an opportunity to start fresh somewhere else? I know I have the apartment above The Book Nook now but I could rent it out. I love nursing but I could get a job in pediatrics anywhere. Or find a brand-new career... and now there's Max."

"It's an awful lot to be chewing on today. Promise me you won't make any rash decisions?"

"Hotheaded and prone to act before I think?" Juliet raised an eyebrow. "Yeah, I promise."

"Thanks. You need to give yourself time to grieve for Pippa. Please don't rush the process—you have some healing to do. I'm praying that you'll know God's presence in a very real way."

Juliet set her jaw. God had abandoned her when she needed Him most. When she needed her prayers for her mom to be answered—but Bella was right, she needed time to grieve.

She reached out and squeezed Bella's hand. "I promise I'll take my time with any decisions and fill you in. Right now, a painkiller or two would be heaven."

At least I can rely on a pill to ease my pain…

* * *

A couple of hours later, Juliet unlocked the door to The Book Nook building and turned on a light. This had been her quirky, fun home since she was five years old and now it felt like a mere shell. Something had shifted. The essence of Pippa Farr—businesswoman, bookworm, ray of light, mother—had been snuffed out. She took a labored breath and stepped further inside.

"Juliet?"

She turned back to Bella.

"You want me to come up to the apartment with you? Adam's not coming back for a couple of hours so I have plenty of time to do my work."

"No, that's fine. You do what you need to down here and maybe join me for some tea before you leave. Ebony will be glad to see you."

"I *am* her favorite." Bella winked.

"Don't I know it." Juliet placed a foot on the first stair and then turned back. "Hey, Bella?"

"Uh-huh?"

"I'm glad that you bought this bookstore from Mom."

Bella reached out and caressed one of the wooden bookshelves. "Me, too. It'll continue to be a dream haven for readers, for sure. I learned so much from my time working with Pippa. It's an honor to carry on her legacy here." Her face broke into a smile. "Plus, you know you can always come on in and remember her fondly."

If I can handle the pain of her not being here anymore. "I know. Thanks. She knew it wasn't something I wanted for myself—but I'm happy it worked out for you. Until you're a best-selling author yourself one day."

Bella chuckled. "We'll see, but I think I'll always want this bookstore. Even if we decide to give it a separate entrance to the apartment someday. For now, I can pretty much check on you any time I like..."

Juliet balked. "I think not, but you *can* come up later for tea." She trudged up the stairs and unlocked the apartment door. "Ebony?"

The black fluff ball leapt with grace from the windowsill and sashayed over to Juliet.

"Did you miss me, girl?" She dropped her purse in the hallway and picked up the cat. There had to be eight vases of flowers in here from the past few days and the air in the entrance was thick with the fresh fragrance of lily of the valley. Sweet sentiments from friends and neighbors who would miss her mom terribly. Just like she would.

"Do you miss Mom, Ebony? I bet you do."

Tears spilled from her eyes and in no time, Ebony was getting damp with them. She squirmed and Juliet let her down to the floor and followed the cat to the kitchen to refill her food and water.

Just like Max had done last night.

She sighed and stood. They had some fun memories here with her mom. All of them: Max, Bella,

Adam, and her. The celebrations, deep conversations, meals shared, decisions made.

Before Max left. Before Mom got sick.

Juliet inhaled. Would this apartment always smell of lavender? Her mom's scent of choice overpowered the floral arrangements in the hallway and permeated the furnishings and even the walls. Yes, it was part of the fabric of this place. Perhaps it always would be. She glanced at her mom's open bedroom door. *No, I can't go back in there yet.*

She went to drop the empty cat food tin in the recycling and saw a crumpled macaroni and cheese packet in the bottom of the bin. *Mom's favorite.* A sob caught her by surprise and she leaned against the counter, undone. Would these random waves of emotion keep coming? She wiped her eyes on her sleeve and realized she was still wearing the clothes from yesterday. From the funeral. *This is not helping... I need to change.*

Juliet headed into her bedroom. The room she had grown up in. She shed her long black dress and dumped it in the laundry basket. Now it would always be her funeral dress. She searched her closet for something warm to wear. A black sweater and black jeans fit the bill. Fit her mood. She put them on along with some fuzzy black socks and stuffed a tissue in her pocket.

What next? A Saturday afternoon in November usually called for a walk on the beach or a shopping trip into one of the bigger towns. It had been a long time since Juliet had done either since caring for her mom had become her all-consuming activity. She wandered into the kitchen and washed a few breakfast dishes from yesterday. From when she was getting ready for the funeral. Her eyes blurred. *Stay busy.* She dried the dishes and put them away in cupboards.

Another look at her mom's bedroom door. *I can do this. I have to go in there and see.*

But first the flower vases needed to be refilled with fresh water. She took her time with each one until she could procrastinate no longer.

Shoulders back, she padded over to fully open the bedroom door. The scent of lavender was heavier in here. Mom had joked she didn't want the odor of sickness to choke the life out of her, so lavender it was.

Juliet surveyed the area. She would need to make some decisions about what to do with all the stuff. Starting with the large hospital bed—it was jarring to look at and caused her chest to tighten. They had attempted to beautify it with pretty sheets but the memory of administering pain medication and fluffing pillows in an attempt to keep her mom comfortable were all too vivid.

Her eyes travelled to the wooden side table stacked with books, her mom's obsession. Reading glasses on a gold chain. A framed photo of Juliet aged six, grinning toothless with hair fiery and wild, as usual. A cozy leather armchair sat in the corner by the large square window. The perfect reading nook. The place where Juliet had spent many sleepless nights keeping vigil over her mom's last weeks. She closed her eyes and let out the breath she had been holding.

There was the walk-in closet, which would take forever to sort through—the scarf collection alone would be a major mission. A veritable rainbow peeked through the open closet door and slammed into her heart. Yes, her mom was all color. Juliet observed her own black attire and fought back a sob. Would she be able to exude color ever again now that her mom was gone?

She walked over to the armchair and fell into it, hugged her knees to her chest, and wept silent tears. How often had she snuck into this room and curled up to read when her mom was working at the store downstairs? It made her feel close to her mom then and somehow, it did the same now.

Yes, she would keep this black leather chair, for sure. The hospital bed would obviously go as soon as possible. She would buy a new queen-sized bed and move into this room as soon as it was cleared. Her old room was small and way too pink, but how could she even think of going through her mother's possessions? It felt like an invasion of privacy. Maybe next week. Or next year.

The apartment door creaked open. "Jules, it's me. Can I come in?"

Grateful for the interruption, Juliet wiped her eyes with a tissue from her jeans pocket. She had become a person who always carried tissues in her pocket. "Yes, I'm in Mom's room."

Bella appeared in the doorway, her face flushed. "I'm sorry to disturb you."

"No, I'm fine. Getting used to it, that's all. Come on in, you look stressed." Juliet beckoned. "The lavender will calm you."

Bella sniffed the air. "Oh yes, it's potent in here still, isn't it? Oh well, at least it's pleasant."

"What have you got there?" Juliet nodded toward the envelope clutched in Bella's fingers.

She pursed her lips. "I don't know if you want this now or not."

"What is it?" Juliet held out her hand and Bella passed it over.

"It's from your mom. I found it in a file she made.

The bookstore business is still new to me so she left diary notes to help me keep track of everything that needed to be done."

A shiver slithered through Juliet's body as she held the envelope. Swirling, black letters written with a fountain pen on smooth, cream paper. Her heart skipped a beat as she traced her name with her finger. "She had such gorgeous handwriting. She wrote me several notes. Letters. She wanted me to read them while she was still here so we could talk about them. All Mom's words of wisdom and advice for my future."

Juliet bit her lip. She would always treasure her mom's encouragement. The messages written with a shakier hand, made weak with sickness yet strong in passion. This one must have been written a while ago. Curious… "Where exactly was it?"

Bella blew a wisp of blonde hair from her forehead. "It was attached to the November diary notes with a paperclip. She must have wanted you to have it after she passed away."

Juliet tilted her head. "I wonder why."

"Should I leave you alone for a while?"

"No." Juliet shifted to one side of the chair. "Come squash in here with me and let's see what Mom wanted to say. We're family, remember?"

"I like that. Sure, but I'll sit on the arm otherwise we'll never get out."

Bella settled herself and Juliet slit open the envelope.

She took a deep breath as she slid the paper out and unfolded it. "Here we go."

"To my dearest daughter, Juliet,"

A sob rose from her chest and she clamped her lips shut. This was too hard.

"Want me to read it aloud?" Bella took the note from Juliet's quivering fingers.

"Maybe."

Bella found her place on the page.

"I can hardly bear the thought of being apart from you, but if you are reading this letter, my time must have come to leave this old world. I have so much still to share with you but will keep it brief.

I'm writing this at the beginning of September, my favorite month. My very last September. I know I haven't much time left—you are taking such good care of me but even your nursing skills can't compete with the random ravages of cancer."

Juliet sniffled. September. *Two months ago. She knew she didn't have long even then.*

"Juliet, I have a story. A manuscript, actually. One I would like you to read when you are ready, and then be rid of it and move on with your life.

I called it The Orphan Beach and it's my life story, my 'before-Juliet' life story. I realize I have always been somewhat vague with details of my past, mainly due to the pain it causes me to this day. Speaking it aloud was too heavy for me to deliver. Too heavy for your young shoulders to bear.

But you need to know everything and even though this is cowardly of me, I wrote it all down many years ago with the intent to leave it with my will. I hope you'll forgive me?

Our lawyer, Edward Johnson, is in possession of the manuscript. He knows I left you this letter and has instructions to give you the manuscript when you meet with him to discuss the estate. Everything goes to you, of course, so there's nothing sinister or surprising there. I would ask that you read my story—only when you are ready—when you feel strong enough to hear the truth about what happened in my life. If you need to wait, that's perfectly fine. It's going to be a tough read but I know you will get through it. God will walk this journey with you."

Bella paused and looked up. "You doing okay?"

Juliet nodded. She couldn't manage words just yet.

Bella squeezed her hand. "She's right. God will walk you through all of this."

Juliet closed her eyes. *No. I can't believe that right now.*

Bella returned to the letter.

"And if I may, could I ask one last favor of you, sweetheart? It's a big ask. Would you burn the manuscript and scatter the ashes under a palm tree on a beach in Mexico? I will leave the exact location up to you, but you will understand its significance upon reading The Orphan Beach.

I hope you will find a way back to the happiness you experienced with Max. (Sorry, but a mother knows these things!) You were more full of life and love when you were with him than I have ever seen. I haven't given up on that young man yet and I don't think you should either. I have been praying, and I have the strongest feeling about the two of you."

Bella peered over the page with wide eyes and Juliet's mouth fell open. Her mom was still determined that Max was the one.

"I love you to the moon and back—and always will,
Mom."

Bella refolded the letter. "Wow."

Juliet closed her gaping mouth and sank deeper into the chair.

Breathe. Again. There you go.

"Are you alright?" Bella handed the letter over and knelt down in front of Juliet. "Did you know Pippa wrote a manuscript?"

"The manuscript?" Good. Avoid the subject of Max. "No. Didn't have a clue. Maybe it was from way back—who knows?" She rubbed her arms. "I wonder why it's going to be a 'tough read'?"

"I guess you'll find out. Don't forget, she advised you to wait until you are ready. No need to rush it." Bella gazed around the bedroom. "You're already dealing with a lot."

"Have you ever known me to be patient with anything?" Juliet glanced at the folded letter with its words about Max and the manuscript. "I don't know whether to be elated that I get to read her story, maybe even learn something about my father at last, or be mad I can't grill her about it all."

"I know what you mean. Remember when I had all those letters from my biological mother? It's an emotional roller coaster."

Of course, this felt familiar after Bella's own bizarre experience. "Did you feel angry?"

Bella squinted. "No. Sort of. I did feel kind of cheated that I would never get to probe any deeper for answers to a lot of my questions, but eventually I prayed about it and gave it all over to God. It was out of my hands and best left in His."

Heat rose up Juliet's neck. "I can't give this over to God. He's already taken enough."

Bella squeezed her hand. "You're hurting. Give yourself grace—and please don't get mad for me saying this, but time *is* a healer. Things will never be the same, but they will get better. I promise."

Exhaustion washed over Juliet like a tidal wave. "Thanks for being here with me. You're a good friend and I know you mean well, but I think I need to take a nap before I say something else snippy about God. I also need to think about what I might discover in this manuscript. Mom warned me it was heavy. I can't imagine it's going to be a happy story if she wouldn't tell me while she was alive."

Bella stood and pulled Juliet up with her. "When you're ready to go and see the lawyer about everything, I'll come with you, okay?"

A smile tugged at Juliet's mouth. "Thanks. I may need you for moral support."

"No problem." Bella's phone chirped and she pulled it from her jeans' pocket. "It's a text from Max."

Juliet's heart sped up. Why did his name still have that effect on her? "He's texting you? That's strange."

"Right?" She swiped to the message.

"What does he want?"

"Oh no." Bella's face paled.

"Tell me. Please?"

"There's been another attempted attack on a nurse by Red, the creepy guy. Happened at noon."

Juliet's mouth went dry. Was it close by? In a neighboring hospital? Would she know the victim? "How bad?"

Bella's eyes flitted over the screen as she scanned the message, her brows knit together. "It sounds like it's not too bad. Although Max is freaking out telling us to stay exactly where we are and lock the doors—and that's not like him to overreact."

Definitely not like him. Max was always cool under pressure. Her stomach churned. This was not good.

"Where was the attack exactly? Does he say?"

Bella gulped and then stared into Juliet's eyes.

"Red is in Florence. At your hospital."

Chapter Five

JULIET CRANKED HER CAR INTO PARK mode, yanked the keys, and bolted from the visitors' parking lot to the hospital entrance.

"Wait for me." Bella jogged to keep up as they hurried through the bustling foyer. Juliet unwound her green scarf and swept her long hair behind her shoulders while she navigated her way past a wall of wheel chairs and an array of visitors and patients.

"Sorry, but I have to check and see who the victim was. I have to know." Her stomach was in knots.

"Max is going to go berserk when he reads my text and sees I brought you here."

Juliet grabbed Bella's arm to keep her moving and marched to the elevator. "*I* brought *you*—and he isn't in any position to tell me what I can and cannot do anymore, is he?"

Bella huffed. "He's concerned about you. So am I."

Once inside the elevator, Juliet pressed the button for her pediatric floor.

"How do you know it was a pediatric nurse?" Bella dug her phone from her purse.

"I don't, but I know Angie will be privy to all the details. She's always in the loop." She glanced at Bella's phone. "Anything more from Max? Not that I care, of course."

"He's on his way here." She grimaced.

Juliet suppressed a smile and squared her shoulders. "Is he now?" *Just let him try to tell me what I can and cannot do.*

The elevator pinged and the double doors drew back. So familiar. Funny how much she missed routine, everyday occurrences after being away for almost two months. Juliet surveyed the area with fresh eyes. Walls were painted bright greens and blues in a long countryside mural complete with trees and clouds and birds. As pleasant as a hospital wall could be.

Bella fell into step alongside Juliet as they rushed down the corridor past a couple of waiting rooms. "I'm not a fan of hospitals, but I have to say the pediatric decor sure takes the edge off."

"They did a good job making it a little less sterile for the kids." They all tried to make this floor as personable and friendly as possible for the young patients. One of the reasons she loved her job so much.

"Shame they can't do anything about the hospital smell." Bella wrinkled her nose.

"I don't even notice it anymore." Juliet squinted as they approached the glass doors up ahead. "I see Angie over at the desk. Come on, I'll let us onto the ward with my pass."

They entered through a secure set of doors and Juliet led the way to the nurses' station. A low buzz of chatter permeated the ward and she waved at a couple of her colleagues en route. All was peaceful.

"Juliet? What on earth are you doing here, lass? I told you to swing by soon but I didn't mean the next day." Angie bustled around the circular desk and smothered Juliet in a tight hug.

Juliet fought back tears.

Mom, I miss your hugs. She pulled back and offered a wobbly smile.

"Hi, Angie." Bella received an equally warm embrace. "Good to see you again."

"You, too. Why don't we step into my office for a sec to have some privacy? Don't want to disturb some of our sleeping beauties here." Angie's gaze flitted down the length of Juliet's hair before she led the way.

She knows. Juliet followed them into a small room in the corner of the ward with large windows on two sides.

"I didn't realize how much I'd missed this place." Juliet sighed. "But you know why I'm here today, don't you?"

"Come, sit."

Bella and Juliet took the two chairs on one side of the desk while Angie claimed the seat opposite.

Angie shook her head. "I'm guessing you've heard about the nasty business with the attempted assault here today?"

"Who was it?" Juliet held her breath.

"The wee lass on the surgical ward. Caroline. You know her?"

Juliet leaned closer. "It was Caroline? Yes. Do you know what happened? Is she okay?" Her stomach sank. Caroline was a tiny thing. Sweet and unassuming. With hair as red as rubies.

"She is."

Juliet exhaled. "Tell me everything."

"Well, your Max—I mean Detective Bennett—he came in first thing this morning to meet with the powers that be downstairs. Then as soon as I arrived for my shift, I was called in and told about this individual who had assaulted red-headed nurses, starting down in

California and making his way up the coast. Argh. I can't believe we didn't know about this before today."

"This is the first you've heard about it then? I wondered if word had leaked out beforehand."

Angie pushed her glasses up the bridge of her nose. "Not as far as I'm aware. They were trying not to cause any panic this morning but, honestly, when we got word there had been an attempted attack on Caroline at noon—well, you can imagine how it caused some serious unrest in this place."

"Do you know any details?" Juliet chewed on her thumbnail.

"Someone was waiting in the parking lot up on the top floor. I hate parking up there. It's creepy at the best of times."

Juliet gulped. That was where she always parked.

"Anyway, someone followed Caroline to her car and tried to grab her from behind."

Bella gasped. "Did he hurt her?"

Angie folded her arms. "He tried. She has a couple of nasty bruises to prove it, but she already had her car door open and somehow managed to slip in and slam the door. The guy ran off immediately and she laid on the horn until security appeared."

What if he had been two steps nearer? "Wow. That's scary."

"Tell me about it." Angie patted her ample hips. "It's given me incentive to get to the gym more often. I swear she only made it safely inside her car because she's so tiny. I wouldn't have a hope."

"I think you're safe." Juliet eyed Angie's gray curls.

"True. Although I used to carry a hint of auburn." She ran a hand over her short hair.

"Is Caroline here now? I don't know her well but I'd like to check on her."

"No. They called her husband, and I'm sure she's tucked up in bed at home recovering from shock by now. Who'd have thought this guy would try his luck here at our hospital?"

Bella cleared her throat. "I hate to ask, but how do we know for sure this is the same guy Max warned the staff about?"

"Lass, do you want to hazard a guess as to the color of Caroline's hair?"

"Oh. I had to ask." Bella nodded. "So, it definitely was Red in action then."

"It seems that way." Juliet's phone chirped. Max. She still had his number listed on her phone. "Uh-oh. I'm in trouble. Guess who's on his way up?" Her cheeks heated and there was nothing she could do about it.

"Max?" Bella checked her phone. "He's telling me to make sure you don't leave."

Angie chuckled.

Juliet snapped her head up. "What?" Had she noticed the blush?

"I'm saying nothing." The smirk said everything.

"Probably best, my friend." Juliet stood. "Come on, Bella, let's meet him in the hallway and get this reprimand over with."

Angie followed them out. "Come back in anytime. The staff miss you dearly."

Juliet smiled at some of the other nurses who were busy with patients. "Thanks. I'll pop back in next week sometime. I want to catch up with everyone and check on a few patients, if that's good with you."

"Sure. Text me to let me know when, and I'll keep you up to date with any news from here. Take care."

Juliet turned to the door and pushed through. Max leaned against the mural in the hallway, hands in his pockets.

"Juliet." He wasn't smiling.

She braced herself for a lecture. "Max. What can you tell us?"

Bella stood between them. "How is the poor girl?"

He straightened and checked to make sure they were alone. "She's brave. I've come straight from her home. Shaken up. He managed to cut a small section of her hair, like the other victims. She's a bit bruised but her quick thinking saved her further injury."

Juliet nodded. "What did she do to avoid the knife? Angie mentioned she managed to slip into her car and honk on the horn."

"Yeah. She was in the parking lot. The top floor you usually use." A vein in his neck pulsated. He was worried.

"I know." This was serious.

"He tried to get her from behind—that's when he cut the hair—and she gave him a swift jab to the gut which must have winded him for a second, giving her chance to get inside her vehicle."

Juliet's mouth fell open. "But Caroline is tiny."

"She took some self-defence course and it was a natural reflex. Impressive. I seem to remember you have a few Tae Kwon Do moves up your sleeve, don't you?"

She blinked. "That was from a few years back. Mom was the pro. She got her black belt. She was incredible."

A sorrowful silence fell over them.

Bella let out a sigh. "Pippa was full of surprises. Might be a good idea to take a refresher, though. Maybe I'll join you."

"Sounds like a smart idea to me." Max stared into her eyes, almost willing her to take every precaution.

Juliet couldn't find her voice. Memories of her mom practicing her Tae Kwon Do forms in the apartment above The Book Nook filled her mind and broke her heart.

Bella reached for her hand. "Hey, let's go home. It's been a draining couple of days and you have some sleep to catch up on."

Juliet groaned. Why did everyone have to make such a fuss?

"Besides, we've found out what you wanted to know. Caroline is okay. Right, Max?"

"I promise she is. We're checking all the security footage at the moment and we're sending out another circular to all staff to be vigilant."

"Especially the nurses with red hair?" Juliet whispered. *Who might be next?*

Max sighed. "For everyone. We can't guess this guy's agenda, but I think you'll be a lot safer at home than here. Plus, you look exhausted."

"Thanks." She narrowed her eyes, well aware they must be puffy from crying and her entire face was void of make-up.

He cringed. "I'm sorry. I just meant you must be tired and some rest seems like a good idea."

Nice backpedaling, Max.

He turned to Bella. "Are you able to stay with her today?"

"Sure. I spoke with Adam and he's picking up some things for dinner and we'll chill at the bookstore. Sound good to you, Juliet?"

"Do I even get a say in anything anymore?" She wound her scarf around her neck.

Bella winked. "Not today. How about you let us make a fuss of you? A nice nap and good food."

"Fine." Juliet saw movement in her peripheral vision and turned back to the ward. Jasmine. One of the other nurses was checking her IV. Her heart sank. Oh no. Jasmine was back in? She had been doing so much better. She had been in remission from cancer and was so pleased her blonde hair had grown back. "I need to say a super quick hello to one of my kids. It looks like Jasmine is back and may need some cheering up. Give me two minutes?"

"Go ahead." Bella settled into one of the padded chairs lining the wall. "I'll wait out here with Max."

Juliet rushed back through the secure doors. The nurse had moved on to the next bed and Jasmine was alone.

Juliet waved.

Jasmine's sweet face lit up when she spotted her—but even her bright smile couldn't disguise the mask of sickness. *Not again.*

"Nurse Juliet, I've missed you."

"I've missed you, too, sweetie." Juliet leaned over the bed and hugged the frail six-year-old. She had lost weight. "Have you been behaving yourself?"

Jasmine nodded. She pointed to her stuffed bunny on the bedside table. "Hopkins has been taking care of me."

Juliet laughed and picked up the bunny and gave him a hug, too. "Hopkins, old friend. You're looking good. How is Miss Jasmine these days?"

She held the bunny's mouth to her ear.

"Oh, she's been a good girl, has she? That's wonderful news. Now I need you to keep an eye on her until I come back. Can you do that?"

"Hopkins says he can, Nurse Juliet." Jasmine grinned. She'd lost a tooth since Juliet saw her last. She was not looking good.

Juliet bit her lip and tucked Hopkins into the bed. "There. He's nice and warm now. I have to go, but I'll be back for a visit next week, okay?" She touched Jasmine's silky hair, the color of sunshine.

Jasmine nodded. "One more hug?"

"Always." Juliet bent over and two skinny arms encircled her neck. How many times had she prayed for healing for this precious child? She closed her eyes to prevent tears. These kids saw too many tears. "Say Hi to your mommy and daddy for me. I know they usually come in at supper time. Won't be long now."

"I will. I'm going to have a nap."

"Me, too, sweetie. Me, too."

Juliet spun around toward the security door. Max watched her through the glass pane. Before he turned away, she caught his eye for a split second. He couldn't hide it.

A solitary tear meandered down his cheek.

Chapter Six

MAX WHIPPED HIS HEAD AROUND BEFORE Juliet could see the wretched tear leaking from his eye. Why did he have to see that precious vignette? Juliet with the child was more than he could handle. It brought the heartbreaking truth to the forefront of his mind again. So much for pushing it to one side.

"You okay?" Bella stood from the chair opposite him and touched his arm as Juliet came through the doorway.

"Yeah. I'll get the elevator." He sniffed and walked ahead of them with purposeful strides.

As they all congregated at the elevator doors, he chanced a glance at Juliet. She cocked her head to one side and stared at him, curious but kind. Perhaps she *had* seen the tear.

Come on, man. Tough guy detective. Don't give anything away.

He cleared his throat. "Want a ride home?"

"No." She shoved both hands in her coat pockets. "We're fine, thanks. I drove here."

Bella placed a hand on one hip. "My driving makes her nervous."

"Sorry. I promise once you've passed your test, I'll come out with you. Until then, I'm afraid Adam has to be the martyr." A hint of a smile played about Juliet's lips. He missed those lips…

Bella pouted and Max smirked. So finally, Bella was learning to drive.

"At least let me walk you out to your car. Everyone's a bit jumpy today."

Juliet held the elevator door open. "You don't think this Red dude is going to strike again today, do you? Wouldn't he guess this place is swarming with cops?"

"Who knows how this guy thinks? This is a huge escalation. Twice in two days? I'm not putting anything past him." With no idea of the perp's mental condition, Max was not prepared to take any chances. Especially where Juliet was concerned.

They filed into the elevator to join several somber visitors and descended in silence.

In the lobby, Max scanned the area and noticed two of his co-workers conducting interviews. He would have to deal with the local news channels this afternoon. Never a fun task. Was anyone spying on Juliet at this moment? Her mane of red hair was in no way subtle, but he wasn't going to suggest a hat or hood. Guaranteed, that would not go over well.

The front doors slid open and they were greeted by a gust of biting cold air. Max zipped up his jacket and had to stop himself from putting an arm around Juliet. Oh, how he missed having her beside him. When they dated, she was a perfect fit tucked under his arm as they ambled along beaches and strolled streets downtown.

Get a hold of yourself.

"I'm over here." Juliet pointed to the silver hatchback parked between a black truck and a minivan. "You must remember my car?"

"Of course. It's still running well?"

"For the most part. You know what she's like. Somewhat temperamental." A glint flashed in Juliet's green eyes. It was good to see some life sparkle in them after yesterday.

He nodded. They used to always joke the car was as stubborn as its owner—and was she ever stubborn. Case in point, the fact that she had driven herself here when he had told her to stay safe at home. Yes, the Juliet he knew and loved was coming back to life.

She pressed the key fob and Bella ducked into the passenger seat. "Bye, Max."

"See you later. Say Hi to Adam for me."

Juliet went to close her door and then opened it again. "Max?"

"Yes?"

"How worried should I be about this maniac? I mean in light of today's attempt. I feel like I'm not thinking rationally this week. You know, with Mom and all." Her face flushed.

Max ran his fingers through his hair and exhaled. "I think you'll be fine at home. We have no reason to believe he's going to any great lengths to locate off duty nurses. Seems he watches for when they are coming off their shifts."

He took a quick glance around. What if he were watching them right now? He might take a shine to Juliet's hair and follow her home…

"All of the assaults have been in the parking lots or parking garages of hospitals, with the exception of one on a side road next to a hospital."

She glowered. "I won't stay in hiding. You know me. It's not who I am. The only reason I'm not working right now is because I've just buried my mother; otherwise I'd be here with my co-workers."

"I know." Man, she was feisty. "But can you at least lay low for a few days? Rest. Hang out with Bella at the bookstore or at their place. Just give this hospital a wide berth until we figure out who this guy is. Can you do that?" His voice was husky with emotion. The thought of Juliet getting hurt was more than he could bear.

She held his gaze for several beats. Memories of their time together surfaced. A time back when he believed their love was forever. He held his breath—and willed his heart to calm down.

She huffed. "Fine, but you have to promise me you'll call with any shred of information."

"I'll keep you in the loop."

"Promise you'll call. Tonight." A thread of steel in her voice melded with the strongest plea.

Whoa. He would have to exercise caution. He wanted to protect Juliet, but in regards to his reasons for leaving, nothing had changed. Watching her today with Jasmine had cemented that fact. "Sure. I'll call you tonight. Promise."

She slammed the car door, started the ignition, and reversed out of the parking stall without giving him a second look. Was she as confused by her emotions as he was? The anger seemed to have dissipated into something soft and hopeful. Or maybe it was all in his head.

Max spent the next three hours at the hospital. Three intense hours. By the time he was free to leave, his head ached and his stomach growled. The press interview went as well as expected, but left everyone asking more questions than he and his team were able to answer. The time would be better spent following any possible leads. He pulled the phone from his pocket to check the time and it buzzed an incoming call. Adam. His body went on full alert.

"Hey, man. Is Juliet okay?"

"Yeah. Just calling to see how it's going."

Max exhaled and paced out through the hospital entrance, surprised to see it was dusk already. Done in, he collapsed onto an empty bench and surveyed the visitors' parking lot. "It's been a long day." People still came and went. This guy could walk right past him and he would be none the wiser.

"You still at the hospital?"

Max waved to another officer who was on his way to the precinct. Poor Rob had been allocated with a mountain of paperwork after today.

"Yeah, I'm finishing up. There's not much to report."

"I saw you on television—nothing new since then?"

Max sighed. "Nope. The footage we have from the parking garage this morning is so grainy we were only able to make out a guy in a hoodie."

Adam snorted. "That narrows it down to about eighty percent of the male population."

"Exactly, and we have a bunch of them on camera from everywhere in the hospital. Where the nurse's car was parked, we can't even be sure he was the right guy. As I said, she saw nothing as he came at her from behind. Just a waft of strong aftershave."

"Too bad. I guess no one else saw anything because there's no description to go on."

"Correct. Male, average height. Caucasian. The fact we're clinging to is that this is the same attacker. Red."

"Because of the nurse's hair color? I suppose it's a bit much to be coincidence."

Max stretched his arm across the back of the bench. "Especially as there had been nothing about Red in the media up to now. No one was aware of the locks of hair being cut. This was no copycat." The thought of anyone jumping on this bandwagon and emulating Red now that it was all over the news was more than Max could think about.

"You still there, buddy?"

"Yeah, just mulling things through. The plan is we keep on following leads and hope he's been sloppy somewhere. Or maybe the other victims think of something new to point us in the right direction."

"Got it. I'll pass it all on to Juliet. I'm downstairs at the bookstore giving the girls some space to chat."

Max changed the phone to his other ear. "How's she doing?"

Adam was silent for a second. "It's hard to say with Juliet. You know how headstrong she is and yet she was so close to her mom, this has been painful for her. We're worried this business with the serial attacker might be too much for her to handle. Don't tell her I said so."

"I know what you mean. I hated having to come back here on the day of the funeral. Talk about bad timing."

"Listen, I don't know what's going on in that head or heart of yours but I do know you were in love with Juliet. You can use the 'work' excuse with others but you wouldn't have left a future with the woman you loved and dropped off the radar for no good reason."

Max squirmed. "Adam—"

"Hey, you don't have to tell me, but I'm looking out for Juliet's heart here. She's acting all nonchalant like she doesn't have feelings for you anymore, but Bella and I both know her better than that."

Really? His pulse raced. She still had feelings for him? But it wasn't that simple. He pinched the bridge of his nose.

"I haven't come back to Florence to hurt her. I promise. Something in my gut said I needed to be here to protect her. Even if it's just until the assailant is locked up and she's safe again."

"Maybe it wasn't your gut. Maybe it was God."

"I agree, and I'm not going to ignore Him."

"I get it, but be careful."

Max rolled his sore shoulders as he tried to get comfortable on the hard bench. "What do you mean? I'm trying to keep it as platonic and professional as possible."

Adam sighed. "She asked me to invite you over for some food in an hour, so can you keep it as platonic and professional as possible tonight?"

Max couldn't hold back a smile. "She did? Sure thing. Thanks. I am kind of starving..."

Adam laughed into the phone. "Man, you're always starving."

***

Max parked his car outside the bookstore. Not *his* car per se, it was a borrowed vehicle from the station. At least it wasn't a police car—that would start the local gossip mill in motion, for sure. Be grateful for small mercies.

He checked his hair in the mirror and then dropped his hand to his lap.

Who cares what Juliet thinks about me? Although she always liked my hair. I was the first blond she ever dated...

A tap on the passenger window startled him. "Max Bennett, is that you?"

Max turned to see his mom's elderly neighbor.

Oh dear, here we go.

He got out of the car and took a few steps to the

sidewalk. "Hi, Mr. Flemming, it sure is me. What brings you into town this evening?"

"Oh, it's Saturday. The missus always lets me out on Saturday to have a drink with the boys. As long as I'm home by eight." He leaned on his cane. "She told me you were back—we saw you on the TV this afternoon. Wait until I tell her I've been chatting with you here."

Max gritted his teeth. *Great. Let the rumors begin.* "I must get going but it was nice to see you."

The old man cocked his head toward the bookstore. "Going to see your lady-friend, are you? The poor girl must be heart-broken. We all miss Pippa."

"Juliet isn't my lady-friend, Mr. Flemming. I'm just checking on her."

"Hmm. We'll see." He gave Max a nod and a wink and shuffled off toward The Blue Anchor.

Max shook his head and paced over to The Book Nook. He noticed a hand-written sign explaining they were closed due to a family emergency. All the locals were well aware of Pippa's passing. She would leave a gaping hole in this tight knit community. He pressed the doorbell and scanned the street while he waited.

The door opened wide. "Hey, come on in." Bella reached up and gave him a quick hug.

Max inhaled something rich and spicy wafting from upstairs. "Thanks. Adam cooking up a storm?"

"You know it." She grinned. "He's trying to teach me his culinary ways but he'll always be the king of our kitchen."

Max followed her up the narrow staircase. "You should leave him to it. It's his happy place."

"True." She walked through the open apartment door. "Max is here."

"Hey, dude." Adam waved from the kitchen.

"Adam, is that a nice frilly apron you're wearing?" Max winked as he slipped out of his jacket and shoes.

Bella nudged him in the ribs. "Don't mock. He's wearing a white shirt and is making tikka masala curry— and I get to do the laundry."

"Got it." He looked around the familiar living space. It was surreal for the four of them to be here together again, like it had been so many times before. Only now Pippa was gone. He bit the inside of his cheek. Her mark was everywhere in this place.

He wandered into the living room. "Hey, Juliet."

She was curled in the corner of the sofa with Ebony on her lap. Her hair was in a long braid and she wore a plum-colored lipstick. Both good signs she was feeling human in spite of the past couple of days.

"Hi. Long day?"

He grimaced. "The longest. Mind if I sit?"

"Help yourself." She gave a small smile and gestured to one of the armchairs. Not the sofa. *Okay, that's fine. Act like it doesn't matter.* "Adam filled me in on the news—or lack thereof. You guys must be frustrated."

He sank into the chair and sighed. "It's early. Hopefully, now that it's out in the media and everyone knows there's a man attacking nurses along the coast, someone will come forward with a nugget of information."

"Do you think so?" Bella settled on the edge of the sofa. "There's not much information for people to go on, is there?"

"It takes one tidbit to get the ball rolling. Someone notices their husband or brother or friend has been acting strangely recently. Something has triggered a change in behavior. They've said something suspicious or been out at odd times. People make mistakes, let something slip, sometimes brag. We have to be patient and field a lot of calls in the meantime."

Juliet groaned. "You must get a whole bunch of false alarms and stuff. I feel sorry for anyone fielding those calls."

He nodded. "Some of the team will be doing exactly that tonight. The phones were lighting up when I dropped into the station on my way here. Most of them concerned citizens, plus a few crazies, but we have to hold out hope."

"Meanwhile we wait?" Juliet's eyes widened. "I'm not worried about me. What about all the other nurses fitting the profile? What if he decides to change his profile to brunettes or blondes?"

"We've got additional security in the surrounding hospitals, a police presence at yours in case he decides to come back, and the team is still following all the leads to determine who he is and why he's on a rampage."

"We're praying." Bella nodded. "We've got our whole church praying and I'm sure the others in the area are doing likewise."

Juliet snorted. "Hooray."

Max noticed her burning cheeks and the hard set of her mouth. Clearly, praying was not on her list of priorities anymore. When had that changed? Her faith was so important to her when they were dating. To both of them. Were her unanswered prayers for Pippa's healing to blame?

Adam removed the apron with a flourish. "Dinner is served."

"Smells fantastic." Max stood and waited for the girls to take their places around the rectangular kitchen table.

Bella sat opposite Adam and Juliet sat across from Max. In their usual spots. Weird to think earlier this year they would gather as couples for dinner. Max passed the rice to Juliet and his fingers brushed hers. Immediate electricity. She peeked at him over the dish and raised an eyebrow. Did she feel it, too?

"Shall I say grace?" Adam reached across to hold his wife's hand and Max slid his under the table. No point in making this any more painful for Juliet than it needed to be. Platonic. Friends.

Adam began: "Father, we thank You for providing food for our nourishment, and we thank You for... friends. We pray Your love and protection over each of us. In Jesus' name. Amen."

Max glanced up and caught Juliet staring at him. Her lip quivered and she excused herself to fetch a pitcher of water.

"We might need two." Adam grinned. "This is going to be hot."

Max took a forkful of the curry sauce and rice. "Whoa." He wasn't kidding. "This is awesome." *And not for the fainthearted.*

The meal was eaten in comfortable silence other than the girls commenting on how Adam should quit his job as an architect and open a restaurant.

He chuckled. "I cook for fun. If I did it for a job, the cooking at home would be down to you, babe."

Bella set her fork on the plate. "In that case, let's stick with Adam the Architect."

"Man, that was delicious." Max took a long swig of water. He stood and collected the plates. "I'll do the dishes. It's the least I can do."

"Actually, Max, I was wondering if the two of us might go for a quick walk. I think I need some fresh air." Juliet blotted her lipstick with a paper napkin. "I know it's dark out but we need to talk, and I don't think it can wait. If you're not too tired."

His heart stammered. Not what he expected. This

could either be a disaster or the best thing for them both. Professional. Platonic. What could he say to this beautiful woman with the imploring green eyes and fiery tresses? Or should he let her take the lead?

"Sure. Fresh air sounds good after being in the hospital most of today, but I can help with the dishes first."

Bella ushered them both toward the door. "I'm on dish duty. It's my turn. Wrap up, guys. It's going to be chilly out there. Stay safe. We'll stick around until you get back."

"Thanks." Max smiled. "And thanks for dinner, Adam. It'll keep me warm for hours."

"No problem." Adam came up behind Bella and put his arms around her waist. "Don't forget to let us know if you hear anything about the case."

"Will do." Max pulled on his jacket and shoes while Juliet slid into her flat boots and grabbed her peacoat.

They descended the stairs in silence. What did Juliet need to talk about? Their break-up? Her mom? The attacker?

She opened the front door and let him pass so she could lock it up. "Where would you like to walk?" He surveyed the quiet street to the boardwalk. A few extra cars parked near The Blue Anchor but nothing suspicious. "We could stay here in town or drive down to the beach? It's well-lit so we'll be fine to take a walk there."

She chewed on her lip for a moment. "Definitely the beach."

"Sounds good. This is my car." He pointed at the blue sedan.

"Max?"

"Yes?"

"You're not going to like what I have to say."

Chapter Seven

JULIET REMAINED SILENT UNTIL THEY REACHED the beach parking lot near the lighthouse. *Deep breaths. Stay calm.* This conversation could give her the closure she needed—or turn her world upside-down. Even more than it was already.

Max stopped the car and took out the key. "Want to talk in here first or walk?"

Juliet scanned the stretch of beach. There was a full moon and the sky was the color of denim. Stars pinpricked the backdrop and the beach seemed well lit just like Max had said it would be. A young couple walked across the sand with a massive dog, which looked more like a small horse. Otherwise, it was desolate.

"It's not too dark tonight. Let's walk." She opened her door and drew the salty air into her lungs.

Max locked the car and fell into step beside her.

"I'm sorry to drag you out here after your stressful day. Bella and Adam have been sweet and are doing so much for me, but I needed to talk with you alone." *And I didn't want to feel trapped by them or by you. I need some freedom.*

"No need to apologize."

Poor guy was probably scared stiff of what she was going to come out with next.

"There's a reason I invited you to dinner this evening. I have a lot of steam I need to blow off and I want answers. It's time for the truth."

Max ground his jaw. "Go ahead."

Don't worry, I will.

"I know you're hiding something and I wish you'd spill it." She glanced at his profile and noticed his throat convulse. "Mom had her own opinions as to why you would take off overnight without giving me a valid reason."

"She did?" He chewed his lip. "Can I ask what she said?"

Juliet lifted her shoulders. "Sure, but don't say I didn't warn you. She was way off base but she never could see any wrong in you." Juliet stopped walking and stared out over the ocean. "Mom loved you. She welcomed you into our family straight away."

He stood next to her, their shoulders touching. "I loved her, too. She was a special lady in so many ways."

"She was, but she thought you were scared."

He turned toward her and she met his gaze. "Scared? Of what?"

Juliet sighed. "Of me. I realize I can be a lot sometimes. I'm stubborn and I can fly off the handle easily." How many times had she prayed for help in this? But that was back when she was a praying woman...

"She thought I was scared of you?" Two lines formed between Max's eyebrows. "You have a bit of a temper to match your fiery hair but you're the kindest person I know."

Juliet shrugged. "She thinks—I mean, *thought*—perhaps I was too presumptuous. She wanted to see us married—she didn't hide that fact."

He gave a lopsided grin. "True."

"But she knew I wanted a bunch of kids, it's been my dream since I was kid myself."

His face fell. "Right."

Was that the problem after all? She continued. "She guessed I scared you off with my talk of the future and having a slew of children." She licked her dry lips. "We did talk about that stuff, didn't we?"

"Yeah. I talked about it as much as you..." He turned back to the ocean. Were those tears glistening in his eyes? Just like earlier when she was with Jasmine at the hospital?

"Was that it? Did I freak you out with my kid-talk? I thought you were into it as much as me, but perhaps I pushed it too hard. I have friends who never, ever bring up the subject of children with their boyfriends because they think it'll frighten them away for good."

A muscle in his cheek wriggled like it wanted to escape. He was struggling to keep his emotions in check.

Max let out a groan and plodded across the beach toward the cave, his head down, shoulders slouched, leaving Juliet at a loss for words.

What do I do now? Follow him? Let it go?

No way. Curiosity got the better of her as she followed him to the large rock he was perched upon.

She stood in front of him and placed her hands on her hips.

"Here's the thing. My mom died." She bit her lip. Would it ever get any easier to articulate? "Plus she left me a weird note."

That caught his attention. He looked up from the sand, his eyes filled with grief. "What kind of note?"

She took a moment. This was harder than she had anticipated. "It says she wrote a story. Her life story. In a manuscript."

"Wow. I didn't know Pippa wrote a book."

"Don't feel bad—I'm her own flesh and blood and lived with her until I went to college and I didn't have a clue."

"Have you read it yet?" Max slid off the rock.

"No. The lawyer is giving it to me when I meet with him on Tuesday."

"How do you feel about it?"

Juliet nibbled on her fingernail. "Kind of ticked she's not here for me to grill her about all the details, if you really want to know."

"Understandable. You don't know much about her past, do you?"

"Nothing. She was always so secretive and it upset her whenever I brought it up, so I stopped asking in the end. Figured she would tell me if I needed to know."

"Perhaps she did after all?" He rubbed his eyes. A sure sign he was beyond exhausted. "This is huge. What does it have to do with me?"

"It's awkward but I'm going to say it anyway."

"Now you sound like your mom." The corners of his mouth turned up.

"She wanted me to give you another chance. In her letter, she said you made me happier than I had ever been before and she was right. I want that joy again. Max, she had the strongest feeling about the two of us."

"Okay." His voice was a whisper.

Juliet couldn't look him in the eye. She felt the heat rise up her neck and flood her face. This was embarrassing. She focused on her boots. "I'm sorry. I can't believe I even had the guts to tell you that. You have no idea how humiliating this is—but I had to tell you. For Mom." She dared to glance up at him. "For me, and for any glimmer of the possibility that you and I have a second chance." *If you would only tell me the truth...*

Max's face paled and his lip trembled. This was a lot to process. A wish from the grave, and all.

"Are you going to say anything?" She reached out and touched his chin. Ran her fingers across his light stubble. The dimple was her weakness. A kiss would be so perfect about now. Why did he have to be so handsome and strong and good?

His silence lingered between them like the horizon as his gaze shifted over her shoulder to the ocean beyond. Juliet's heart caved in on itself and she dropped her hand. He wouldn't answer. What did she expect?

Stupid. Stupid. I've opened my heart up again on the whim of my deceased mother.

She took a step backwards. "You know what? Forget every word I just said. Blame it on my grief or my lack of sleep or the fact some lunatic could kill me at any point. You left and you had your reasons for not wanting me in your life. If you won't tell me why, then I guess it's something I have to live with. For the record, it's not cool."

"Juliet, stop." He pulled her toward him, smothered her in a hug, and held on as if for dear life.

She circled her arms around his body and inhaled the smell of him, a hint of musk aftershave and fresh air on his jacket. As his hand stroked her hair, she was almost transported back to the times her mom had done the same, when she had awoken from a nightmare or skinned her knee or had an argument with a friend.

This.

This was where she wanted to be more than any other place on the planet. It felt like home.

I've missed being held in these arms.

Strong, protective arms. Tears coursed down her cheeks and were absorbed into the fabric of his jacket, and it felt so right. Yet it wasn't enough. Something was missing.

Her gut told her this was not a romantic gesture filled with promise. It was safe and secure. That of a friend. He was not capitulating to her mom's brazen request, after all. They would have no second chance. Why had she gotten her hopes up this afternoon anyway? For whatever reason, he'd moved on and left her behind. Rather than live with false hope, she was going to have to let him go as well. If only he could explain why.

"I'm sorry." He whispered the words into her hair. "So sorry for everything. For all the loss."

Juliet wriggled from his embrace. Nose-to-nose, a breath apart, she memorized every inch of his face one last time before she accepted they had no future together.

She stared deeply into his eyes as they stood frozen like statues. Souls searching. Hearts hunting.

Don't speak. Don't ruin this, whatever it is.

A cool breeze ruffled Max's hair but still, he didn't break eye-contact. Juliet realized he was holding her hands. Gentle. Whisper-light. Now their breathing matched, she sensed her shoulders rise and fall in time with his. Her heart soared within as she recalled the love she had for this man. It was still alive and well. She could see it in his sky-blue eyes—he felt it, too.

A smile tugged at her lips, a life of its own. "Max?"

Before she could form another thought, he leaned in and kissed her. It was as if she'd never been kissed before. Sweet, gentle, true. All sensibilities flew from her brain and she allowed herself this moment of joy. How long had it been since she felt joy?

"Juliet."

She opened her eyes and saw a tear escape down Max's cheek. *Please let it be tears of joy to match her own.* No, pain was etched on his face. What grief was he carrying inside?

"What's wrong?"

He stepped back and leaned against the rock, pulling her along with him and turning her so they both faced the ocean. She nestled into his side. *Home sweet home.*

"I shouldn't have done that. I had no intention of coming back here to hurt you again, I promise."

No. Please don't say it was a mistake.

He exhaled. "I still have feelings for you..."

"Do you still love me?" She held her breath as she watched the waves batter the giant boulder in front of them, over and over. Like he was battering her heart. *Why did I allow myself to hope?*

"Yes. You must know I still love you. I always will."

She braced herself. There was a *but* coming...

"But it's not that simple. I truly wish it was."

"It can be. I know it can." She turned to face him and pulled on the front of his jacket. "If you explain the issues, we can work things out. I would never beg you to come back to me—you know it's not my style. If I thought you were over me or there was someone else involved, I would never pursue this. Pursue you." She exhaled. "Am I making a complete fool out of myself here?"

"No." He stroked her cheek and she melted. "Please don't ever think that. Love is always worth a risk. I'm not making much sense here but I have to let you know. It's not you, it's me. One hundred percent my fault, my own issues. You are perfect in my eyes."

Juliet grunted.

"Almost." He squeezed her arm. "You are the most fascinating, beautiful, captivating woman I have ever met."

"But not enough to see a future with?" Something died inside. He was giving her the "let's be friends" speech.

"*NO*. It's not you, I promise."

She'd never heard him raise his voice like that before. This was serious.

He let out the deepest sigh. "It's me. Don't you get it? *I'm* not enough. I'll never be enough."

"What do you mean?" She had to get to the bottom of this.

"I didn't want to tell you. I'm a coward. I'm not even—"

The loud trill of his phone interrupted the tirade.

He swiped at his face and pulled the phone from his pocket. "Sorry. I have to take this. It'll be about the Red case."

He cleared his throat and she watched the detective façade replace the passionate man. Their conversation was over.

"Yeah, this is Max. Sure, Rob. I'll be right there." He disconnected the call and stared at her. "I'm so sorry." Their eyes met and his face fell.

Juliet's heart fell further.

Chapter Eight

"I FELT LIKE SUCH A JERK."

Max cradled the steaming mug of black coffee on the table before him. It was Sunday morning, a perfect time for confession. Even if it was in The Rich Brew coffee shop.

Adam shook his head. "It wasn't your fault you got the call from the station. Yeah, the timing was off, but that wasn't up to you."

Max waited until the cappuccino steamer finished hissing from the counter.

"But poor Juliet. You didn't see the disappointment written all over her face. I fully intended to go for professional and platonic but it backfired. I can't seem to stop hurting her." *And I couldn't exactly blurt out the truth in the car on the way home*. He took a swig from the mug. The coffee scorched his throat and he flinched.

"Listen. You have to focus on your case right now if that's why you came back to Florence, right? I mean, the personal stuff between you and Juliet you can figure out later, after this guy is locked up and Juliet's safe again."

"I agree, but..."

"I knew it. You're not over her, are you, buddy? Not one bit." Adam settled back into the chair and folded his arms. "I could tell at the graveside on Friday."

"How?"

Adam leaned over the worn wooden table between them and lowered his voice. "I saw the way you watched her when she wasn't looking. It wasn't a detective protecting a possible victim. It was the look you always get when you're with Juliet. Totally besotted."

Max rubbed his hands down his face. "I can't help it. I thought I'd been gone long enough for my feelings to subside but who am I kidding? The distance hasn't made an iota of difference to me. I know she feels the same way. Did she speak with you guys last night after I dropped her off?"

"No details. She insisted she was fine and sent us back to The Lighthouse because she wanted to get an early night."

"Yeah. The work call was lousy timing. We were right in the middle of something. I was ready to explain it all to her, until my phone went off." It had been the perfect opportunity to get everything out in the open. To come clean.

"Seriously? So, you took the call and just quit talking to her?" He cringed. "Man, no wonder you felt like a jerk."

"I know, but this case has to be a priority after the attempted attack yesterday. Except, when the phone call broke the moment, I grabbed her hand and we marched across the sand to my car. She always used to marvel at how well I compartmentalize things. In this instance, I think I did it a little too well. Got my head into work zone and drove her back in silence." *Plus, I didn't come to my senses until I fell into bed later on and realized what I had done. What was I thinking? She deserves better than me.*

"Juliet's a tough girl and she's going through a terrible time, but she has her mother's strength and tenacity." Adam drained his coffee. "Can you tell me what was so important about the news from the station?"

Max took a deep breath. The strong coffee aroma he loved made his stomach curdle. He was sick with regret for the way he treated Juliet last night and this case sickened him even more. "We're hoping it's something big. I have to head down the coast soon to meet a nurse who was attacked by this Red guy last winter when she was working at a hospital in southern California. One of his first. We could be barking up the wrong tree, but I'm willing to follow up on anything my team deems important enough. I can't give you details yet, but pray it'll put us on the right track."

"Will do. I guess you won't be coming to church this morning then?" Adam bit into a gooey cinnamon bun.

"Afraid not. I would have liked to catch up with friends and get some much-needed wisdom from the message, but I'll have to pray on the road instead."

"Don't close your eyes, man."

"Cute."

Adam offered his cinnamon bun. "This thing is ginormous. Are you sure you don't want half? I don't think I've ever known you to turn down the offer of food."

"Thanks, but I can't handle the thought of eating anything. Last night talking with Juliet threw me for a loop. I'm still feeling pretty nauseous." He rubbed his stomach.

"Wow. This *is* a big deal, isn't it? I know it could be awkward with me being married to Juliet's best friend and all, but you have to know I'm here for you. You've got a lot on your plate and if you need to talk, please call. I'm praying for you. You know that, right?"

Max tapped his fingers on the tabletop. He had to unload this on someone. Who better than his oldest friend? He picked up the mug and then put it back down. "I appreciate it. More than you know."

He studied the man who had known him in every season of his life. Through high school, college years, and when he went off to Seattle to follow his dream of protecting and serving in the police force. He knew Adam prayed for him when he was going through his rebellious phase and then when he came to know Jesus as Lord. Adam had even re-introduced him to Juliet. He was the most trustworthy friend a person could have. A peace settled over him. It was time...

"Remember when I quit Seattle about eighteen months ago?"

Adam nodded. "You said it was burnout. I could tell you were done in, man."

"I took my job way too seriously and allowed it to overtake my entire life. My priorities were all out of whack. I was a wreck, to be honest. The idea of moving back to Florence was appealing. More laid back, less crime, fresh ocean air, great seafood."

"Amen to that." He raised his cinnamon bun to the seafood restaurant across the street.

Max grinned, and then released a sigh. "I remember when I saw Juliet. You called me to come check on Bella when she was having those weird packages delivered."

Adam shook his head. "That was the most bizarre month of my life, but yeah. You had no clue Bella was sharing an apartment with Juliet at the time."

"Right. We had a bit of history from her training in Seattle the year before. I kicked myself for not pursuing her then, but our schedules never meshed." He shrugged. "Maybe that was for the best."

"Shame you never gave her the time of day back in high school. She would have been good for you."

"I was too busy working on my macho image and pumping iron at the gym." While she was the beautiful redheaded bookworm.

Adam chuckled. "You were so into yourself back in the day."

"Tell me about it." *I was looking for love and acceptance in all the wrong places.* "But the point is, when I saw Juliet in their apartment that day, I was smitten. I knew I wanted to at least try to make things work with her."

"You don't have to tell me. Bella and I both called it."

Max felt his face flush. "Well, you know the rest. We started dating right away and it was progressing so well. We had a few minor issues but nothing we couldn't figure out. Like back in Seattle, a nurse and a cop are always going to have challenges matching their schedules and shifts, but we loved our respective vocations. Faith was a priority for both of us, my mom thought the world of Juliet, and I got on great with Pippa."

How was he going to explain this? He eyed the giant-sized clock on the cafe wall and realized he didn't have long until he needed to leave for his appointment, but he had to finish what he started here. He swallowed his fears and studied the table as he continued.

"One of the things I love most about Juliet is the way she is with children. Her face lights up when there's a kid around, whether it's on the beach, volunteering in the church nursery, or at hospital in her pediatric unit. She adores babies and children. You know how some people are completely natural with them?"

"Sure. That's Juliet."

"Anyway, we talked about what our future might look like together. We dreamed of having a family. Lots of kids. We're both only children and always wished for siblings. It felt like our happily ever after could be right around the corner. I even started searching for engagement rings."

"Doesn't surprise me. You were one of those couples who you expect to marry and do the family thing. That's why we were all so confused when you left."

"I know. I was so sure about our future up until then." He licked his lips. "But before I could make that kind of commitment to a woman who dreamed of starting a family with me, I knew I should get tested. Except I kept putting it off and putting it off." *Like I've been putting off telling Juliet ever since.*

Adam's brow furrowed. "Tested for what?"

Max took a deep breath. "Because it took my own parents so many years to get pregnant with me, I guess I always wondered whether I would have similar issues. I had a horrible feeling I might be infertile." He swiped at his eyes. "Turns out my instincts were right. Without going into all the medical details, I'll never be able to have my own biological children."

"Oh man, I'm sorry." Adam shook his head. "That's intense news to bear on your own. Does anyone else know?"

"Nope. I couldn't tell Juliet. You know how tender-hearted she is. She might pretend she was fine with it and let her compassion take over. I can't handle her sympathy on this, but even more—I can't be the reason why she doesn't have her own biological children. She deserves more. She deserves her own great big family. Even if we got married, she would come to resent me eventually for crushing her dream. I couldn't live with that."

Max blew out a long stream of air and sat back into his chair. Saying it aloud was even worse than keeping it bottled inside. He glanced at the other tables and noticed a family out for Sunday breakfast with something he would never have. He averted his eyes. This was painful.

"But don't you think you should let Juliet decide what she deserves?"

"What do you mean?"

Adam frowned. "I understand this is heartbreaking for you, I do. There were years when I couldn't handle the thought of being responsible for fathering a child after what happened with my baby sister."

Max winced. Adam had been a kid himself when he babysat his sister and she choked to death. So devastating. Yet he was better now. Healed. Max would never be healed from this.

"I know what you're getting at, but it was the kindest thing to do for Juliet. To remove myself from the equation and let her find someone who can give her what she wants most in life. What she craves more than anything. Don't you agree?"

"No."

Max sat up. "Why not?"

"You think you know Juliet but you don't know her heart. Not really. You didn't see how she plummeted after you left."

Max ached at the thought of her in pain.

"Trust me, there has been no other guy on her radar since. I've got to be honest with you, it's unfair for you to make this decision for her."

"Ugh." Max checked his watch. "I don't know what I think anymore. I thought I was doing the right thing by her, but last night threw me off guard and now I'm not sure."

"You said you were about to tell her, right? Before you got the call that interrupted you?"

Max nodded. He had been so close to sharing the news with her. Perhaps Adam was right. Perhaps he needed to lay all his cards on the table and allow Juliet to make the decision for herself.

"Thanks for listening. You're right. I need to finish the conversation with her, and I'll do it as soon as I can." He shot another look at the clock and stood. "But first, I have to go and see if we can crack this case wide open."

Adam wrapped the massive slab of cinnamon bun in a napkin and handed it over. "Take it. You need to be doing some clear thinking today. On all counts. I know you don't function well without food."

"Thanks." Maybe a snack for later. "I think I'll know where I stand soon—with everything."

* * *

Juliet couldn't bring herself to get ready for church. Her attendance had been sporadic of late anyway and the thought of the congregation offering condolences and giving her the pity-look was more than she could handle. They would understand her absence. Instead, she made herself a huge mug of strong coffee and settled onto the sofa next to Ebony.

"Am I going to become a weird cat-lady?" She reached across and stroked the soft fur on Ebony's back. "It's you and me now." *After last night, I don't think*

82

there's any hope of a future with Max. "Perhaps I'll become a recluse. Get a bunch more kitties. We have plenty of books downstairs and we could get food delivered. What do you think?"

Ebony purred like a tractor and twitched her velvety ears.

Juliet noticed her mom's Bible on the side table. She should pick it up and read it. Wouldn't she receive some measure of comfort from its words? From knowing it was her mom's lifeline in those final months?

No. I won't. I'm sorry, God, but I'm mad at the moment. Mad at You for taking Mom too soon. Mad at Mom for leaving me. Mad at Max for coming back...

Her phone rang out from her cardigan pocket and she groaned. Did she have to talk to another human being today? Except it could be news from Angie. She pulled it out and saw Max's name on her screen. Her traitorous heart skipped a beat. She set her mug on the coffee table and cleared her throat.

"Max?"

"Hi, Juliet. I hope I didn't wake you."

"No. I didn't sleep much." Nothing new there.

Silence. Then the sound of his windshield wipers. He was driving.

"Where are you? Sounds like you're out in the rain." She glanced at the window. Yes, it was pouring. She hadn't even noticed.

"I'm heading down the coast following a lead from last night's call."

Her mouth dropped open. "About the attacker?"

"Hopefully. We got a bunch of information in since yesterday but this one sounds authentic. It's one of his prior victims. Let's pray she has something fresh for us."

Juliet grunted. "I'm not into praying these days, remember?" She turned her back on the accusing Bible on the table.

"Sorry." His voice was tight. Juliet could hear his tension. "And I'm sorry about last night. It was the worst timing for work to intrude and I know you must be disappointed we had to cut our conversation short."

Disappointed? Try devastated.

"If it means catching the guy who's trying to hurt my colleagues, I'm willing to wait for you to find time to finish your confession."

"Confession?" He sounded surprised. What was she supposed to think?

"Max, you have no idea how many different scenarios ran through my imagination last night when I was trying to sleep. About what you were so close to telling me."

"I apologize for leaving you in the dark. You don't need this added stress at the moment."

She sank further into the sofa and pulled a cozy throw over herself. "I guess it's given me something else to think about other than how much I miss Mom and our little family."

The windshield wipers swooshed for several beats. "Then let's meet this evening?"

Did she really want to face him when she was running on so little sleep? Maybe she needed a day to gather her strength. "No. Today I promised myself rest. I'm going to nap and read and eat."

"Can I send some food over for you? I could get take-out delivered."

"That's sweet, but I have enough casseroles to feed an army. Thanks anyway. Let's meet tomorrow after you finish work. I'm sure I'll be climbing the walls by then."

"Okay." He let out a sigh. Was that relief or frustration? Perhaps he was anxious to finish what he started last night. She lifted her chin. He would have to wait. "But will you promise me something?"

"Depends." She wasn't going to back herself into a corner.

"Stay inside. If you need something, call me or Bella or Adam. This guy could still be local. If you are worried about your safety at any time, for goodness' sake, call the police. They're on high alert and can be with you in minutes."

A shiver ran up her spine. How safe was she? Her mind went back to the time Bella had been stalked right here. Perhaps this was her turn.

"Juliet?"

Caroline's attack was only yesterday. It was a little too close to home to ignore. She should go ahead and capitulate. "Fine."

"In the meantime, I'll text you if I have any news to share. I'll see you tomorrow."

"Drive carefully."

"I will. Get some rest."

Juliet dropped her phone onto the arm of the sofa and stared into space. She had too many issues swirling in her head. She needed to grieve for her sweet mom, finally understand if there was any chance of a future with the man she still loved, and stay safe from a maniac running loose in her own town targeting nurses. Specific nurses. She ran her fingers through her long hair and turned to the window.

He was targeting her.

Chapter Nine

MAX TURNED OFF THE RADIO. HE needed to concentrate on driving as the rain lashed against his windshield. He checked the time on his dashboard. Almost twelve. He should put a call in to Rob again to see if there were any updates.

His phone rang and he hit the button on his hands-free. He glanced at the display. "Rob?"

"Yeah, is this a good time?"

"Perfect. I was about to call you. Any news?"

Paper rustled. "We've had a few more calls to check out but this Brianne Hodges you're going to meet seems the most solid lead so far."

"Good. I have her address and I know she's there until two, right?"

"Correct. You going to make it in time? The weather may slow you down a bit."

"It's not too bad. I should be there in an hour. There's not much traffic out so I'll take it steady. At least I don't have to go all the way to southern Cali to talk with her."

"Yeah, it could be worse. Looks like she ran from an abusive ex-boyfriend and moved up the coastline."

Max grimaced. "She's had a rough time of it."

"She sounded fearful when I spoke to her last night."

Max slowed down at the sharp bend in the road. "You couldn't get her to say any more over the phone?"

"No. I tried but she requested to see someone in person and I get the feeling she may suffer from agoraphobia or something. She doesn't go out on her own."

Max squinted. "But she's a nurse?"

"*Was* a nurse. Like I said, she got messed up after the assault."

"Oh, man." This guy might not have taken her life but it sounded like he had robbed her of a future, confidence, and calling. "I'll give you a shout after the interview. In the meantime, you let me know if there are any other developments, alright?"

"Sure thing. Drive safe."

Max gripped the steering wheel tighter. This guy had to be stopped. He had ruined too many lives already and it seemed as if he had a taste for it now. He had killed once, he could do it again.

This could be the lead that breaks the case.

God, would You give me wisdom as I speak with this victim? I pray that she'll have courage to tell me what I need to know to stop this man in his tracks, and would You please protect Juliet? Watch over her and heal her grieving heart...

For now, he pushed thoughts of Juliet to one side and focused on the task at hand. If there was one thing he was good at, it was his job.

An hour later, Max held his detective identification up by his face and peered through the crack in the front door. This woman was cautious—for good reason. "Miss Hodges?"

"Yes. Are you from Florence?" Nervous green eyes looked back at him from behind gold-framed glasses. A brunette. Interesting.

"Yes, ma'am. Detective Max Bennett. You spoke with my colleague last night and I believe you may have some information for me."

The glossy, black door closed and Max heard the rattle of a chain as she released the lock, and then opened the door wide.

"Please come in." She stood back and allowed Max to walk into the apartment. It was contemporary and immaculate. Perhaps her own way of maintaining control in one area of her life.

"Thanks. Where would you like to talk, Miss Hodges?" It was important they had this conversation on her terms. He could see fear in her eyes as she adjusted her glasses with trembling fingers.

"Come into the living room. The fire's on and you must be freezing. Please, call me Brianne."

She took his jacket——which was drenched from walking from his car to the apartment entrance——and he slipped off his shoes.

"Thanks. Sounds great. It's been pouring all day and it doesn't seem like it's going to stop anytime soon." Nothing like talking about the weather to put someone at ease.

Brianne led the way and settled on a sleek love seat. She gestured to the matching couch for Max. "I'm sorry to have dragged you all the way down here today. I'm sure there are other things you need to be doing."

"No worries at all. If your information helps us with this case, it will be time well spent. We need to stop this guy—and soon."

"I had no idea he was a serial attacker until I saw the news report yesterday." She tucked a strand of her short hair behind one ear. Was she a natural redhead? Her complexion was pale with a smattering of freckles…

"Neither did we. Not until recently."

"Would you like some coffee?" She nibbled on her bottom lip and glanced toward the kitchen. "I can make some."

Max smiled. "I'm fine, but thank you. Try to relax and remember as much as you can, then I'll be on my way." He pulled out a small notebook and a pen.

She exhaled. "Sorry. I never used to be this skittish."

"No need to apologize. Can I ask how long you've lived here?" *Start with the safe subjects. See if we can get those hands to stop shaking.*

"About nine months."

"It's a beautiful apartment. You like Gold Beach?"

She nodded. "I do. My mother lives here in town and I always loved visiting her when I lived in California. Never imagined I'd want to leave my busy city life for this, but I'm grateful. It's a five-minute walk to the ocean." She stared at her hands. "Not that I go anywhere on my own these days."

"Can I ask why? I know you were a nurse down in Cali."

"I was. I loved it. It was my life." She looked up, her eyes filled with pain. "Until he attacked me. I don't expect you to understand. I don't understand it myself. I ended up in the hospital as a patient after he tried to... kill me. Ever since then, I can't bring myself to even visit a hospital. I need someone to be with me when I go anywhere. My mom's wonderful but I hate being a burden. He's ruined my life in so many ways." Her chin wobbled.

Max clenched his fist around his pen. This was devastating. "Take your time, Brianne. I don't want to push you or rush you, but I still want to get a full picture.

Can you maybe take me back to earlier on the day it happened? We'll go from there."

She plucked a tissue from a box on the side table and clutched it in her hand. "I had finished my shift on the surgical ward and was walking out to my car, which was parked in the staff lot outside the hospital. It was just before five in the morning and still dark. Cold. Colder than it ever usually gets down there. I had my hands buried deep in my pockets."

Max squinted. "Were you wearing a hat?"

"No, and in case you're wondering, I *am* a redhead. I've since cut it short and dyed it. Now I realize I was a walking target with my long red hair blowing in the breeze."

Like Juliet. Max cringed. "There was no one around at that time?"

"No. Just empty vehicles. I remember being surprised it was so eerily quiet but then realized it was because I had finished my shift about fifteen minutes early. I was coming down with a cold and feeling rough. If only I had waited until everyone else came out to their cars…" She drew in a ragged breath.

"I'm so sorry. Just carry on when you're ready."

She focused on her hands. "I was about to dig the keys from my purse, and he jumped me from behind. He must have followed me. Or been hiding behind a vehicle. I don't know." She shuddered.

"Take your time."

"He put a hand over my mouth to muffle my screams and pulled me to the ground between two cars." She was shredding her tissue. "I tried to scramble away but he was strong."

"Big guy?"

She wrinkled her nose. "Not huge, but he was strong and I didn't stand a chance. I told the police all this when they interviewed me. I don't remember much after that. He didn't say a word. He was still behind me when he grabbed my hair and I caught sight of his black ski mask before he slammed my head into the ground—which is when I blacked out."

Max made a few notes. "You received a nasty concussion then."

"Yes, and I broke my wrist when I landed on the ground. I think it was because my one hand was still in my coat pocket. Anyway, I was in the hospital for a couple of days recovering. I was devastated to know this man hadn't been caught."

"Who found you?"

"A doctor. Thank goodness. He must have scared the guy away. Who knows what he may have done given more time with me. Apparently, I was lying next to the doctor's car when he came out to drive home. There was no sign of that monster." Her shoulders slumped. "He was free to carry on his rampage, so it seems."

Max bit the end of his pen. He had done his homework and read the report himself, along with the collection from the other victims. So, why had she called the hotline last night? Something wasn't adding up. There was more.

"Is that all you remember?"

Tears filled Brianne's eyes, and she dabbed at them with her mangled tissue. "I could have prevented these other women being attacked—one nurse was killed—I could have helped catch him before." She bit her lower lip. She was trying so hard to be strong but something else about this case had been haunting her.

Max went with his gut. He had to find out why he was really here. "What *didn't* you tell the police back then?" He forced himself to stay calm. He couldn't spook her. "You can tell me now—it will help us. It's not too late." Juliet. It could save Juliet or any number of other nurses.

She sniffed and met his gaze. "You have to understand I was in a bad relationship at the time. My boyfriend had been charged with drunk driving and was walking a fine line with full-on alcoholism. He'd become abusive—not in a physical way, but he would rage and threaten me. I needed to get away but he had me where he wanted me and I was a soft touch."

Max's winced. How often had he heard the same story from girls who believed they had no way out?

"Anyway, when he discovered what had happened to me in the parking lot, he came to the hospital and was there when I came around after surgery on my broken wrist." She closed her eyes. "I thought he was there to comfort me, but as usual he was looking out for himself. He made me promise I would be as vague as possible about the attack. Get rid of the police ASAP so they wouldn't go snooping into our relationship. Into his business—he was into some scam I chose not to ask about."

"He wanted you to brush it all under the rug." Max nodded. Now they were getting somewhere.

"He did. To move on. So I moved on in every way. My mom came down to help and we moved my stuff out of the apartment when he was out drinking and I left my whole life behind. My job. My ex. My memories of the attack."

Max leaned back. "You're courageous."

"I don't think so. If I was courageous, I would have gone back and told the police something I chose to omit. I led them to believe it was random. I didn't tell them about the chunk of hair he cut before he left me on the ground."

Max's shoulders slumped. This was nothing new. "A trophy of sorts. We know he did the same with the other victims, too, Brianne. It's okay. Some of the other nurses didn't realize until later either."

"But I knew straight away. Well, as soon as I was coherent again in the hospital. It was from underneath by the nape of my neck and he took a decent amount. With a knife, I think. That's not all. There was something about his appearance I never shared. I know I should have." Her voice broke.

Max's ears perked up. They had nothing to go on so far. Zero. He always wore a black ski mask. "Go on."

She turned her wrist around. "Here on the inside of his wrist—I'm not sure which one, it changes when I remember it in my nightmares—he had a tattoo."

"A tattoo?" This was hopeful. Now if only she remembered the details. *Give her a moment. Let her share in her own time.*

She stood and walked over to the dining table and picked up a sheet of paper. "It's been etched on my mind for the past year. It's the last thing I remember seeing before I passed out. The tattoo literally flashed before my eyes when his black sleeve rose up his arm. Here it is." She thrust the paper into Max's hand as if ridding herself of the awful memory.

He studied the image. "Two interlocking hearts." Not the generic type. This was intricate. Custom designed, perhaps.

"Yes." Tears trickled down her smooth cheeks.

"Brianne, this is good. Excellent, in fact." He looked up from the paper. "You can't recall whether it was on the left or right wrist?"

"I can envision it on either one. Trust me, I've tried to be accurate. It all happened so quickly and I was struggling and he was strong…" Tears pricked her eyes.

He slid his notebook and pen into his pocket and stood. "Don't worry. You've done well. Thank you for coming forward. It was brave of you and it's certainly not too late. I hope you're able to let some of this go now and move on with your life."

She hugged her waist. "Me, too. My counsellor is hopeful and I would love to return to nursing one day. To helping others heal."

"Perhaps baby steps? A smaller clinic?" He shrugged. "You need to heal first—and I think you're going to be able to now." *I'll be praying.* He tilted his head. "You ever hear from your ex?"

She shook her head. "I'm safe here. At least I hope so."

"I'm sure you are." *I'll be looking further into his case. This woman has been through enough and if I can offer her some closure, I will do everything in my power to see that it happens.*

She drew back her shoulders. "Detective Bennett, I need you to go and catch this man before he hurts any other women."

Max stood. "That's my plan." He lifted the paper into the air. "Thanks so much for this. It could give us the break we need to find him." He strode to the door.

I only hope we can do it before he strikes again.

Chapter Ten

JULIET'S EYES FLEW OPEN. *WHAT WAS that noise?* She checked the alarm clock on the bedside table. Six in the morning already? Scraping. It sounded like fingernails on her window.

She lay still as she got her bearings. She slept in her old pink room and Ebony was curled up on the beanbag in the corner. The curtains were drawn but there was a slight gap. *If someone is actually out there, they could see me lying here.* She dared not move.

More scraping.

Her mouth went dry. Could it be Red? Had he seen her at the hospital on Saturday, done his research, and discovered her address?

Juliet grabbed her phone from the table and hesitated. Who to call? Bella lived too far away and Max—well, she wasn't sure about anything with Max. The police. She punched in 9-1-1 with trembling fingers.

"Nine-one-one, what's your emergency?" A calm, female voice.

She pulled herself up against the padded headboard. "I think someone is trying to get into my apartment. It might be nothing but I don't want to take any chances." She kept her voice as quiet as possible.

The scraping again. Now it was continuous.

"What's your name and address, please?"

Juliet rattled off her information. "You should know—I'm a nurse with red hair. That's why I'm being extra cautious."

"Yes. I understand. I'll dispatch someone immediately. Which room are you in?"

"I'm in the apartment above The Book Nook in the smaller back bedroom above the shed. It sounds like someone's scraping the window and I know it's possible to reach it by standing on top of the shed roof."

How many times had she snuck out using that route in her teens? Ebony pounced onto the bed, her sleep interrupted by the phone call.

"Should I go to the window and see what's going on?" *I can do this. The police are on their way.*

"Stay where you are, please. I'd like to keep you on the phone to make sure all is well. Is there anyone else in the apartment with you?"

Juliet's eyes burned. "I'm alone." Utterly alone. "With my cat." Which sounded even worse.

The steady scraping stopped. Juliet froze.

"Juliet, are you still there?"

"Yes." She dropped her feet over the side of the bed.

I have to check it out. Just two steps.

"It stopped. I'm going to look..."

She sidled along the wall until she stood to the side of the window, flat against the curtain. She still clutched the phone to her ear. "I'm there now. Taking a peek..." She braced herself, then pulled the curtain fabric to one side and craned her neck. Bare branches like old man fingers splayed against the glass.

"Oh." She exhaled and her entire body relaxed. "I'm so sorry."

"What is it, Juliet?"

"You're not going to believe it but a random branch has found its way to my window. Strange that I've never heard it scratching against the glass before."

She glanced up and spotted other branches still attached to the trunk, now swaying in the wind. "It must have broken off the larger tree above our roof." Her face heated. "This is embarrassing."

"Not at all. A nasty windstorm is passing through which explains the branch. Given the circumstances, I'm glad you called. It's an unusual case for this town." The voice on the other end of the line sounded so kind, Juliet almost started blubbering. "An officer has now arrived outside your place so I'll get him to check the premises to be sure."

Juliet pulled a robe from the end of her bed, scurried through the living room to a different window, and peered down to the main street below. "I see the officer."

"Juliet, would you like him to come and check inside?"

She wiped a hand down her face. "No. No, thank you. Please don't trouble him anymore. Again, I'm sorry about this." She chewed a thumbnail as she padded back to bed.

"No problem. You have yourself a good day."

"Thanks." Juliet flung the phone to the end of the bed and buried herself under the covers. Hot tears escaped and soaked the sheet. How dare the Red creep make her a bundle of nerves in her own home? The adrenaline faded, leaving her weak and exhausted.

This is not who I am. Or maybe this is the new, broken version of me...

***

After another long and lonely day, Juliet parked her car at the beach and turned off the ignition. Max had balked at her driving alone but she needed to feel some semblance of control in her life.

Silence filled the space. With her windows shut, she couldn't hear the crash of the waves or the seagulls squawking overhead. Just her own breathing, a reminder she was alive—and her mother was not.

She turned the ignition back on and cracked open a window for some fresh air and some sounds of something. Anything.

She massaged her temples with her fingertips. Mondays used to be her favorite, the start of a fresh week. Juliet could never understand people who berated Monday mornings like they were something to dread. Yet today had been tough.

The false alarm with the police first thing hadn't helped and she'd been jumpy all day after that. As soon as it was a decent hour, she had made a point of texting Max to explain the situation, knowing he would have been briefed on the false alarm from a redheaded nurse and been on her doorstep in a flash. She had managed to assure him she was fine and that she didn't want to stand in his way when he had a killer to catch. That did the trick.

So, this was the first Monday after the funeral, the start of her new normal. A life on her own. *Just me, myself, and I.*

She leaned back against the headrest. When had all her joy evaporated? Unmotivated—that was it. She was unmotivated for the first time in her life. She couldn't bring herself to do anything productive. She had no energy. Classic depression symptoms. Perhaps she would chat with her doctor if it persisted. Or perhaps she would wait and see.

The day had been a complete write-off spent in bed. Other than Bella popping up from the bookstore with a bowl of homemade tomato soup at lunchtime, all had been quiet. Too quiet.

Will I ever feel like myself again?

She pushed up the wrist of her peacoat to check her watch. She was five minutes early. Max would be here any second. He was nothing if not punctual. Would they be able to pick up where they left off on Saturday night? He had been so close to telling her the truth about why he'd left. She knew it. Her overactive imagination resulted in fitful sleep since the abrupt termination of their intimate conversation two nights ago—the dark circles beneath her eyes told the tale. She glanced in her rear-view mirror and smacked her lips together. A little lipstick and some blush offered a slight improvement. Not enough. Max would know she wasn't sleeping. He knew her too well.

Would his mind have been rehashing their conversation? Or was he consumed by the case? Perhaps he had news. There was the lead he was following yesterday when he called from his car.

Although wouldn't he have told me if it were good news?

She gnawed a thumbnail. Probably a false alarm. Maybe someone had come forward with fresh information. Wouldn't a person know if they were living with a killer? Or working with him? Or was a neighbor? Why hadn't anyone found Red yet? He must be smart. His victims were spread out and he never left any evidence behind. He could still be here.

The hairs on the back of her neck prickled. She locked her doors and closed the window just in case. She checked her watch one more time, and then dug her phone from the bowels of her purse. No new messages.

He'll be here any minute. Should she have taken Max up on his offer to pick her up from the apartment? He was only trying to protect her from the monster.

Thoughts of Red caused a shiver down her spine. She swivelled in her seat and took stock of the handful of early evening oceanfront visitors. The windstorm had given way to glorious sunshine and now several hikers made their way toward a trail up by the lighthouse that would lead them through lush rain forest and afford breathtaking views of the sunset. A young couple were taking a romantic stroll, hand-in-hand at the edge of the water where the sand was solid.

Her heart twisted. What was Max going to say? This could be the beginning of something special she knew she wanted more than she was willing to admit—or it could be the final nail in the proverbial coffin. Coffin. Mom. Tears sprung to her eyes.

A blue car tore into the parking lot and Juliet recognized it as the one Max was using.

I can do this.

She glanced in the rear-view mirror and dabbed at her watery eyes before getting out.

Max pulled in next to her as she slung her bag over her shoulder and slammed the door.

"Hey. Am I late?" Max jogged around his vehicle to join her. He hadn't shaved this morning—she knew the speed at which his stubble grew. His hair was a little dishevelled and he smelled like delicious musky fresh air. Great, just what she needed to keep her heart detached.

"No, I was early. You're right on time." She blinked. "Of course."

He smiled. "Want to go for a walk before it gets too dark? Looks like the wind has died down."

"Sure. It turned out to be a nice sunny day." Wow, they were resorting to talking about the weather? Lame. "So, can I ask if your afternoon yesterday was productive with the lead you had?"

They walked across the parking lot toward the beach. She chanced a look at his profile and noticed the frown.

"Oh. Was it a waste of time?"

He shook his head. "No. It was helpful. She had some new information."

"But you can't tell me the details?" Juliet knew the drill but couldn't help being curious. Her hair blew across her face, and she attempted to tuck it behind her ears.

"I'm sorry, you know how it is. I can tell you we are following through on this lead and also a couple of others. I'll need to check in at the station later tonight to get the latest updates, but I'm cautiously optimistic. The woman I spoke with yesterday has given us a new angle, for sure." He rubbed his eyes. This case was a heavy load for him to carry.

Her heart squeezed and the temptation to reach out and touch his arm was almost too hard to suppress. She tucked her hands deep inside her coat pockets.

"I wish I could share more. I know how much you being hate being kept in the dark." He nudged her arm with his elbow. Yes, he knew all too well.

She nodded. "It's fine. I understand." Talking about being kept in the dark. "Max, we need to finish our conversation from Saturday night before we get interrupted again."

He slowed his steps and concentrated on the sand in front of them. "Yes. We do. I'm sorry to drag this out. I'm ready to explain."

"Then let's stop procrastinating, shall we?" She nodded toward a painted bench. "This will do. I'm not getting up from it until you tell me what you need to tell me. I mean it. I'll sit here overnight if you get called away again."

Max opened his eyes wide. He knew she wasn't bluffing. "Fair enough. Let's sit."

* * *

It's now or never.

Max bit the inside of his cheek. Should he look Juliet in the eye, or gaze out toward the ocean? Keep his focus. Avoid the pity or anger or disappointment her face was sure to portray when he revealed his sad secret.

"Look at me?"

Juliet made the decision for him. He turned to face her. Shifted his body at an angle and stretched one arm along the back of the bench.

"Thanks. I want pure honesty here. No more lies." She took his other hand. "Your eyes always give you away."

He nodded as he cringed on the inside. "I hate that I was never brave enough to tell you this. So, I need to start by apologizing. Again. It was unfair of me, I see that now. I was a total coward."

She squeezed his fingers. "Tell me."

Here goes nothing.

"Like you were saying before work interrupted with that call, we were at a place in our relationship where we were starting to plan ahead. Thinking about a future together. I was shocked at how fast and how hard I fell for you, but it seemed like the most natural thing in the world. I was on board with our talks about a future family."

"You mean *I* talked about a future family." Juliet raised an eyebrow.

She couldn't blame herself for this. "No, we both did. We're both only children and I thought the idea of having a bunch of kids was appealing to us. It didn't freak me out one bit, I promise. I always dreamed of having a sibling, and was jealous of my friends who had several. My parents tried for many years to get pregnant, and when they had all but given up hope, I happened."

Juliet nodded. "I kind of guessed that, with your mom being a bit older."

"You know my dad died when I was at college—even though it was a heart attack and a real shock, he was pushing seventy. My point is, they had… infertility issues." His mouth went dry.

"Okay." Her compassionate green eyes willed him to continue.

"I guess in the back of my mind, I always feared it might be something genetic, the trouble they had with getting pregnant and all."

Her head tilted to one side and she frowned. She was dying to offer her medical opinion. He knew it. Somehow, she was reining it in so he could finish.

Spit it out.

"I decided to get myself tested. To avoid any nasty surprises later on down the road. It wouldn't have been fair to you—and I discovered my suspicions were spot on." He blinked back moisture and lifted his eyes to the gathering gray clouds above. Seeing her initial reaction would be more painful than receiving the doctor's report. "I can't have kids, Juliet. I'll never be a daddy to my own biological children." His voice cracked. "To yours." He cleared his throat. "It's hereditary. I'm sorry."

Silence settled between them like an invisible barrier until Juliet buried her head in his chest. He let out the breath he had been holding and put both arms around her. As her silent sobs racked her body against his, he allowed his own tears to fall.

In that agonizing moment when nothing else mattered, Max wept for the children they would never have together.

Chapter Eleven

WRAPPED IN MAX'S STRONG EMBRACE, JULIET attempted to keep her emotions in check but failed. She felt every beat of his breaking heart against her body, and it almost wrecked her. She longed to take away his pain. See him healed. All she could do was cry alongside him.

She hadn't seen that revelation coming. Not for a minute had she ever considered Max's explanation would be a confession of epic proportion like this. Infertility was the furthest thing from her mind.

I don't know what to do with this.

Her emotions threatened to overtake her sense of reason. *Think.* So, it wasn't her fault he'd left. She hadn't messed things up at all. She was innocent. After all the guilt and confusion and frustration where she had guessed the wildest of scenarios, this *predicament* had not even come close to being on her radar. This was why he abandoned her?

Slow breaths. Calm down. She pulled back and wiped her eyes with her sleeve.

"Oh, Max."

His cheeks were wet. This was huge for him. He would never have a son with his bright blue eyes or a daughter with his thick, blond hair. She delved into her purse and pulled out tissues—one for each of them.

I've never seen him cry before.

"Thanks." He took it and dried his face before stuffing the tissue in his jacket pocket. "Sorry."

"Don't be sorry. Tears remind us we have feelings. Trust me, I've shed more in the past week than I have in my entire life."

He groaned and sat up straight, one arm still draped around her on the back of the bench. "You don't know how I longed to tell you everything and dreaded it at the same time. I know now I should have shared the news as soon as I found out."

"Why didn't you? Tell me the truth."

"I thought I was protecting you."

By breaking my heart? I think not. Always the protector... "Because that's what you do?"

When he looked at her she saw truth and sincerity. "I guess, but it's no excuse. I panicked when I got the results and I messed up. Big time."

Juliet pushed her windswept hair from her face. She had to gauge his reactions. "This is a lot, so forgive me if I process it out loud and ask questions."

"You can ask whatever you like. I can't guarantee it'll make sense. I've had months to think about my actions and I still second guess myself." He leaned back and she missed his closeness.

"Did you pray about it?"

His eyes widened. "Yes."

"You prayed about whether we should stay together?" She held her breath.

He cringed. "I prayed God would comfort you when I left..."

"But did you pray and ask God if you should leave me? Be honest because I need to know." She dabbed damp eyes with her tissue. "My faith has taken a beating this past year. It's no secret I was devastated when you left and Mom got sick. I gave up praying. I guessed God didn't care anymore, and now I need to know if you believe He told you to leave me."

Max closed his eyes. "No."

"No?"

He clenched his fists. "I made that particular decision all by myself. I decided you would be better off with someone who could give you the children you want and, no, I didn't pray about it." He tightened his jaw.

"Why?"

Max took a moment to answer.

"Because I was scared He would ask me to stay. It seemed easier to go." He opened his eyes and looked deep into hers. "God did *not* tell me to leave you, Juliet. I understand that you're mad at Him for taking your Mom, but please don't blame Him for my decision. That was all me."

Juliet nodded. She *had* blamed God for Max leaving. Presumed it was another test of her faith or something. She had failed the test and would need to process it all later. For now, she had more questions for Max...

"You said you dreaded telling me—what did you think I would say if you told me the truth back then? Am I that heartless? Did you think I would dump you on the spot or something?"

He shook his head. "No. The opposite, in fact." He took her hand again and rubbed the back of it with his thumb. "You have a heart of gold. You always root for the underdog, go out of your way to help others, and you're full of kindness and compassion. That's the problem."

"Why is compassion a problem?" She squinted. Concentrate. The guy was pouring out his whole heart.

"It's a beautiful thing. It's one of the things I love most about you, but I also feared you would take pity on me and insist we'd be fine without kids. I couldn't let you give up your dream. I know it's your heart's desire and what you want more than anything else in the world."

What? She let his words sink in. He'd left and broken her heart because she'd wanted kids more than anything? "Oh, you know for a fact, do you?" She gritted her teeth.

"Yes, I do. You love kids. You work with them and you're like a magnet to any child you come into contact with. You'd even picked out names for your own." His voice dropped to a whisper. "Don't pretend you would be fine not having children, because I know you better than that."

She let out a joyless laugh and pulled her hands away. "Are you serious? You *know* so much about me. It might have been nice to be given the option. To be allowed to make a decision for myself rather than you decide for me." Her voice was at maximum volume and she didn't care who else might hear her words carry on the wind. "What makes you so sure I ever wanted to give birth? I'm a nurse and I've seen the birthing process up close."

He lifted one shoulder. "I assumed—"

"There you go. You assumed. Did you even consider the option of adopting kids instead? Fostering? You do know my good friend Madison has an orphanage in Mexico where babies are longing for forever homes, don't you? Or that here in the States there are thousands of children needing to be loved and given a family?" Her face was hot. Burning.

Calm down, girl.

An elderly gentleman walking a Poodle stopped in his tracks, lowered his head, and took the long route around them. Wise move.

Max reached up and touched her cheek. His fingers were cool against her angry skin.

"I'm sorry." His voice was husky. "I'm sorry for all of this. I would change it all if I could. I would have given you the world—but what I wanted most was to give you children. You can claim you don't want your own biological kids until you're blue in the face, but *I* didn't want to be the reason you had to make that choice. I didn't want you to settle. I hope you can understand. I wanted to release you in the hope you would find someone else. A man who could give you everything you desire. Everything you deserve. I didn't think I was enough."

"Wait—you hoped I would find someone else?" Was he serious?

"It was the hardest decision I've ever made. Saying goodbye. Turning my back on our future." He clamped his mouth shut.

She gazed into his watery blue eyes and melted. He didn't have a clue about her feelings. *Seems my noble protector needs protecting from his own misguided heart.*

"Did you ever consider for one moment that I might choose you anyway? That I might be content having a future with you and you alone? That I would prefer to be loved by you than end up being alone and sad? You couldn't guarantee I would find a perfect human being to do life with, could you?"

"No. No, I couldn't. At the time, I honestly believed I was doing the right thing. Now I see what a jerk I've been. I've put you through so much heartache and that was never my intention."

You have no idea.

Juliet took his face in both her hands and kissed him hard on the lips. They were salty. Safe. Her breath caught in her throat. How could she trust him not to break her heart again? He didn't know her at all. She pulled her hands away from his face and stood.

"I'm sorry you think I'm so shallow. I'm sorry you decided to play God and took away my one chance of happiness with the man I loved more than life. I'm sorry that in thinking so much of me you ended up thinking so little of me."

Run. She turned in the direction of the parking lot and willed her legs to move. Faster and faster. She was running. Running from her wretched life.

The wind stung her face as the sky darkened.

Along with her heart.

* * *

What have I done?

Max jumped up from the bench and followed her. She wanted space to think but he felt compelled to watch over her. He had said his piece, and now she needed to process the news and the ramifications on both their futures. He scoured the beach to make sure no one was watching Juliet as she bolted to her vehicle.

She didn't even turn around to see if he pursued her. Simply unlocked her car door, hopped in, and the engine roared to life. What had that kiss meant? Would she consider having him back after all? *Or have I lost her trust forever?* His heart constricted.

By the time she raced out of the parking lot, Max was in his own car. He would follow her home until he saw she was safe in her apartment. Red could be anywhere at this point, and given the escalation between attacks, there was a good chance he would strike again soon.

Max peeled away from the beach, the golden orb of a setting sun in his rear-view mirror. That wasn't *closure,* was it? Was that the final sunset on their relationship? Or perhaps there was still a glimmer of hope.

It was up to Juliet now.

He focused on her silver car ahead. What would life be like without her? He'd had a taste of it this past six months. Pure misery. She brought so much light into his life when they were together. Even when they fought. The temper flashing in her green eyes with her fiery hair only made her more beautiful. Made him want to wrap her in his arms and kiss her until she calmed down…

His gut ached. No, his *heart* ached at the thought of not being able to see her again. Not being able to love her. One thing he now knew—he wanted her. Without a shadow of a doubt, he wanted her back and he was willing to do whatever it took to prove that to her.

Lord, I love her so much it hurts. I would do anything to have Juliet in my future. I've made a monumental mistake and I hate that she may have even blamed You for my foolish decision. I know You're in the business of forgiveness and restoration—but is Juliet? Can she see a way back to me after this? She needs You now more than ever. It's like a part of her is missing. She used to be so on fire for You, Lord. Can You reach her in her pain? Can You find a way for us?

As the road hugged the coastline on their way back to Florence, Max spent the entire time praying for the woman he loved, wishing she would consider his confession and think about what she truly wanted her life to look like. Hopefully, she would also find her way back to the Lover of her soul.

God, give her faith and give me wisdom.

He had to tread carefully and remember she was at risk in the case he was working. He needed to keep his head. Keep his cool. Be professional.

Not only did he long to protect her heart, he needed to protect her physically from a killer with a sick affinity for nurses.

Chapter Twelve

"Are you ready to go in?"

Juliet chewed on her thumbnail and winced. It was bitten down to the quick after another fretful night worrying about Max and their conversation at the beach. "Give me a sec?"

Bella had already asked twice. They must have been sitting in the car for at least ten minutes. The office building parking lot was full, everyone into the swing of their Tuesday morning.

Bella checked her watch. "I'm sure we can reschedule with the lawyer if you're not feeling up to it. It may be too soon for you."

Juliet grimaced. "Why is everything such an effort? I feel like I'm wading through molasses each second of the day." She turned to her friend. "Please tell me it's going to get better."

"It's going to get better. I promise." Bella gave a sad smile. "Have you heard anything from Max yet today?"

Max. How could she gather enough energy to deal with him? She had vented to Bella on the phone last night about his confession and her confusion. She was still no clearer on what to do about the situation. Or what *he* wanted to do.

"No. He's probably got his game face on with the Red case. Maybe now that he's shared his reason for dumping me, he'll move on with a clear conscience. If that's what he really wants. Except I can't stop going over our conversation in my mind. It was horrible. Half of me wants to hug him and offer comfort and the other half wants to strangle him for keeping it a secret." Her stomach churned as compassion warred with indignation. "You're with me on this, right? You think it was unfair for him to decide what I did and didn't want for my future?"

"Of course. Like we said last night, he made a mistake, and he may live to regret it for the rest of his life. Unless you can see a way past it and are both willing to try again." She dug her phone from her purse. "Personally, I don't think it's an impossibility. You guys had something special."

"Easy for you to say." Juliet inspected her gnawed fingernails. She should paint them now that she had time in her schedule. It might be an improvement. "My head is a chaotic jumble of Mom, Max, and this manuscript."

"Shall we at least strike one thing from your to-do list?" Bella put her hand on the passenger door handle.

"Yes. Come on. Let's get this over with."

A light rain drizzled from a bland sky as they half-trotted from the parking lot to the door of the office tower. Juliet led the way to the elevator, and they found the sign for *Edward Johnson, Lawyer* on the second floor.

Her insides churned as they exited the elevator. "I feel sick."

Bella opened the door to the lawyer's suites. "You can do this. I know you can."

Juliet allowed Bella to report in at the receptionist desk while she found a padded seat to collapse into. This constant state of exhaustion was frustrating.

"She said Mr. Johnson will be out in a minute." Bella sat in the adjacent chair. "You sure you want me to come in with you? I don't mind waiting out here."

"No, please come. It's not like we have any secrets."

Unlike Max and I.

"Juliet Farr?"

Juliet's head snapped up and she met the gaze of a jolly gentleman in a three-piece suit. Her mom's lawyer?

Trust Mom to find a Santa lookalike to handle her estate.

She stood and grabbed Bella's arm.

"This is my friend, Bella. Is it all right if she comes in?"

"Of course." Mr. Johnson stroked his soft, white beard.

She almost expected him to belly-laugh a ho-ho-ho.

"Come with me, ladies."

Bella shot her side-eyes and silently mouthed, "Santa?"

Juliet smiled as they filed down a small corridor into a corner office. Until she remembered she was here because her mother was not.

"Please come in and take a seat, both of you."

The lawyer lowered himself into a chair on the opposite side of the mahogany desk and then proceeded to offer his condolences and explain the legalities of the paperwork set before him. Juliet bit the inside of her mouth in an attempt to hold in her emotions. All she could think about was the mysterious manuscript and how much she longed to hug her mom one last time. Was her mom's story in this pile of papers?

I hope Bella is paying attention to all this because I'm not.

Mr. Johnson slid several sheets of paper across the desk along with a pen. The pen was red with his name in gold lettering. *Festive.* Thankfully, he had placed tiny sticky tabs at various places where she needed to sign.

"And so, it's all routine, with you being the sole beneficiary."

She nodded.

"Do you have any questions at all?"

Probably, but there was only one she could think of at this moment.

"Mom left a letter for me saying you had a manuscript? Something she wrote. Something she wanted me to read."

His cheeks reddened. "Ah, yes. The last thing on the agenda. I have it here."

He opened a desk drawer to his left and picked up a package. "Your mother insisted I tell you to take it home and read it. In your own time, she said. Only when you are ready." He placed it on the desk between them and it landed with a soft thud.

"Wow." Bella's voice was a whisper.

"This is the manuscript?" Juliet reached over and pulled the large envelope toward her. It had to be a half-inch inch thick. "I wasn't sure what to expect. Mom wasn't a writer, as far as I knew. I had no idea it would be this long."

"I suppose she had much to say, Miss Farr." Edward Johnson stood and walked around the desk.

Juliet rose and hugged the manuscript to her chest. Tears escaped but something joyful welled within. This was a part of her mom and now she was about to discover the circumstances that shaped her life.

"How well did you know my mom, Mr. Johnson?"

He stood before her and smiled. His eyes twinkled.

"We met several times over the years for legal matters, but Pippa always made me feel like I was a long-lost friend."

"Yes, she did that a lot." Juliet nodded and put out her hand. "Thank you. Thank you for being her friend."

He took her hand in both of his. "The pleasure was all mine. You know I'm here if you have any questions at all. Even later down the road once you have a clearer head."

Juliet's face heated. Was it that obvious that her mind had strayed elsewhere while he had been talking? She nodded her thanks and sensed Bella guiding her out through the reception area and back into the hallway. She had a death-grip on the package as they waited for the elevator.

"Jules, do you want me to drive? That was intense and now you're shaking. I should have thought for us to grab a taxi or something."

Juliet winced. "I love you to bits, but the thought of being driven home by you right now is more than my nerves can handle. I hate to be blunt, but I would rather walk."

Bella balked. "Thanks a lot. I'm not that bad."

"But you know I'm fragile at the moment."

The empty elevator arrived and they stepped inside.

"True. Why don't I call a cab then? We could wait downstairs in the cute coffee shop and figure out how to pick up your car later with Adam. I could really do with a cup of coffee. How about you?"

Coffee was a good idea. "Sure. A latte would be lovely. Maybe I could use a few minutes to gather myself—unless you're in a hurry to get back to The Book Nook?"

"Not at all. We can call a cab once we've finished."

Juliet patted her purse. "Oh no. I left my phone in the car." She wasn't thinking clearly these days. Max may have been trying to call about the case. "I'll go grab it while you line up for our lattes."

Bella bit her lower lip. "I should come with you."

"No need. You can practically see my car from the coffee shop. No sense in us both getting wet if it's still raining. I might as well pick up my umbrella while I'm there."

"Okay, if you're sure. I'll go ahead and put our orders in."

The elevator pinged and they went in opposite directions. Juliet exhaled as she left the building. She had done it, and the jolly Mr. Johnson made the final closure way more comfortable than she had anticipated. The air smelled faintly of forest as she walked across the parking lot in the rain. It was falling in earnest now and she clutched the manuscript to her body to protect it. No way was she allowing this treasured package to get wet.

She delved into her pocket for the key and pressed the fob to unlock the door. The rain pelted her back as she ducked her head inside the car and leaned in for the phone.

Her entire body spasmed as her arm was wrenched backwards. She screamed and turned to face a guy in a baseball cap. What? Was this Red? Had he come for her in broad daylight? Where was the ski mask?

He lunged for her purse, but it was secured over her shoulder and across her body. He grabbed at the envelope. *No way.* She held tight and screamed again. Frantic, she looked around for help. No one. Not a single person in sight. *Think.* A swift elbow to the nose and her assailant cried out in pain. A knee-jerk into his groin and he was down.

Juliet took that moment to pull herself into the car and lock the door. She rammed her hand onto the horn and kept it there while she caught her breath. The man stumbled onto his feet and she watched in her rear-view mirror as he hobbled between other cars and out of sight. Blue jeans, black jacket, black baseball cap. Sandy hair. Heavy build. Young. Maybe in his early twenties at the most?

A rap on her window caused her to jump. Bella.

"Juliet, what's wrong?" She yelled and pointed to the steering wheel.

She still had her hand on the horn. She pulled it back as if it were on fire. She was okay. The manuscript was safe. The guy had gone.

"Open the door?" Bella's eyes were wide and she was soaked to the skin.

Juliet obliged. "You're drenched."

"What happened? You're white as a ghost. I heard someone honking a horn and came running—I dreaded it would be you."

Shaking. Juliet was trembling, barely able to keep hold of the envelope, still clutched in her left hand. "A guy tried to attack me."

Bella's jaw dropped and she looked around, frantic. "Seriously? Wait—oh my goodness. Was it Red?"

Juliet lifted her shoulders. The effort was monumental.

"We need to get you inside. Now. Come back in. We'll go up to Mr. Johnson's office and call the police. Yes, I should call Max."

"Max?"

Please, not Max.

Bella half-pulled Juliet from the vehicle. "Do you have your phone now?"

Phone?

"Don't worry, I see it in the console." Bella dipped her head into the car and retrieved it. "Quick, let's get inside. I need to find out if any of these gawkers saw anything."

Juliet lifted her eyes and spotted half a dozen spectators watching from the foyer peanut gallery. Raindrops splattered her face. "Why didn't anyone come and help me?"

"Who knows? I need to get you somewhere safe. Run."

* * *

Max clenched his jaw. Bella's phone call was almost his undoing, and it shouldn't be. He was a detective, used to way worse scenarios than an attempted assault or robbery—but this was Juliet Farr, and they had a killer on the loose with a penchant for redheads.

God, help me out here.

He took the stairs two at a time up to the second floor and the law offices of Edward Johnson. He was a solid guy, respected in town and with the police force. Juliet was in good hands.

"Max." Bella met him at the door to the office. She was drenched, her long blonde hair stuck to the sides of her face.

"Where is she?" Max scanned the reception area. An elderly couple and a businessman sat in a row.

"In Mr. Johnson's office. Come with me."

He followed her down the hallway in silence. The door to the office was open.

"Detective." Edward Johnson stood and walked around to shake Max's hand. "Come on in. Miss Farr had a nasty fright. You carry on. I'll wait out in reception." He disappeared through the door, leaving the three of them to talk.

"I'm fine." Juliet sat ramrod straight in a chair, her face pale. She was as soaked through as Bella.

"Can you tell me what happened?" Max took the chair next to her. Should he hold her hand? Hug her? He wanted to in the worst way but she appeared fragile. Breakable. Not to mention the elephant in the room, namely their conversation yesterday. "Start at the beginning?"

He grabbed a notebook and pen from his inside jacket pocket, and observed her every move. Professional over personal. This could be a clue in the case.

Come on, Juliet, I have to know if this is Red.

"It wasn't him." She stared at a huge envelope on her lap. Bella moved behind her and put a hand on her shoulder.

"Red? How do you know for sure?"

"I've been thinking about it, playing it back in my mind." She met his gaze. "He wanted my purse. Or this manuscript, although I can't imagine why. He tried to grab both. He wasn't interested in me or my hair." She reached up and smoothed a wet lock from her face. "Max, he was a young punk. Not a calculated murderer. He didn't wear a ski mask or anything. He wore a baseball cap pulled down low."

"How did you get away?"

"I tried the same moves Caroline used at the hospital the other day. It worked."

The corners of his mouth twitched. Yes, she was feisty. He gestured toward the envelope. "Is that Pippa's manuscript you told me about?"

She nodded.

Her attacker messed with the wrong woman. "You did well. I'm proud of you."

She raised an eyebrow.

"I'm relieved you're safe. Are you hurt at all?"

She rubbed her shoulder. "Nothing a long, hot bath won't cure."

"Sure you don't need to get checked out?"

"Which one of us is the nurse again?"

He nodded. "Fair. Did you get a decent look at him?"

"Late teens to early twenties, blond, sandy hair stuck out from a black baseball cap. Average height, chunky build. Blue jeans, black jacket. Clean shaven."

She had a good eye for detail. *Not our guy.*

"Good. I think you're right, it doesn't sound like Red. We're after someone in their thirties at least, strong and lean. Not interested in stealing purses." He turned to Bella. "Did you see anything at all? I know you said you were inside when it happened."

She shook her head. "I was in the coffee shop waiting in line when I heard someone laying on a car horn. I ran out to check on Juliet since she was out there getting something from her car. He'd disappeared by the time I got there."

Max scribbled down the order of events. "I'll phone this in, and then can I give you both a ride home?"

"No thanks." Juliet stood, her envelope a shield at her chest. "We'll grab a taxi."

Bella glanced from Juliet to Max, confusion clouding her features.

He chanced touching Juliet's arm. "Please let me help? I'd like to get you home safely. You've been through a lot today."

She shook her head and walked past him to the door. She turned back and looked over her shoulder, her eyes on fire. "You have made one too many decisions for me, Max. *I* make the decisions from now on. Not you."

His mouth fell open as she disappeared. Was she walking away from him for now or forever?

Juliet's angry footsteps echoed down the hallway, each one stomping on his broken heart.

Chapter Thirteen

"YOU'RE STARTING TO GET A BIT of color in your face again. Here, this should help you feel a little more human." Bella set a mug of hot chocolate on the side table next to Juliet, along with a toasted bagel and cream cheese. It smelled wonderful.

"Thanks. I'm feeling much better. I didn't think I was hungry but this looks delicious. You're getting all domesticated now that you're a married woman." Juliet managed a half-grin and picked up the steaming drink. "Marshmallows, too? You're spoiling me."

Bella perched on the end of the bed and folded her arms. "Thanks, but it's not rocket science. It's a bagel. You deserve to be spoiled after all the craziness."

"Running me a bubble bath helped. I'm finally warm."

"I am, too. Thanks for the loan of the cardigan. I'll pop it back up here before I head home this evening." Bella squinted. "You sure you don't want some company? I could stay up here with you this afternoon. I have help in the bookstore for as long as I need it today."

"I'm good. Thanks, though." She stared at the envelope on her lap. The jarring events of this morning paled in comparison to the task at hand. She wouldn't be able to focus on anything else until she learned the true story of Pippa Farr. "I think I need to do this alone. Here in Mom's room. Mom's chair. It feels right."

Bella nodded and stood. "I get it. I'll check on you later. Holler downstairs if you need me?" She padded over and squeezed Juliet's hand.

"Yeah. Promise."

"I'll head on down then." Bella left and Juliet picked up half the bagel and nibbled on it.

What am I going to learn from reading this?

Either her whole world was going to implode or it would bring some measure of closure to questions she had regarding her heritage. Her father, in particular.

She took a huge bite of bagel and dumped the rest back on the plate.

Here goes nothing.

With trembling fingers, she ripped open the end of the package and slid the contents out onto her lap.

Breathe.

Sure enough, it was a printed manuscript held together with a bulldog clip. Page numbers were on the top right corner. Good. If she muddled the pile, it would be salvageable.

Juliet exhaled and blinked to clear watery eyes. In the center was the title: The Orphan Beach. Underneath was simply: Pippa Farr.

Oh, Mom. When did you create this? Why aren't you here so I can ask you about every single sentence?

She flipped to the back page to make sure it was complete. Not to see how it ended—her mom hated when anyone did that with a book. It was sacrilege. No, she would savor the entire thing in order. She sank deep into the armchair and stretched her legs out onto the ottoman. She pinched the bulldog clip open, placed it on the side table, and then began reading her mother's words. Wow. These were her mother's actual words...

"It started early, wearing this cloak of rejection. My first memory is gnawing on the edge of my wooden crib, standing as tall as my pudgy toddler legs would hold me. Watching. Waiting. I didn't know who it was I watched and waited for at the time. I simply yearned. Little Pippa Farr needed to be loved by someone. Anyone... and so it began."

Juliet stopped and pulled a tissue from the box. This was going to be gruelling. One paragraph in and tears flowed like Niagara Falls. She knew her mom began her life in an orphanage in California and had never known her biological parents. That was the extent of her knowledge and now she realized why her mom had never shared more. She was a brave, independent woman, and would never want pity from anyone. Including her daughter. Although her heart already broke at the thought of a lonely baby gnawing on a crib.

As she read on, it was as if she were reading some fiction story rather than the factual information from her mother's early years. Her childhood was heartbreaking. As it unfolded, Juliet learned her mom had been deposited at an orphanage in California as a baby, where she remained until the age of sixteen. Over the years, other kids were accepted for adoption, but she was never chosen. In fact, she was bullied and picked on as one of the smallest. Juliet's heart squeezed at the thought.

There was no mention of any special childhood friends, but books had been her greatest companions, allowing her to escape and dream—yes, that made perfect sense. The Book Nook was an extension of her passion, allowing others to share in her greatest love.

Mom, why didn't you ever tell me all this before?

Juliet took another bite of bagel as her eyes flew across the pages of the manuscript. She needed sustenance. She didn't want to miss anything and drank in each and every word, yet was anxious to get through it in its entirety, to make sure there were no hidden skeletons about to jump out at her. She had dreamed up a multitude of horrific scenarios over the course of the weekend.

She slowed as she came to the part where life changed for her mom:

"I knew there would be no Prince Charming to sweep me off my feet and carry me away from my miserable existence. I made the best of each day, but my teen years were an ugly melding of insecurity and rejection. Until one afternoon in June.

I was sixteen years old, and knew my time at the orphanage was coming to an end—I would be kicked out as soon as I turned eighteen. I was drawn to a crowd of misfits in school and although I was smart, I was not one for following rules. As a result, my hopes of graduating were slim to none, but everything came to a screeching halt when I met Dan."

Juliet's shoulders tensed. Was Dan her father? This was surreal.

"He was ten years older than me and drove a cool, sky-blue convertible. I had a part-time job at an ice-cream parlor and he worked in the office building next-door. I would flirt with him when he came in for his hot fudge sundae on Fridays after work, and he would give me a huge tip. One afternoon, he handed me his cash and a hand-written note. He wanted to take me for a ride in his car.

After a life of rejection, this seemed like a dream come true. He was rich, not bad looking, and he liked me. So just like that, my life changed on a dime. He wined and dined me, and promised me the world. I quit bothering to go to school at all and planned to move in with Dan. When he told me he loved me, I would have done anything for him—and I did.

He rented a tiny apartment in the city and I said farewell to orphanage life forever. It was my Cinderella moment. He stayed with me on occasion, but I basically had the place to myself, which was a massive change from sharing a dorm in the orphanage. I was clueless and naive, but I was happy to be a kept woman. Until the beatings began..."

Juliet gasped. What kind of monster had her sweet mom encountered? One who was both possessive and abusive. She read details through a blur of tears—the unpredictable violence, the fear, the glimpses of happiness, the confused teenage girl yearning to be loved and accepted. This Dan had some sort of hold on her mom for two long years. Two years?

And then he took her to Mexico for a long-promised vacation. There he lavished attention and romance on her, until his jealousy flared up and the rages continued. She covered bruises on her face by wearing floppy hats and sunglasses, but her soul was being pummelled along with all remnants of self-worth. Her greatest joy was time alone when Dan was sleeping off the effects from the previous night of drinking and she got to sit on a beach.

"Orphan Beach became my favorite place to be. The locals named it so because an orphanage was

situated amongst dense foliage at the far edge of the sand. Whenever possible, I would find a spot in the shade and sit on a towel while the children spilled out from the dilapidated building for their play time. It happened each morning at ten, before the heat became too intense. I watched, enthralled by their simple joy. Simple play. I considered the stark contrast to my own experience growing up in an orphanage. How I would have savored a day at the beach, splashing in waves, building sand castles, carefree, knowing fun. I was happy for them, sad for myself.

Until one morning, when I took courage and moved my towel closer to the children. Some of them came up to me, shy, curious. I was paler than pale and had long auburn curls—they were fascinated. It was then I saw the truth in their faces, their eyes especially. They yearned, too."

Juliet looked up from the page. She was also yearning for love—now more than ever before. Without her mom, without Max, without God. Orphaned. She was feeling orphaned in so many ways. She dropped her gaze back to the page to read more.

"The lap of waves on shore replaced the lap of a loving mother.

The sand pies they fashioned were a poor comparison to apple pies baked by a grandma.

The screech of seagulls overhead should have been a gentle call of a parent.

They wrapped themselves in scratchy beach towels when they craved the arms of a mother wrapped around them.

They were me. They, too, needed to be loved."
Tissues. She needed more tissues. This was heart wrenching. Juliet set the manuscript on the table, pulled herself up, and trudged to her mom's en suite, where she pulled a wad of tissues from a box on the counter. She caught her reflection in the mirror, eyes red-rimmed and hair a hot mess. Her life had been a cake-walk compared to her mother's. It put her troubles with Max into perspective somewhat.

No wonder you wanted Max for me, Mom. Kind, tender, protective.

She took her stash of tissues back to the armchair and curled up again.

I have to get through this. I have to know if Dan is my father... or if Mom went on to find real love in her life.

"The seagulls enthralled me. I regarded them in their easy flight—swooping low, flying high, soaring carefree with no boundaries. I realized I was jealous. Jealous of these small birds flying wherever the mood took them. I knew in one singular moment of revelation, I needed to flee.

Flee from the prison of my toxic relationship with Dan, the physical and mental abuse, the fear of what each day held. I wasn't living, I was merely existing. Always had. Get through the day. Unscathed, if possible. I needed to breathe. To live free as a bird.

Dan had been my escape route from my first prison—the orphanage—and I had been gullible and desperate. Then on the beach that day watching the seagulls, feeling the warmth of the sun on my face and the gentle breeze lift my hair, I knew I was ready. I knew the beach would always have my heart, and I would always gravitate toward it. It showed me the possibility of freedom. Of hope. Of childlike joy, the like of which I had never encountered."

Yes, the beach… no wonder her request had been to bury the ashes beneath a palm tree. She took a sip of cooled hot chocolate. Details about her own life were dropping into place in light of her mom's story. Juliet's childhood was full of fun memories enjoying the freedom of play. She had been given that gift because it had been denied to a young Pippa Farr.

Her mom had been determined to make Juliet's childhood fun and free, always giving her the attention she needed and entering into the world of games and make-believe with gusto. Even as a single parent, she somehow juggled work and bills and the stress of the everyday so Juliet never gave any of it a thought.

Mom, you were the best.

She would have been a phenomenal grandmother, too. Fun Granny. Juliet's mouth twitched with a smile. Her dear mom had been cheated out of that privilege by cancer—and there would have been no biological grand-babies even if Juliet *had* ended up with Max.

You were way off base with that one, Mom.

The thought of Max made Juliet glance over at her phone on the table. She'd silenced it earlier to allow her full concentration on the manuscript. Perhaps there had been some news related to the punk from this morning. She set the manuscript and the mug on the side table and picked up the phone. Sure enough, there were missed calls and three text messages from Max, all of them identical:

JULIET. STAY WHERE YOU ARE. DO NOT LEAVE THE APARTMENT.

RED STRUCK AGAIN.

Chapter Fourteen

BEFORE JULIET COULD MOVE, THE THUD of footsteps sounded from her staircase below. She held her breath as the apartment door flew open.

"Jules, it's me. Did you get Max's message?"

Bella. She exhaled and emerged from the bedroom. "Yeah, I just read it this second. What's going on?"

Bella raced across the living area, one hand over her mouth. "I'm not sure. Max phoned me when he couldn't get hold of you. Told me to close the store and lock up until we heard otherwise. There's been another attack."

Juliet clutched the phone to her chest. "When will this nightmare end?"

"I know. It's awful, but we're safe here." She clasped Juliet's arm. "We'll find out details soon. There's nothing else we can do but wait."

"I hope whoever the nurse is, that she fought back." Juliet clenched her teeth at the thought of all his victims. "I can't believe this creep is still on the prowl."

"It makes my skin crawl." Bella shuddered. "But we don't know anything yet so let's hope she's not injured. Whoever she is."

"I wonder if she was from my hospital." Juliet processed a list of redheads in her mind. There were only a couple more she could think of.

"Come and sit." Bella led her to the sofa by the window. "I'm going to wait here with you until we know what's going on. In the meantime, how's it going with the reading?"

Nice try with the distraction.

Juliet pulled her phone from her chest, turned on the volume, and texted Max a quick message asking for the victim's name.

Come on, Max. I need to know my colleagues are okay.

"Have you read much of it yet?"

The manuscript. "It's hard to read, I'm not going to lie. I had no idea Mom's life was so devastating growing up. I knew she'd been an orphan but I can't believe all she went through." She checked her phone again to see if he had responded. Nothing.

Bella held up her phone. "Want me to try calling Max?"

Juliet sighed. "No. I just texted. You're right. He'll let us know what's happening. I should never have silenced my phone. I always keep the volume up in case of an emergency." She pulled her hair to one side. "But I wanted to concentrate on Mom's story. It's compelling, for sure. Now I'm itching to find out where I come into the picture."

She set her phone on the table and exhaled.

"Then you should carry on reading since it'll keep your mind occupied. Did you leave it in the bedroom? I can get it for you."

"That would be great." Juliet pinched the bridge of her nose. *So much to process.*

Bella reappeared with the stack of pages in her hands. "Looks like you're halfway through already." She set the pile on Juliet's lap. "You carry on. I'm going to text Adam and fill him in on the latest." She picked up Ebony from the floor. "I'll give this fur ball some attention while I'm here."

"Thanks." Juliet gnawed on her thumbnail as she focused on the next page and lost herself in her mom's story again.

"By the time we returned to California, I realized two things—-firstly, I could no longer live as Dan's part-time partner and punching-bag, and secondly, I was pregnant."

"Oh, Mom." Her skin prickled. This was it. This was her beginning.

Bella looked up from her phone. "Not what you expected?"

"I don't know. I was kind of hoping she had a happier story. That she had a beautiful romantic start on some level. This is awful. This guy must be my biological father."

"Perhaps things improve—you still have a long way to go."

The bagel wasn't sitting well in Juliet's stomach. "I guess so. I need to see the whole picture." She picked up the page again.

"In my naivety, I decided to give him one last chance. The opportunity to start being a decent human being again, perhaps even romantic and generous like he was in the early days. I dreamed that maybe the threat of me leaving would cause him to smarten up and he would buy a house with a white picket fence for the three of us and everything would be perfect.

But when I told him I was pregnant, he punched a hole in the wall and then laid into me. When I begged him to think of our future, he broke the news to me—he was, in fact, already married. Married. How did I not know?

Then the rest of the pieces of the puzzle fell into place. The reason why he only spent certain nights of the week with me, the way he constantly checked his watch, the rules about never showing up at his office or meeting anywhere in town, which I presumed were because he was ashamed of my upbringing in the orphanage. When I thought he was being extravagant taking me to remote locations for dinner and to Mexico, he was, in fact, keeping me as his sordid secret."

A tear slid down Juliet's cheek as she scanned the page and absorbed the truth. Her poor mother. She's been lied to and bullied.

"Before he could humiliate me further, I grabbed my purse and ran into the night. He didn't come after me at first. I never looked back. I had nothing other than a few dollars, and all I remember is the rain soothing my freshly-bruised face. I guess I allowed my memory to lead me back to my old neighborhood and I took shelter in the doorway of my orphanage. The exact place where I had been abandoned as a baby—and that's where it happened. He had followed me after all and then attacked me… and left me for dead."

Juliet gasped.

NO.

She couldn't exhale the breath back out. Her hand trembled over her mouth and bile rose up her throat.

"What is it?" Bella's concerned face came into focus and Juliet forced the air from her lungs. "What's wrong?" She wiped the tears from Juliet's cheeks.

Can't speak.

Juliet handed her the sheet of paper and watched Bella's face contort as she slipped a page to the back of the stack and read the narrative.

"I don't know what to say." Her eyes brimmed as she shook her head. "Poor Pippa."

"This is worse than I imagined." Juliet swiped at her tears.

Bella bit her bottom lip. "Want me to read on for you?"

"I have to know. Go ahead." She hugged a pillow over her churning stomach.

"The next morning, the orphanage administrator found me unconscious and I was rushed to the hospital with a broken nose, cracked ribs, and too many bruises to count. Yet my baby was fine. My strong daughter. My miracle."

Juliet rested her chin on top of the pillow. Did her mom really see her as a miracle? The ray of light in a living nightmare? She was always the glass-full optimist. Perhaps that was her mode of survival.

"An old friend allowed me to stay at her place to recover—I'll never forget her generosity. I was scared and broke, but I had my unborn babe to think about and to love. So I channelled my affection for books by working at a bookstore and saved as much money as I could before my daughter came along. Then my life was forever changed..."

"Wow." Bella shook her head. "Your mom was incredible. I always knew she was strong but this takes it to another level."

Juliet shivered. She pulled the knitted throw from the back of the sofa and wrapped it around her shoulders. How was she supposed to react to a story about her own life? Her dreadful beginning. Her horrid father.

"Can you carry on?" Her voice came out as a whisper.

"Of course." Bella found her place on the page.

"This exquisite young life in my care, this sweet baby girl with a shock of red hair and a cry loud enough to wake the dead, she was mine. Mine. Someone to love. Someone who would love me back. I would protect her with every bone in my body. Every fiber of my being.

Three days after birthing my Juliet, we left fear and misery in our wake and headed north. I cared not where. I had all I ever dreamed of right there in my arms."

"That's beautiful." Juliet sucked in a sob. "But I think I want to leave it there for now." She took the manuscript in her hands and held it to her chest. Warmth trickled through her veins like honey. Her mom had saved her, and in a way, she had saved her mom. Given her purpose. Someone to love and care for.

"And it all makes sense now." Bella shifted to face Juliet on the sofa. "You remember how Pippa helped hide my mother when she was on the run and pregnant? It's no wonder she went out of her way to help. She had lived through it herself and come out the other side. She understood and that's why they bonded."

Of course.

Juliet rubbed her sore eyes. "That's true. She was always thinking of others. It must have been so hard to keep her whole past a secret, though. Not only from me, but from her friends, too. I wonder if she ever opened up to anyone."

"She never had another serious relationship with a man, did she?" Bella reached down and stroked the cat as she strolled past. "She must have been so burned."

"By my father." Juliet shuddered. Had she inherited her temper from him? What other characteristics did they share? "Is it possible to hate someone you've never met?"

Bella reached over and squeezed Juliet's arm. "Hey, you mustn't let this define you. You are your mother's daughter and that's enough. Not to mention you have a Heavenly Father who loves you and always wants the best for you."

Right.

"I'm struggling with both of my fathers at the moment." Juliet shrugged free from the throw and stretched her arms above her head. Her shoulders were in knots.

Bella let out a long sigh. "Remember, I can identify with you more than most. My biological father was bad news, too."

"We have more in common than we ever imagined, don't we?" Conflicting emotions raged through her body.

Bella smiled. "The closest thing to sisters we are ever going to get. I'll take it."

Juliet's phone chirped and she picked it up. "Max?"

"Yeah, it's me. Are you okay?"

"Why shouldn't I be?" Juliet bit her lip. Too curt. "I mean, what's happening? You said there's been another attack?"

"Yes, I'm sorry. The good news is that the nurses are all on high alert so this one also jumped into her car in time."

Juliet exhaled. "Thank goodness. Who was it?"

Max rustled some paper on his end. "Zoe Waterstone. She's fine. I'm at the hospital now." His tone softened. "Do you know her?"

"No, I don't think so, but I'm guessing I know her hair color." She held up a section of her own red locks and cringed.

"Right. Although he failed to cut any hair from Zoe."

He's not going to be pleased about that. "Did she have any extra information for you to go on?"

"She got a half-decent look at him in her rear-view mirror. Definitely not your young guy from this morning. This is an older man, she guessed mid-thirties, six feet tall, slim build but strong."

"The ski mask again?"

"Yes. Black. He slipped away, but something tells me he's getting gutsy. More regular." Max paused. "And there's more."

Juliet's stomach flipped. "More? You mean another nurse?"

"No, what I mean is he's done his homework."

Juliet set the unfinished story on the coffee table. She stood and plodded to the bay window overlooking the street below. She didn't want to know. Yet needed to know…

"Would you spit it out?" She raised her voice. "I can't handle your riddles today."

Bella cleared her throat.

Juliet turned to her and put a hand over the phone. "Sorry, but he's being all detective-like and I need clarity."

Max grunted. "Listen, Juliet, this didn't happen at the hospital."

She gripped the phone with both hands. "Then where was it?"

"On the street outside her house. He knew where she lived."

Juliet gasped. "He followed her all the way home? That's awful."

He let out a sigh. "I'm afraid it's worse. She was coming *in* for her shift. Somehow, he knew where she lived and came to her home rather than waiting for her to arrive at the hospital."

"Where does she live?" Juliet's throat was bone-dry.

"He was in your neighborhood. She lives less than a mile from The Book Nook."

Juliet moved away from the window. He could be down there now, wandering the streets.

"How did he know where she lived and what her shifts were?" Her voice was small now, defeated. She leaned her back against the living room wall. Her knees were about to buckle with tumbling thoughts of the guy this morning, her mom being beaten by Dan, and this maniac stalking her friends. Maybe even her.

"We're guessing he got hold of staff records somehow. With pictures, if it's the red hair he's drawn to."

Silence. What could she say? How could this even be possible? This man could have Juliet in his sights even now. Her blood ran cold and she dropped the phone to the floor.

Ebony mewed and Bella was there in a flash. She steered Juliet back to the sofa and picked up the phone.

"Max, it's Bella. Yeah, she's a bit shaken. For sure. Yes. I will. Bye."

"Did you hear all that?" Juliet's hands trembled. "This killer has our hospital staff records. I don't understand..."

Bella wrapped her in a hug. "I know. I wonder if they have any clue as to his identity yet? Did Max mention anything more about the lead he was chasing?"

Juliet shook her head. "Probably still investigating it. I can't believe this is happening. The staff at work must be so worried. I should go in and check how Angie and the girls are doing."

"No, you will not." Bella looked her straight in the eye. "Now is not the time for you to be hotheaded. We have to think smart and stay safe. By all means call Angie if it'll put your mind at rest, but she wouldn't want you endangering yourself. Plus, Max is at the hospital and he'll go nuts if you show up."

"I'm not worried about what Max thinks." Juliet folded her arms across her chest.

"Really?" Bella tilted her head to one side. "But you don't want to distract him while he's doing all he can to find Red and protect the other nurses, do you?"

Juliet huffed. "No. Fine, I'll let him do his job, but I don't like him telling me what to do. It's getting old."

"Why don't *you* make the decision to come back to The Lighthouse with me for tonight? You can bring your manuscript to finish and you'll have company if you want it. Bring Ebony with you. Let Adam feed you. You know it's his thing. I think it's spaghetti tonight, and no one makes a Bolognese sauce like my guy."

"Yeah, I have to admit, he is real good in the kitchen."

Mom used to love it when he helped her make dinner.

Juliet's heart sank. "But I don't feel up to socializing. You understand?"

"You can have all the privacy you need. Hole up in the guest room and read this—I'll even bring your dinner in there for you."

Why did Adam's Bolognese have to be so irresistible? Juliet's stomach gurgled on cue. "Okay. Thanks. You're too good to me. As long as you guys don't mind me being totally unsociable. Because I'm going to take you up on the offer of being a recluse in the guest room."

She gathered the papers into a neat pile and wandered back to her mom's room for the clip and the envelope.

"No problem." Bella called out. "I don't blame you one bit. I wouldn't be able to sleep until I had read the whole enchilada, either."

"Right?" Juliet returned to the living room, stuffed envelope in hand. "As heartbreaking as it is, I'm also learning so much about my mom. It makes me miss her even more."

"Of course, it does." Bella checked her phone. "Adam texted. He's swinging by here on his way home." She chewed on her bottom lip. "Oh dear. Guess who he invited over for dinner tonight?"

Juliet put a hand on her hip. "Not Max? Are you kidding me?"

"Sorry, I didn't know. Will you still come?"

Juliet pouted. "I seem to have lost my appetite."

"No. You have to eat. You can still stay in the guest room. You don't even have to speak to him if you don't want to." Bella squeezed her arm. "Come on. It'll save you thinking about food. Not to mention the fact you were attacked this morning and there's a madman on the loose with your address, in case you had forgotten."

Like that was possible. "I'll defrost one of my many frozen casseroles and eat it in bed. I'm sure I'll fall asleep reading anyway. I just want to get everything finished so I can move on."

"I can't leave you here alone."

Juliet tightened her jaw. "Alone is my new normal and I refuse to be scared in my own home."

"I understand, but I want you to be safe."

Sweet Bella. "I'm safe here with the locks on my doors and the phone by my bed. I promise I'll call if I get spooked about anything. There's nothing to worry about."

Other than the nurse-killer on the prowl who now has my address...

Chapter Fifteen

JULIET GROANED AS EBONY POUNCED ON her head and began kneading her long hair.

"Really, kitty? You couldn't let me lounge in bed a little longer after the night I just had?" Her sleep had been peppered with nightmares featuring a young version of her mom running for her life on a tropical beach. Disturbing on multiple levels.

She extracted Ebony and sat up. Pages of the manuscript littered the pink bedcover. It had been a rough night. She tied her hair back with an elastic from her wrist and leaned against the padded headboard. Ebony gave a soft meow and leapt onto the floor.

"Sorry. I'm lousy company even for a cat."

Alone. I'm completely alone.

Reality had hit in waves over the past few days, and each time it hit harder. Deeper. Every muscle ached and she was not motivated to do anything. Even to go back to work, and nursing had been her greatest joy. It was what made her tick. It was in her DNA.

What else is in my DNA?

An odd detached feeling flowed through her at the thought of Dan.

My biological father.

A wretched human being. He was everything she detested—unfaithful, abusive, a liar, violent, manipulative, and cruel. Perhaps he was dead by now.

I hope so.

The mere thought of trying to find him turned her

stomach. With no solid details to go on, it would have been difficult to say the least—but now there was no desire. Childhood dreams of one day discovering a long-lost loving father had been crushed. He had intended to kill her when she was in her mother's womb—and probably hoped her mom would perish, too, after the beating he gave her.

What if she carried something of him in her genes? She had a temper, that was no secret. Hotheaded. Violent? No, never. Although was it possible she might pass something sinister onto her own children? She shuddered, and then a picture of Max popped into her head.

If—and it was a big *if*—they got back together, it may not even be an issue since they wouldn't have biological children. Before even reading the manuscript, she had mulled around the possibility of adoption. It would be one way of knowing for sure her father's DNA would not be passed down.

She massaged her temples. She was going around in circles and her head ached.

I'm being ridiculous. Even if I ever adopt, there's no guarantee the child's parents would be healthy in a physical or mental capacity.

Who knew what kind of parents would create an escalating stalker or murderer like Red? Her eyes drifted to the locked window.

Ebony pounced back onto the bed and Juliet almost jumped out of her skin. The nurse-killer case was turning her into a nervous wreck. She ground her teeth at the thought of the madman terrorizing her colleagues, terrorizing her. He was nothing but a bully.

A psychopathic bully.

Like my own father.

"Oh, my goodness."

The realization caught her off guard and she wrapped her arms around her middle. Her father was like this murderer. Just as evil. Just as dangerous. What other atrocities he had performed in his lifetime? Her mom could have been one of many victims. What about his wife or other girlfriends he had along the way?

Her chest tightened and she braced herself for more tears. Nothing. She was dry. Empty.

She stared at the strewn pages, her heart heavy.

Am I anything like him?

Bile rose in her throat.

No, my daughter, you are fearfully and wonderfully made.

Juliet sat up straight. The answer to her question came as clear as a bell. It wasn't audible but it resounded in her being. From the inside out. A snippet from Scripture and an overwhelming sense of peace like she hadn't known in a long time.

She closed her eyes. God. He was still here with her. Even though she had done all in her power to push Him aside and quiet His voice. Those familiar words from her favorite Psalm filled the emptiness in her heart. God saw her and knew her—even when she was being formed. Even when her earthly father wished she were gone.

Her phone chirped and she reached over to the bedside table. Seven o'clock. Bella was checking on her. Again.

Juliet cleared her throat. "Morning."

"Sorry, did I wake you? I wanted to make sure all was well. It was the deal, remember?"

"Do you think I have any of my father's traits?"

Bella was silent for a beat. "Whoa. What? No. I

know where you're going with this, and no. From the part of the manuscript I read, that man was everything you are not. You're a nurse, Juliet. You're gentle and kind and compassionate. Your heart's desire is to offer healing, not inflict pain. You've been dealt a blow with this new knowledge but please don't let it seep in and make you question who you are."

Bella's words brought a measure of comfort but it was nothing compared to the amazing feeling of God's presence within her. Juliet studied the ceiling. "I think God spoke to me a moment ago."

"He did?"

"It was a first. Nothing weird and there were no lightning bolts but I know He spoke words. I felt it in my soul, and it was crystal clear."

Bella let out a tiny gasp. "Sometimes He gets our attention more effectively with His still, small voice. Can I ask what He said?"

She sighed. "He called me His daughter and said I was fearfully and wonderfully made."

"Oh, I recognize those verses—Psalm 139?"

"Yep."

"Thought so. I love that whole Psalm. He called you His daughter... isn't it comforting? I find incredible peace in that truth. You know my story, and I've come to terms with the fact I'll never know my earthly father. I have my Heavenly Father and He's all I need."

"I guess." *She's right. I don't need or want to meet Dan even if I had a clue where to find him.*

"Does this mean you are back on speaking terms with God?" Juliet could hear the smile in her friend's voice.

"Not necessarily." She lifted her eyes to the ceiling again and remembered the unanswered prayers for her mom's healing. They hadn't made it past that barrier, had they? "I still have a lot of stuff to work through."

"But you can't doubt He's walking through this entire journey with you."

"Maybe." Juliet yawned and attempted to collect the pages into a pile. "Anyway, I should get up and feed this cat. She's getting all needy on me and I think I've confused her after being awake reading for most of the night."

Bella chuckled. "Did you get to finish the manuscript?"

"Yeah. At about three this morning, and then I lay awake steeped in my swirl of thoughts until sleep claimed me at some point."

"Oh. In that case, I'm *really* sorry to phone you so early." A coffee maker beeped in the background. "How was it? Did you get some answers at least?"

Juliet pinched the top of her nose. "Yes, I think so. The rest was the story of how Mom made ends meet when we arrived here in Florence, and then how she raised me. I had no idea. Absolutely no idea. She hinted at how hard it was when I was young, but somehow, she always made it sound like an adventure. Like we were privileged to get to be just the two of us."

She glanced at the dresser. A photo of them both smiling as they made sandcastles at the beach. "And now it's just me."

"You have us. You have your church family and your nurses at the hospital. You're not alone. I promise."

That's not how it feels. One more glance at the ceiling. Would she hear His voice again?

Juliet took a calming breath. "Thanks. I know. I guess it's cool to hear my story in Mom's own words."

"I'll bet. What a gift."

She picked up the framed photo. "A gift. Yes, I love that. I cried my way through reading it, but I'm grateful she documented it all for me."

"Are you going to be okay with letting the manuscript go?"

Juliet paused. "I hate the thought of burning it to ashes but I have to. It's what Mom wanted. I can't help thinking in her wisdom she believed it would be more healing for me if I destroyed it once I knew the truth. Moved on from it rather than dwelling on the past." *Perhaps it will be a chance for me start fresh like Mom did.*

Her phone vibrated in her hand and she checked the screen.

"Can I call you back? Angie's on the line and I want to see what's going on at the hospital."

"No problem. Speak to you later."

Juliet answered the other call. "Angie?"

"Hey. How are you?" Angie's voice was somber. Hushed.

Juliet swung her legs over the side of the bed. "What is it? What's happened now?"

"I'm sorry, love. I have some bad news."

Juliet clutched the phone and braced herself. Had Red struck again? Surely Max would have contacted her? "Please don't say another nurse has been hurt."

"No, it's not a nurse. It's not about that maniac at all." She let out a whimper. "It's wee Jasmine. I'm afraid she took a turn for the worse."

"NO." Please, God. No. I prayed so many times…

"She passed away in her sleep last night. It was very peaceful. I knew you would want to know. I'm so sorry." Angie sniffled on the other end of the phone.

They all loved the sweet girl and had been with her through a horrible journey. "Her parents wanted me to thank you for being so kind to her. You know you were her favorite."

No more tears. She couldn't even cry. Her insides were hollowed out, and she had nothing left to give. That darling child. She closed her eyes and recalled the last memory of Jasmine from Saturday as her fragile arms had wrapped around Juliet's neck. Her sweet smile as she lay in her hospital bed snuggling her stuffed bunny, Hopkins. Then that tear running down Max's cheek.

"Juliet? Are you still there?"

Why, God? Why? Haven't You taken enough?

She swallowed the boulder in her throat. "Yes. Yes, I'm still here. It's a shock, though, isn't it?"

"It is. We weren't expecting it. Listen, I have tomorrow off work. Why don't I come over to see you in the morning? I can bring some breakfast and we can talk. What do you say?"

Juliet squeezed her eyes shut. She had been debating her next step in the early hours that morning and now knew what she had to do. Hotheaded? Maybe, but she would not be talked out of this decision.

"Thanks, but I won't be here."

"No worries. Can I come some other time then?"

"I don't know when that would work. The thing is, I've made a decision. I'm going to Mexico."

"Mexico? When?"

"Tomorrow."

Chapter Sixteen

"MEXICO? WHEN?" BELLA'S VOICE WAS FRAUGHT with anxiety.

"Tomorrow. As soon as I can snag a flight. I have to do this."

Juliet balanced the phone between her shoulder and her ear as she pulled a suitcase from beneath the bed. Might as well start getting stuff ready. The phone call with Angie had ignited a fire in her belly and she had to act on her conviction before it was quenched by exhaustion and common sense.

"Do you have to do it so soon? I mean, you're still grieving. I'm not going to lie—I'm worried about you."

"I'm sorry but I have to get out of here. I feel like the walls are closing in on me, Bel." Now her laptop was dead. Just great. She plugged it in to charge the battery. "It doesn't even feel like home here anymore. I can't explain it exactly. It's like my entire life has shifted and I can't find my bearings." She sank onto the bed next to her suitcase. "I've lost my sense of home and I'm floundering. I don't like being out of control."

"I know you don't, but I hate seeing you so lost."

Juliet hugged her knees to her chest. "On top of everything else, Angie gave me some terrible news and I don't know how much more I can take."

"Not about the nurse who was attacked?"

"No. No, it was my patient, Jasmine. She passed away..."

Bella gasped. "I'm so sorry. I know how close you two were. I wish there were something I could do to help you with all this."

"There is. Don't try to talk me out of going away. Please. I have to do this for me before I go crazy. I have to do it for Mom, too."

"The manuscript ashes?" Bella's voice was soft.

Juliet walked into the kitchen and filled Ebony's dish. Poor, neglected cat was frantic. She hated suitcases.

"Yeah, the ashes. The manuscript is heartbreaking and beautiful. Part of me longs to hold onto it forever, her words, her soul, her story." It would be like reliving the funeral all over again. Her chest constricted at the memory. This time charred ashes instead of white rose petals…

"It's going to be hard to part with, isn't it?"

"The hardest thing ever, but I need to do this."

"I'm sorry. I get it. You want to respect her wishes."

"I have to. She was so specific: read her story and then burn it. Bury it beneath a palm tree in Mexico. Anywhere in Mexico, it doesn't matter. It's the principle of the thing."

Bella sighed into the phone. "I understand, but don't you want to read it through a few more times? There's no clock ticking telling you when you need to part with it. I don't want you to make a rash decision you may later regret."

"I know what you're thinking. I'm prone to act before I think things through but I feel in my gut this is the right time." *And it beats sitting around here depressed and lonely.*

"Do you believe Pippa wanted you to do this now?

You knew her better than anyone else and I can't argue if you think she intended you to react this fast."

"I knew Mom and she knew me. She would have guessed I wouldn't sit on this for a long time. I can't help believe she was thinking of me in making her request. I need to bury the past, the ugly bits at least. I thought about what you said—the stuff about my father doesn't define me. I've been this version of Juliet Farr all my life and hearing about my mother's awful past isn't going to change anything."

"I agree, and I think it's brave of you to go, but why now? Especially after hearing this sad news about Jasmine. Why not wait a week or two until you're feeling more like yourself again?"

Juliet blanched. "I don't think I'll ever feel like myself again. That's the problem. I don't even know who I am anymore. What my future is going to look like."

She walked through the living room over to the window, pulled back the sheers, and peered down onto Main Street. Life was going on as usual. Except a murderer was on the loose. She released the sheers and turned on her heel.

"I have some big decisions to make and I need some headspace. I'm scared if I stay here, I might allow the loneliness to swallow me whole."

Bella waited a beat. "Want me to come with you? You hate flying."

"To Mexico?" Juliet smiled. "You're a good friend, but I think I need to go on my own. Call it a spiritual journey or something. Could I get you guys to take me to the Eugene airport first thing tomorrow though? I can let you know what time as soon as I've booked a flight. It's a big ask on short notice. Otherwise, I'll grab a taxi."

"No, of course we'll take you. Adam can drive on the way and then I'll get some practice on the way back. Can't get you all jittery before you even begin."

"Thanks. You're the best." The cat wrapped her fluffy body around Juliet's legs. "Oh, the cat. What am I thinking? Would you take care of Ebony for me while I'm gone?"

"That's a given. I'm more concerned about what Max is going to say when he finds out. He's worried about you. You should have heard him last night at dinner."

Juliet huffed. "I can imagine."

"He still loves you something fierce, you know."

The look in his eyes on the beach had been confirmation: even after their time apart, he was very much in love with her.

"I still love him, too. I always will, but I need to figure out our relationship and I need some distance to do that. My head feels like it's stuffed with cotton balls at the moment and I'm scared stiff I'll make a mistake when it comes to Max." Mexico sounded more appealing by the minute.

"You know I'm praying for you, don't you?"

Juliet gritted her teeth. "A year ago, it would have been such a comfort, but the way I feel at the moment, it doesn't hold much weight. I simply don't trust God." She glanced at her mom's bedroom. There were too many unanswered prayers.

"In your relationship with Max, you mean?"

"With anything at all. Look at my life. Mom, Max, and even this madman on the loose." She let out a sigh. "When I was starting to wonder if perhaps He *did* care after all..."

"You mean the voice you heard earlier?"

"Yes, but then Angie tells me Jasmine's precious life has been taken and I'm back at square one with trusting Him. Why does He keep taking away the people I care for? I know better than to trust my emotions when it comes to faith but I don't understand anything anymore. I have to go. I'm too close to the pain here."

"I'm sorry. Really, I am. Please don't run away."

Juliet winced. "I'm not, I promise. I'll be back." Her eyes roamed the familiar rooms she had grown up in. She would come back, wouldn't she? "Listen, I'm going to get showered and make some calls. Turns out I have a lot to do today, after all." It felt good for a change after days of numbing apathy. "Are you coming into the store soon?"

"I'll be there in an hour or so."

"Great. I'll come down and fill you in on the details. See you later. Thanks for being there for me."

"Always. Bye for now."

Juliet closed her eyes.

Am I running away? Mom ran from a horrific situation but am I running from my feelings for Max? Running from God? Or is this part of my journey to find the freedom I need to move on with my life?

* * *

Juliet threw back her shoulders as she walked down the stairs and entered the bookstore. She had to assure Bella she was making the right decision in flying off to Mexico, so she plastered on a smile as she turned the corner…

"Hey."

"Max? What are you doing here?" A flush crept up her face as she froze in place. Where was Bella?

"I wanted to see you." His bright blue eyes danced as he set down a colorful picture book on pigs. Juliet's heart squeezed at the image of him reading a kids' book in light of his issues. "Bella will be back any second. She went to grab doughnuts."

"She left you in charge?" Juliet walked toward him, his musky aftershave a vivid reminder of happier days.

"She knew you were only a shout away."

"Did she tell you my plans?" Juliet lifted her chin.

Max stood and met her in front of the desk. "She said *you* should tell me." He narrowed his eyes. "Is it as ominous as it sounds?"

Juliet broke his gaze and extracted a black cat hair from her cream sweater. "I'm going to Mexico. Don't try to stop me."

"Whoa. I didn't see that coming. When?"

She looked him in the eye. "Tomorrow morning."

He gulped. "Can I ask why?"

She pulled herself up onto the desk and let her jean-clad legs dangle. "You know the manuscript my mom left for me?"

"Yeah. Bella said you were reading through it last night. It must have been difficult."

"It was a lot to take in. A lot for her to write, but she requested after I read it, that I would burn it, take the ashes to Mexico, and bury them under a palm tree."

Max's brow furrowed as he tried to follow the logic. "That's specific. Why Mexico?"

"It's a long story." Her shoulders slumped. "It was on a beach somewhere in Mexico where she began to make sense of her life, where she got her brave on, and chose freedom."

"You want to do likewise?"

Did she? Perhaps. Perhaps she needed to go there to make sense of her own life now. Maybe she *would* get her brave on—and find the freedom she craved. Freedom from this ache of abandonment. Freedom from loneliness. Freedom from fear...

"Yes. Yes, I really do. It's where she wants her story buried so that's where I'm headed."

He raked his fingers through his blond hair. "Whereabouts in Mexico?"

The bell above the door jangled and Juliet almost jumped out of her skin. Her head whipped around to the entrance and Bella hurried inside the store, bringing a gust of wind with her.

Juliet exhaled as her pulse returned to normal. "Hey. I was about to fill Max in on my Mexico plans." And having her friend as a buffer was a sudden relief.

"Good, I didn't miss anything. I have doughnuts." She set the paper bag on the table and peeled off her plaid scarf. "Help yourselves."

"Thanks." Juliet pulled out a pink frosted treat and offered the bag to Max.

He shook his head.

Weird. He never turned down food. Doughnuts were his favorite.

"Do you have a flight booked?" Bella hung her coat on the back of the chair.

"I do. I'm going via L.A. My flight leaves at eight in the morning."

Bella nodded. "That's fine. We can go to the airport before work."

Max cleared his throat. "We?"

"Adam and I are going to drop Juliet off."

"Right." His face fell.

Should she have asked him instead? No, this was

the right decision. They needed space. She needed space. Having him see her off at the airport could result in further heartache and more confusion. Or another kiss.

Bella interrupted her thoughts. "Where are you going to stay? Did you decide yet?"

"Yes." Her face broke into a smile. The plan had come together in a matter of minutes and now she wouldn't be alone in a foreign country. "I spoke with Madison this morning and—"

"No way. 'Madison-and-Luke' Madison?" Bella grinned. "I wondered if you might head in their direction. That does make me feel less worried about your safety." Her grin faded and she bit her lip. "Although after all you've been through and with Red on the loose, I'm still not sure you should travel alone."

Juliet held up her hands. "It's all arranged and there's nothing to worry about. They might not be the greatest flights since it's last minute, but I'll be fine. I'm flying out early with a hefty layover in L.A. and by Friday afternoon I'll be at their orphanage in Sonaja. They have a room for me and said I could stay as long as I needed. Of course, I'm sure they'll put me to work with the children, but it's my happy place and I think it'll be a great distraction. I miss the kids at the hospital."

Max reached over and touched her arm. "Bella told me about your patient, Jasmine. I'm so sorry. I know she was special to you." Juliet recalled how upset he had been as he watched on, and now she knew why. She studied his hand. Strong. Protective. Warm.

Max, I miss you.

"Yeah. It's heartbreaking for everyone." She met his gaze. "Another reason for me to make this trip tomorrow. I can't take anymore." She bit her lip.

"I can't begin to imagine what you're going through." Max gave her arm a gentle squeeze before shoving his hands in his pockets. "But I wish you weren't travelling alone."

"Are you offering to come along?" She clamped her mouth shut. Did she just ask that out loud?

His face lit up. "Would you even want me to?"

Juliet didn't answer for a moment. Did she want him to come with her? Or did she need this time alone to figure out her life and prove to herself that she was capable of making decisions? To discover a way to fill the emptiness and see what the future might hold?

"I don't know." Her voice cracked. At least she knew he was willing. That he would even consider leaving work and the Red case behind to be with her.

He let out a small sigh. "Right."

"I guess we can feel better knowing you'll be with Madison and Luke—and all those sweet kids." Bella sank into the chair. "I hated the thought of you wandering the streets of Mexico searching for the perfect palm tree. Although my offer still stands, if you want me to come with you. Plus, I'd love to see Madison and Luke again."

She had to do this by herself. She hadn't felt this purposeful in weeks. "You guys are both kind, offering to put your lives on hold for me. I'm fine though. You'll know where to contact me at the orphanage." Juliet nudged Max's leg with her foot. "I'll leave their number with you, too. To be honest, I have a feeling I might be safer down there than here at the moment. You'll keep me posted with the Red case?"

Max rubbed his jaw. "You bet. I have to agree on that count. I'm sure you'll find spending time with the kids healing, too." He lowered his eyes.

Would the subject of kids always bring him pain? He had seemed comfortable enough reading the picture book when she walked in. Perhaps it was more the thought of *her* with kids that hit home. Their kids. Juliet's heart melted.

"But will you allow me to do one thing for you before you go?"

"Sure." Juliet bit the inside of her cheek. What was she agreeing to?

"I'm guessing you need to burn this manuscript sometime today so you have the ashes ready to go."

"Yes. I hadn't thought that bit through yet." Tears burned behind her eyes at the mere notion of destroying her mom's words.

"Could I do it with you? You shouldn't be alone. Physically or emotionally. We could head down to the beach, make a tiny bonfire and have a moment for Pippa before you leave. I can finish work a bit earlier. What do you say?"

Juliet tilted her head. "I say it's the sweetest thing you could have suggested. Can you meet me there at five? It'll be getting dusk and not many people will be around at that time. It'll give me chance to run errands beforehand."

"Please let me come with you to run your errands?" Bella's blue eyes begged. "That way Max won't be stressed about you being alone, and I'll get to hang out with you before you leave."

"It'll make me feel better." Max lifted both his eyebrows. "Please?"

The walls were threatening to close in on her here. That plane couldn't take off fast enough with her in it. "Fine. You can babysit me this afternoon."

"Awesome, and then Adam and I could drop you at the beach at five after he comes to pick me up?"

She nibbled her doughnut. This was smothering but their concerns were valid. "I refuse to stay cooped up in here the whole time but, yes, I'll take you up on your offer. Thank you. I'll admit I am kind of skittish."

"I can't say I blame you." A muscle twitched in Max's jaw. "Everyone seems on edge in town at the moment. I can drive you home afterwards and make sure you're safe and sound. I'm guessing you'll want to get a good night sleep before your travels."

Juliet forced a smile. "Sleep's hit and miss these days, but I'll try to have an early night."

"Great. I know you hate having your wings clipped but you only have to humor me for a few more hours." He slid his phone from his pocket and grimaced. "I'm needed back at the station. I'll see you at five."

Juliet picked a sprinkle-covered doughnut from the bag and handed it to him. A peace offering of sorts. "One for the road."

She was rewarded with a lopsided grin. "If you insist."

Juliet watched him leave and then threw back her head. "That guy is killing me. Why does his smile still make me weak at the knees?"

"He's a good man. With a good heart." Bella chuckled as she opened her laptop on the desk. "And it's got your name written all over it."

Does it, though? I need some time away, for sure. Perhaps absence will make the heart grow even fonder.

The bell over the door jangled again, and a young couple strolled in.

Juliet hopped down from the desk. "I'll leave you to your customers. I should dig out some beach attire and finish packing my case."

"Now *that* makes me jealous. Sunshine and palm trees. Are you sure you don't need a travelling companion? Last chance." Bella wiggled her eyebrows.

"Next time."

"Fine. Go pack. Give me a shout if there's anything I can do for you from here."

"Will do. Thanks." Juliet's heart skipped a beat as she headed upstairs to her apartment. She felt alive for the first time in weeks. Was she emerging from the suffocating blanket of fog weighing her down?

I sure hope so.

Maybe it was the anticipation of sunshine on her shoulders. Or escaping the danger lurking in her hometown. Or perhaps it was simply the anticipation of sharing a special moment with Max that evening...

Chapter Seventeen

Five. He was right on time for Juliet—and there she was, her long hair blowing wild in the ocean breeze.

Max tucked the metal bin under his arm and jogged across the beach toward her, glad he had remembered to pick up some kind of receptacle.

He scanned the beach for Adam and Bella as he got closer—they were supposed to be here with her. No way should Juliet be on a beach by herself with Red still at large. He spotted them standing hand-in-hand at the water's edge, and breathed a sigh of relief.

Slowing his pace, he checked for other visitors. Just a couple of families out for a stroll. He drew his attention back to Juliet.

She was perched on an enormous, flat rock by the beach caves. The same one they had sat upon for their conversation on Saturday evening. He flinched at the memory, but the location was wise—secluded for the bonfire. The wind less violent.

She hugged a stack of papers to her chest, and he had a flashback to their high school days when he would see her marching down the hallways clutching her schoolwork. He'd been intrigued but too full of himself to take time to get to know a bookworm.

What an idiot I was back then. Didn't give her the time of day.

"Juliet?" His voice carried on the wind.

She turned around and offered him a smile.

His heart flipped as he approached the rock. "Hope you haven't been waiting long."

She shook her head. "It's fine. We just got here, and it's a perfect evening."

"It is." The sky was almost golden as the sun made its descent. "Perfect."

Bella and Adam must have heard the conversation because they soon joined them by the cave entrance.

"Hey, man, I see you came prepared." Adam pointed to the bin in Max's hands.

"You bet. I wanted to be safe and thought this was the best way to salvage the ashes."

"It's a great idea." Bella touched Juliet's shoulder. "Are you going straight back home afterwards?"

"If that's cool with my ride." She looked up at Max and blinked. "I suppose you still want to play bodyguard and drive me home?"

"Yes. Absolutely." He wasn't taking any chances with a lunatic on the loose. Perhaps she would be better off in Mexico after all—and perhaps he could end their time here on a positive note for their future. Maybe even a goodnight kiss.

Juliet nodded. "I hate it but I do appreciate it. Thanks for bringing me here, you two." She winked at Bella and Adam. "And for running me out to the airport tomorrow morning. I really am grateful."

"Our pleasure." Adam slid an arm around his wife's waist. "We'll pick you up at five-thirty in the morning. Should give us plenty of time."

Max gritted his teeth. He would have been happy to give her a ride. If only she had asked.

"Thanks." Juliet's hair blew in front of her face and she attempted to push it back with one hand still holding the papers. "Text me when you're outside The Book Nook."

Bella gazed up at Adam. "We will, but we should leave you both to it. Call me if you need anything tonight?"

"I promise."

As Bella and Adam headed back to their jeep, Max placed the bin on the hard sand in front of him and leaned against the rock next to Juliet, watching her face. Her eyes were wide and her hands trembled. She appeared much younger than her twenty-six years.

I wish I could hold you tight. Tell you how much you are loved.

No, he had to give her the space she had asked for… but she had to know he was here for her.

Juliet glanced down at the pages in her arms and he watched deep emotion cloud her features. Her green eyes brimmed with unshed tears.

"Are you one hundred percent sure you want to do this now? You can still go to Mexico. You could even burn the front cover or something if you want to keep a hold of this. I can imagine how priceless it is to you."

"I have to do it." She looked down at the crumpled pages in her arms. "I don't like it but it's what Mom wanted. I have to respect that, don't I?"

"It's your decision. I support you either way."

Juliet raised her chin and gazed out across the ocean. The sound of waves slapping the gigantic rock formations before them was like a symphony of sorrow. Letting go of Pippa's words forever would be like losing another part of her, wouldn't it?

"Mom loved the beach. That's one reason why I have to go and find a palm tree in Mexico. Thank you for suggesting we burn the papers here." Her voice was a whisper.

"I know you both spent a lot of time at the beach together. Especially when you were younger." She had shared many childhood memories with him when they were together.

"Even with our red hair and freckled fair skin." Juliet slid down from the rock. "We had so many sunburns, but we loved it here."

"I can't remember Pippa with red hair." Max tilted his head to one side. The Pippa he knew had silver-gray hair, short and trendy.

"It was a beautiful auburn color but then she went gray when she got cancer the first time. It suited her." Juliet's mouth quivered. "She was always gorgeous."

"She was." Max stretched an arm out and Juliet nestled herself into his side.

A perfect fit.

He felt her shoulders shaking. She was crying. It was time.

"Mind if I pray?"

She hesitated for several seconds and then shook her head. "Go ahead."

"Heavenly Father, thank You for the beautiful memory of Pippa. We can't pretend to understand Your ways, but we're leaning into the truth that You are sovereign and You know best. Always. Thank You that Pippa is now with You, pain-free… and until Juliet can be reunited with her mom in Heaven, I ask for Your love and peace to fall over her in the most comforting way possible. Thank You for this gift of a manuscript with a story to give Juliet some answers. As we carry out Pippa's wishes, would You fill Juliet's heart with hope for her future? In Jesus' name. Amen."

"Thanks. That was lovely." Juliet wiped a lone tear from her cheek, took a deep breath, and stepped from

Max's embrace toward the bin.

Max slid a box of matches from his pocket and set the lid on the sand. "I can put the lid back on if the ashes start flying away. Are you ready?"

"Yes." She pushed her wayward hair behind her ears. "Let's do this." She leaned over, placed the pile of papers in the bottom, and stood back.

"It won't take long." Max lit the match and touched it to a couple of different spots before dropping it on top of the manuscript. He turned and took Juliet into his arms. She needed him and it felt good.

Lord, I want to love this woman and care for her. Is there a way? Can we ever work through our issues? Does she really think adoption could be a possibility for us? She mentioned it, but then left... I'm so confused.

Max held her close into his side, grateful they could be together to watch the burning process. He listened to the crackle and smelled the acrid smoke as it escaped into the chilled air.

"Max." Juliet gasped. "The ashes are flying away."

He released her, grabbed the lid, and was about to slam it down on the bin when Juliet caught hold of his arm. "Wait. Let's watch a few of them float."

Max froze and observed particles of Pippa's life dance pirouettes on the ocean breeze as they rose into the graying sky.

He found his voice. "It's... magical." He glanced at Juliet's profile and saw a look of awe and pure wonder as she watched the ashes dance.

"It's *so* Pippa Farr." Juliet smiled, her head back, eyes closed, arms wrapped around her middle.

Max crouched down and secured the lid on top of the bin, saving the remaining ashes.

She needed some quiet to ponder and reflect. Time to release. This was a special mother-daughter moment and he had no desire to intrude.

The ashes cooled.

"Thank you." After a few moments, she took his hand and pulled him to his feet. "It wasn't easy but it was the right thing to do. I'll never forget it."

"Me neither." He looked into her eyes and wiped a tear from her cheek with his thumb. "You're a brave lady."

"I don't feel brave, but I'm trying. For Mom."

He dug into his jacket pocket with his free hand. "Here. This is for you. To carry the ashes." He presented the little mahogany box he had picked up from the jewelers in town on his way.

A smile split her beautiful face. "Max, this is lovely." She held it with reverence, turning it in her fingers. "The carvings on it are gorgeous. I'll keep it always. It's perfect to take to Mexico."

"You might want to put it in your case rather than your carry-on. I'd hate for these ashes to get confiscated in security for some reason."

She nodded. "I hadn't even thought of that. Good idea. It's a decent step up from the ziplocked bag I had planned on using."

"You deserve special. Can I fill it with the ashes for you?"

"Please. I'll take one last look at the ocean. I can't believe I'm soon going to be staring out at a warmer version."

"Go ahead. Catch the last of that spectacular sunset. I won't be a minute." Max watched as Juliet trudged down to the shoreline, hugging herself against the elements. He knelt in the sand and transferred the ashes from the bin to the box with as much precision as possible—no easy feat with the breeze blowing.

Done. He smiled at the small slip of paper he had pulled from his pocket and inserted underneath the ashes. Hopefully Juliet would spot it when she was under the palm tree and it would encourage her heart.

Use these words, Lord. Your words...

"Thanks for doing all this." Juliet stood over him. "I appreciate it."

He got to his feet and handed her the filled box. "You know I'm here for you."

She cocked her head. "What does that mean?"

Good question. What did he mean? He couldn't go throwing those words to a vulnerable, hurting young woman unless he intended to back them up with his actions. If only he was enough for her.

"Are you here for me as a friend or something more? Will you still be here when I get back from Mexico? Even if your case is wrapped up and there's no danger to protect me from?" Her chin wobbled and she took a deep breath. "Do we have any hope for a future together?"

Why couldn't he choke the words out? Yes, he wanted to marry her. Yes, he wanted a future together— but what about children, having a family?

"Yes. Yes, to all of it, but we still have so much to discuss." Could she really love him for a lifetime knowing he was not whole? "We need to decide if you can be happy without your dream family. You have to understand it's just not that simple."

Her mouth dropped open. "It's not that simple? What you mean is *you* haven't decided what I want or what I need yet, have you?" Her face reddened. "Thanks for your help tonight, but I've got it from here." She spun away from the caves and walked away in the direction of the parking lot.

Taken aback, Max watched for a moment. Something about the way she braced against the blustering wind, hugging her middle, head down, made her look broken, alone, and in pain. His heart squeezed.

"Wait. Juliet, can we talk about this before you leave?" He picked up the still-warm bin and fell into step beside her.

"No. I have to get home to finish packing."

"Do you want me to come in with you? I don't mind helping you pack."

"You mean be my bodyguard and decide what I should pack? No thanks. I'm fine on my own." She shot him a look.

Stubborn. If she wouldn't listen to him as a friend, she needed to listen to him as a police detective. She could be in serious danger. "I don't want to scare you, but this Red guy could have your personal details from your file. He could have your address. You know that, don't you?"

"Which is why I'm better off in another country. Don't you think?"

"You may be right, but I hope you'll be cautious in Mexico. I still think it's extreme."

She stopped and turned to him. "I'm not running away." She licked her lips and hesitated a beat too long. Did she believe that? "You know why I'm going to Mexico. This is about Mom."

"I wish you'd wait." He regretted the words as soon as they left his mouth. His decision-making was not a popular topic.

"You don't get to wish." She continued marching. "I don't know how long I'll be gone. I signed off at work for another month."

"A month?" The thought of not seeing her for that long made his chest ache. He could even be moved on to another case by then.

"Maybe more." When they reached his car, she sighed and leaned a hip against the vehicle. "I don't know what you want from me anymore. I'm confused and frustrated on so many levels. I have to get my life in order. I have decisions to make about my job, my faith, and my future. I think I'll find some answers in Mexico. I have to. I feel like I'm going to either implode or waste away here."

Max nodded. This was about more than just their relationship. She had a great deal to work through and he would pray for her. She needed God's wisdom in this. "Just be careful. Please? I'll notify you about the case, but will you let me know when you've arrived at Madison and Luke's place?"

"Fine." She puffed a strand of hair from her face, and with that, Storm Juliet had blown over. "Hey, I'm sorry. I get that you're worried about me but I have to do this. I promise I'll stay in touch and let you know when I've found the perfect palm tree for the ashes." She rubbed the top of the mahogany box. "You had a part in this, after all."

"Thanks. I'll be praying for you, Juliet. I know you're struggling with God at the moment, but He can take it. He'll still be there for you when you're ready. You're missing your mom like crazy, but you're His child, too. He loves you more than you can begin to imagine and He's not going anywhere."

She let out a sigh. "We should go."

There was nowhere she could go where God was

not. He would hold onto that promise.

"Please stay safe while you're away from me." *I hate the thought of not being around to protect you.*

He pulled her into a hug, and held on for as long as he dared. Her hair smelled of lavender and he ran a hand over the length of it.

Oh, Juliet. Please take care of yourself, sweetheart.

She seemed to melt into his embrace, and before he knew what was happening, his lips found hers for one last, desperate kiss. One lasting memory to savor.

She drew back and stared into his eyes. "What are we doing, Max?"

"We're going to figure it out. Don't give up on us." He opened the car door and surveyed the surrounding area as she climbed in.

She bit her lip. "I won't, but would you do one thing for me while I'm away?"

Was she kidding? "Anything. Name it."

"Catch this guy before he hurts anyone else. Please, catch Red."

Chapter Eighteen

"Ladies and gentlemen, please be seated and check to ensure your seat belt is securely fastened."

Juliet felt for the metal clasp with trembling fingers. Yes, she was more than ready for take-off. She clenched her jaw and sank back into the seat as the plane taxied toward the runway.

I hate flying.

Travelling was fun, flying was not. Take-off and landing in particular. At least now she had an aisle seat with room to stretch and no one to inconvenience if she needed to use the bathroom.

She had been lamenting the fact that she was stuck with a middle seat to Bella earlier that morning due to the last-minute booking, and then—a perfect gentleman had restored her faith in humanity.

He caught her eye when she arrived at their row, and right away he offered her his aisle seat. He then moved over to make sure she had enough room to stow her carry-on under the chair in front. She couldn't help noticing how different he looked from Max. He was equally handsome but with hazel eyes, dark brown hair—a little longer on top, and a trimmed mustache-beard combo. He wore smart jeans and a navy collared shirt. Thirty-something. He looked safe and respectable and like a decent travelling neighbor.

And no wedding ring. Yes, she had peeked.

She tried not to notice but he also smelled delightful. The elderly lady by the window had already made mention of the delicious aftershave. Poor guy.

The plane began its roll down the runway, and Juliet forced herself to take deep, cleansing breaths. People did this every single day. It wasn't a big deal. Flying was just another layer of stress to add to her burdens of sorrow and grief.

Don't think about the mass of metal about to launch itself into the wild blue yonder.

"Are you all right, Miss?"

Juliet cracked open her eyes and turned toward her neighbor. "Yes, don't mind me. I'm not a fan of flying, that's all." She clenched and unclenched her fingers on the armrests.

His eyes shone. "Can I tell you a secret?"

She shrugged. "Sure."

"This is my fiftieth flight this year."

"Fifty?" She wrinkled her nose. "Are you a pilot?" Who else would do this voluntarily?

His laugh was deep and warm. "No, nothing as glamorous, I'm afraid. I'm in sales and get to travel way more often than I would like."

"Oh, and you don't mind it?"

He leaned back into his chair with an easy smile. "I used to hate it. Trust me, it's the sort of thing you get used to. I haven't experienced any plane problems yet. Delays, yes. Crashes, no. They say it's safer than driving around town. I tend to believe them."

Juliet released her death grip on the armrests and wiped her hands on her jeans. "Makes sense, I suppose."

"Do you drive?"

She nodded. "I love driving. I don't ever think about crashing my car. I'd never go anywhere if I did."

The plane began picking up speed and Juliet needed to concentrate. She shut her eyes tight and clasped the armrests again. This was the worst part...

"I lost my wife in a car crash."

Juliet's eyes flew open. "Excuse me?" Had she heard him correctly?

"My wife. She died in a car crash. It's probably why I prefer travelling by plane." He stared straight ahead.

Juliet's hand flew to her mouth. "That's awful. I'm so sorry."

"Thanks. It was a long time ago. Almost six years now." He let out a ragged sigh and Juliet's heart squeezed.

"My mom just died." There. It was out. She hadn't planned on sharing her grief with a complete stranger. Usually, she would pray about the situation but she was in non-communication mode with God at the moment and went with her gut instead.

His hand covered hers on the armrest. "Really? My heart breaks for you. I'm sorry for your loss, too."

"Thanks." The weightless sensation of take-off fluttered in her stomach. Totally unrelated to his touch, right?

She stared down at their hands. *How do I feel about this? Uncomfortable, but not altogether unacceptable. How many times have I comforted a stranger as a nurse?*

He followed her gaze and pulled his hand away. "I know how lonely grief can make a person feel."

She nodded. "Sometimes it feels easier opening up to a complete stranger than those closest to you." *Is that normal?* Since life had turned upside-down, she had no idea what was normal and right anymore.

"Perhaps it has a lot to do with timing." He let out a quick chuckle. "Here you are, trapped in a plane with nowhere to hide and the opportunity to unload on someone you may never see again. Nothing to lose."

"Hmm. Maybe you're onto something there. Although I'm not sure you want me to unload everything." The plane might be lifting freely into the sky but her soul was heavy with grief and pain.

"Lots of baggage?"

"I should say, and not just what's in the cargo hold."

He nodded. "You and me both. Do you want the good news?"

"Always."

"You survived the take-off and we are now on our way to sunny L.A." He broke into a grin.

Juliet leaned forward and peered through the sliver of window. "I barely noticed. Thanks for the distraction."

The dozing woman on his other side stirred for a moment.

How could she sleep through take-off? "I should stop my chattering before I wake up our friend here."

"I think she's out for the count already." He shared a smirk with Juliet.

"Wise woman." Juliet dug into the seat pocket for her novel.

"Before you get lost in your book, can I ask what takes you to L.A.?" Those warm, hazel eyes pierced her soul.

Wasn't expecting that. Is he interested in me? Like romantically? Maybe he's merely curious and likes to chat if he does a lot of travelling. She adjusted the collar of her soft gray blouse.

"I'm on my way to Mexico. Which means another take-off before landing at my final destination." She checked her watch and cringed at the thought of another flight after a six-hour layover.

"No way. I'm heading to Mexico, too. Vacation?"

"No, it's a long story. I'm visiting friends who run an orphanage there. I'm hoping to get some down time, too, though. How about you? Is this one of your many work trips?"

He shook his head. "No, this is vacation time. It's been a manic year and I'm in desperate need of some sunshine and rest in Colima."

"That's where I'm going, too." What were the chances?

"No way." He wiped a hand down his face. "That's bizarre."

She angled her shoulders to face him. "Have you been to Colima before?"

"Several times. You're going to love it."

"I've never been to Mexico at all."

"Not much for travelling?" He raised an eyebrow. He already knew how much she detested flying.

"I went to Hawaii with my mom when I was in high school, but otherwise, I've only travelled in the States. I have to admit, I'm looking forward to seeing Mexico and getting to know the area where my friend lives now."

"She's at an orphanage, hey? Fantastic."

"Yeah, she married a missionary and ended up joining him in his work in Sonaja."

He nodded slowly. "Sonaja. Must be an amazing experience. Especially at an orphanage. I love kids." His eyes filled. Was he thinking about his late wife and the family they never had?

"Me, too." Juliet sighed. Max. Every time she thought of children, she thought of Max and the fact he would never have biological kids of his own. It wasn't the end of the world, was it? Evidently, it was to him. At least so much that it meant the end of the road for them as a couple. What was he feeling now? She had some serious processing to do.

She rolled her shoulders.

I need this break. Some time away for me to decide if I want to have biological children or could consider a family made through adoption. Or no kids at all. Also, to consider my future and if it can include Max. Or someone else.

Perhaps she would be a pediatric nurse for the rest of her life and care for other people's kids instead. Thinking of nurses, how were Angie and all her friends back at the hospital? How were Caroline and Zoe? Could there have been another attack already?

Oh, Lord...

She stopped herself short. Praying had always been such a natural part of her life, it was proving difficult to keep from crying out to God even when she wasn't officially talking to Him.

"Can I ask what you do for a living?"

Her neighbor cut into her thoughts. She should put a name to his handsome face. "I'm a nurse. Pediatrics. Hence the love of kids. Can I ask what your name is? I feel like we've done a lot of sharing for two people who are nameless."

The grin again. "Sure, it's Richard." He reached out a hand and shook hers. "Pleased to meet you. For the record, I guessed you were a nurse."

She wrinkled her nose. "You did?"

"You have a caring yet confident air about you, your nails are clipped short, and you don't wear nail polish. Plus, you check your watch in a particular manner."

"I'm impressed. I'm Juliet, by the way." This was going to be a long shot, but she had a hunch. "I hope you don't mind me asking, but was your wife a nurse, too?"

Pain etched his features and he nodded. "Am I that transparent?"

"Not at all. You know nurse things. Usually people aren't that observant."

"I guess so. Some things you don't forget. When you marry a nurse, you marry into a lifestyle. It's an admirable vocation." He tilted his head. "Are you married?"

"No." She blinked at his question and peeked at her bare ring finger. Would it ever be graced with a gold band? "No, not married."

I really don't want to expound on my relationship woes...

"Would you like anything to drink here?" A flight attendant flashed a smile at them as she tended her cart of beverages and pretzels.

Juliet pulled down her tray. "Water for me, please. No ice."

"Same here, thanks." Richard pulled down his tray, too.

Their third member of the row was now snoring, oblivious to her surroundings.

Must be nice.

The attendant passed two plastic cups filled with water and Juliet sipped from hers before placing it on her tray. "Thank you."

"Snacks?"

Juliet eyed the toddler-sized pretzel packet. "No, thanks."

After the attendant turned her attention to the opposite row, there was an awkward silence where Juliet didn't know whether to continue chatting with her new friend or to start reading the book she had been dying to crack open all week.

Richard made the decision for her when he pulled a pair of earbuds from his pocket and slipped them on. He plugged them into the armrest jack, settled back into his chair, and pushed the button to recline. Yes, he was a comfortable flier.

Juliet read the first paragraph of her book and then had to go back and re-read it. Why was it so hard to concentrate these days? And now she was more than aware of the man sitting close beside her with his eyes closed, still smelling delightful.

Her curious nature was desperate to know what had happened to his wife. Had he been driving? Had someone else crashed into her? How old was she? Did they have kids?

Why do I even care?

She squinted at the page and tried again.

***

The seat belt lights illuminated and the captain's voice came over the loudspeaker announcing their imminent descent. Richard righted his seat and Juliet slipped her book into her bag.

"Ready for the landing?" His eyes glinted. Was he teasing her? Not funny.

"I kind of have to be." Juliet pushed her long hair behind her ears and forced her shoulders to relax.

"Want a mint? I find it helps with the ear thing." He pulled a packet from his shirt pocket and offered it to her.

"Thanks." She popped one in her mouth.

"What happened to your mom, if you don't mind me asking."

Juliet opened her mouth to speak and then shut it. This was hard.

"Sorry if it's too personal. I've been wondering as I listened to my jazz."

Juliet sighed. "Cancer. It was cancer that killed her." A lump formed in her throat. Would it ever get easier to say out loud?

He gritted his teeth. "It's a beast. I'm sorry. It got my girl, too."

What? Juliet whipped her head around. "Wait, I thought you lost your wife in a car crash?" Why would he lie about that?

He nodded, his face like granite. He was doing well at masking his emotions. "Correct, and then I lost my young daughter to cancer."

It felt like a punch in the gut. Juliet was lost for words. Which rarely happened. She saw children battling cancer and all manner of awful sicknesses at work, but this one hit hard. It reminded her of Jasmine. Sweet, brave girl. She would be missed by everyone.

The downward pull on her body as they descended in the plane seemed to affect her heart also. To lose a wife and then a daughter way too soon was unbearable. He couldn't be more than thirty-five, tops. No wonder he travelled so much. Kept himself busy. Was it healthy to go on vacation all by himself?

Why do people have to go through this pain, God?

"I don't know what to say." She uttered the pathetic words with tears in her eyes.

"I know. It stinks. There's not much to say."

Juliet's entire body jolted as they hit the tarmac, snapping her out of their cocoon of grief. So much for a smooth landing.

"Are you going to be okay?"

He was asking *her*? "Yes, yes, of course."

Fellow travellers gathered bags and children as they readied themselves to disembark. She spotted a blond guy with a sleeping baby over his shoulder and her thoughts were drawn to Max. Again. He would be a wonderful father, no matter how it happened.

"Wouldn't it be something if we were on the next flight together?"

Juliet turned back to Richard. "You never know." She put out a hand, which he shook with care.

Please don't let me be blushing.

She looked down and noticed a tattoo on his wrist where the shirt cuff rose. "Take care, Richard. Thanks for helping me to not lose my flying cool."

"The pleasure was all mine."

She grabbed her bag, turned, and followed the stream of passengers down the aisle.

I hope I meet Richard again.

The thought was followed by a wave of guilt. She scowled as she shuffled along. Was it a bad thing? What about Max? He had occupied that portion of her heart for so long—even while he was away—it seemed as if she were cheating on him to even consider an attraction to another man.

I don't know what I want anymore.

One thing was for certain: she needed space.

But she couldn't shake the intrigue stirring within her after meeting the kind man with the devastating story and two hearts tattooed on his wrist.

Chapter Nineteen

"OH, MY GOODNESS, YOU'RE HERE, FOR real."

Juliet turned from the yellow taxi, one bag slung over her shoulder and a rolling suitcase at her side. "Madison, are you ever a sight for sore eyes." She looked wonderfully tanned in her bright yellow sundress, her dark brown hair tied in a topknot.

Before she could move, Juliet was enveloped in a warm hug from her dear friend.

"Welcome to *Esperanza*, our humble abode." Madison pulled back and shook her head. "This is surreal. Isn't it?"

"I can't believe I'm here." Juliet looked up at the high stuccoed walls at the front of the property. She knew from her cab ride down the hill that the beach was close behind the orphanage. Through the front gate opening, she could make out the single-story white painted building and a thrill of excitement spread through her. The children.

She turned back to Madison and squeezed her hand. Tendrils of dark curls fell about her pretty face and her eyes were bright. Alive. *Things must be going well.* "You look amazing. Mexico suits you."

"Thank you. It's home for me now. It's yours, too, for as long as you need it. You must be exhausted. Come on inside and let's get you settled."

"Thanks. Exhausted. Yes. Although the cab ride was exhilarating, to say the least." Juliet allowed Madison to take the case from her and followed her past the open iron gate and up a wide gravel path. "I can't believe how hot it is." She pulled her blouse away from her clammy skin and squinted up at the bright sunshine filtering through surrounding palm trees. Palm trees. The reason she was here…

"It's cooler in the mornings. Siestas are the best invention ever." Madison winked. "You'll see."

"Sounds good to me." Juliet stopped to smell one of the huge cerise blooms on the lush foliage at the side of the path. It was sweet and heady. "I couldn't get over all the exotic flowers I saw on my drive here."

"I know, it's gorgeous. I'm sorry you had to catch a cab. I was hoping to pick you up from the airport myself but we couldn't swing it this afternoon. How were the flights? I know it's not your favorite mode of transportation."

Juliet continued walking in the direction of large double doors and wrinkled her nose. "Not too bad, to be honest. I met this guy…"

"Wait. What?" Madison's eyes bugged. "So, are things still on hold with Max?"

"Calm down, I met this man on the plane and he was just a kind travelling companion who helped soothe my nerves, that's all." *He gave me courage to handle the second flight by myself, no problem.* "As for Max— let's just say it's complicated." Even after mulling everything over on her journey, she was no closer to finding answers than when she left.

Madison put a hand on Juliet's arm. "I'm sorry, and I'm heartbroken about your mom. Goodness, we have a lot to talk about, don't we?"

The orphanage doors opened ahead of them.

"Where's our favorite nurse?" She recognized Luke's voice.

He came through the doorway, a huge grin on his face and two little girls wearing bright, flowery dresses in his arms. They giggled as they peeked at her from behind long, dark hair.

"Now this is what I've been looking forward to. Seeing you guys in action and meeting the children. Hola, everyone."

Luke set the girls on the ground and they both gazed up at him. He nodded and they left him in the dust as they ran bare-footed and embraced Juliet from either side.

She couldn't help but laugh. "This feels good."

"Let Miss Juliet come inside, you two." Madison stroked the taller girl's black, silky hair. "Our guest is tired after her journey."

The girls scurried off into the building.

"They speak English?" Juliet joined Luke and gave him a hug.

"They do. Other than the baby, of course, all twelve of the children are doing well with the language. In fact, they're like sponges when it comes to learning anything, and English is something we've been working on. If they speak and write it, they will have a huge advantage when they leave school and go into the workforce."

Juliet blew a stray hair from her face, grateful she had braided it between flights when she was waiting in L.A. "Thank goodness. My Spanish is lousy. I was dreading the thought that I'd have to resort to miming for communication."

"It's so great to have you here." Luke took the case from Madison. "Let's get out of the heat."

Juliet exhaled as she walked into the building. The coolness was an instant relief. "Do you have air conditioning in here? It's so nice and cool."

"No." Madison closed the front doors behind them. "The thick stone walls help, but we manage to keep it comfortable with a few fans and by closing the curtains. If you do get too hot, we have a quick fix."

Luke grinned. "You're going to love it. You ladies carry on, I'll go put your case in your room. Shall I take your bag, too?"

"Thanks so much." Juliet gave him her oversized purse and Madison grabbed her hand.

"Walk this way." She ushered Juliet down the whitewashed corridor to the rear of the building. "Open the door to your own personal slice of paradise." Pride and joy colored her voice as she stepped aside.

Juliet pushed the heavy wooden door open and gasped. The spacious yard was surrounded by tall iron railings draped with deep green foliage and it sloped down to the beach in all its glory.

"I knew the beach was close by but you are literally on it here. It's fabulous." The heat hit her again as she stepped outside.

Madison followed and closed the door behind her. "This is our play area for the kids." A basic playground lay out on their left as they walked toward the beach. "On the right is our vegetable garden, where we're trying to grow some onions, peppers, and whatever else I can manage. It's a learning curve after living in Seattle. Also, of course, we have coconuts up in the shady palm trees."

"I absolutely love it." Juliet walked to the gate at the bottom of the yard and peered through the railings to the ocean view. "This is perfect. The sunshine alone helps." She sighed and turned back to Madison. "Thanks so much for letting me come on short notice."

"It's our pleasure. Let's sit for a minute while it's quiet. It won't last for long. The older kids will be home from school soon and siesta time is almost finished for the little ones." She slid two wooden stools from beneath a patio table. "We haven't had many visitors yet. Chloe and Nathan came out, but they want to start a family soon so we may not see them out here again for a while."

"Really? That's exciting for them." Juliet forced a smile. She was pleased for Madison's younger sister and her husband, yet it burned. Why did her kid issues with Max have to put a damper on everyone else's joy?

Madison frowned. "You okay?"

No, not at all, but I'm not ready to dive in with Max details yet. Juliet pulled her braid to one side in an attempt to cool her neck. Thick, long hair was going to be a challenge here. "Sure. I'm fine. Tired and hot. I may be tempted to cut this mane off after a couple of days in Mexican humidity."

"Don't you dare." Madison took a stray tendril of red hair in her fingers. "It's your one beauty."

Juliet batted her eyelids and they both burst into laughter. The *Little Women* quote had been a standing joke between them since they first met.

"No worries, I won't do anything drastic. This red hair of mine is more of a curse than a blessing at the moment." She frowned at the thought of her nurse friends at home and made a mental note to text Angie and check on how everyone was doing at the hospital.

"What do you mean?" Madison leaned forward.

"It's one of the reasons I jumped on a plane in a hurry. You know I told you on the phone about this guy on the loose targeting nurses in our area?"

"Yes." Madison shivered. "Sounds so creepy."

"Creepier still, he's only attacking nurses with red hair."

"What?"

"I know. Enough said. It's been stressful on top of Mom's funeral." She drummed her fingers on the table. "Then Max turned up again out of nowhere."

"Which you have to tell me about. When you're ready." Madison put a hand on Juliet's arm.

She nodded. "I will. Promise."

Where do I begin?

"Drinks, ladies?" Luke came outside with a shy little boy in his wake, who clutched Luke's leg as he walked. "We have mango juice. Our specialty here at Esperanza."

"Thanks. It looks fantastic." Juliet waved at the boy, accepted the sweating glass, and took a long sip. The cool sweetness slipped down her throat with ease. "Wow. It's delicious. So refreshing."

Luke bowed his head. "Why, thank you. I poured it from the carton myself. Now prepare yourself because siesta time is over and this serene moment is done for another day." He cringed. "Sorry in advance."

The next second, the playground was invaded by screaming children as they streamed through the door behind Luke. There were maybe seven of them clamoring to go down the plastic slide or take a turn on the swings. Luke headed back indoors and a blonde woman around Juliet's age took his place. She walked over and offered a hand.

"Hi, I'm Carla. You must be Juliet." Her face broke into a huge grin.

"Nice to meet you." Juliet stood and shook her hand. "You must be the Canadian Madison told me about."

"Guilty." Carla adjusted her trendy purple glasses on her nose. "I've been here almost as long as Luke. They can't get rid of me, I'm afraid. I'll catch up with you later." With that, she was dragged toward the swing by the shy boy.

Madison laughed. "She'll be pushing those swings for hours. The kids adore her."

Juliet sat back down and caught the eye of one of the young girls she had met at the front door earlier. She beckoned and the girl grabbed her tiny friend. They wandered over and stood either side of Juliet's chair.

"Hello, again. What are your names?" On closer inspection, they could be sisters they looked so alike with their rosebud lips and button noses.

"Lola." The younger one, maybe four years old, whispered her name and then stuck her thumb in her mouth.

"My name is Rosa." The older one made the announcement in a bold voice and gave Juliet a confident grin.

"Pleased to meet you both. I'm Juliet." She reached over and gave each of them a gentle hug. They both touched her red hair before erupting into giggles and retreating to the playground.

"You made their day." Madison blew a kiss to one of the little boys who was watching the grown-ups with wide eyes. He blew one back and ran to the slide.

"Tell me about the girls."

"Lola and Rosa are sisters."

Juliet nodded. Her suspicions were on track. "How old?"

"Four and six. They've been at the orphanage since Lola was a newborn. There's no one else to care for them."

Juliet's heart broke.

Just like Mom's experience.

Luke appeared again, this time with a chunky baby boy in his arms. "Who wants Angel-time?"

"Who is this darling?" Juliet put out her arms to accept the bundle.

"Angel. By name and by nature. He's our newest family member here and likes to be cuddled whenever possible." Luke deposited the baby and was commandeered by the other kids.

"Suits me fine. I like to be held, too." Juliet pulled back his sunhat and looked into huge, adoring eyes. "Oh, I think I've fallen in love."

Madison chuckled. "I know what you mean. Those eyes make me melt into a puddle."

"Such long lashes. Most women would kill to have lashes like these." She stroked his downy cheek and sighed. "How old is our sweet Angel?" He stared up at her as he sucked on a pudgy thumb.

"He's ten months."

"Ten months?" It didn't add up. Juliet would have guessed five at the most. "He seems small for his age. How long has he been with you guys?"

"Nearly two months." Madison bit her lip. "He came to us from an unfortunate situation. He's thriving now, believe it or not. You should have seen him when he first arrived." Her eyes flashed. "It was heartbreaking, but we're hoping he'll catch up and start wanting to crawl around on his own soon. He seems content to be held close by us for now, so we're taking it one step at a time."

Juliet snuggled him into her chest. "Consider me signed up for Angel duty whenever needed."

"That would be a massive help. We could always use more hands on deck, especially with Angel. He almost needs one-on-one care, which stretches us pretty thin. I can't stop thinking God knew we needed you here with us."

Juliet squirmed. *I can't handle talking about God. I don't want to hear how He is always faithful and knows what we need. Not now.*

"What?" Madison cocked her head.

"Let's just say my faith is also on my list of issues to be sorted out."

Madison stood with a smile. "You know I'm here for you whenever you want to talk. I'll be praying for you, regardless."

"Fine."

"Before you get sunburned, let's go inside and meet Maria, our wonderful housekeeper, cook, and general lifesaver. You'll love her. Then I'll show you to your room. I'm sure you want to change out of those jeans and you're welcome to have a rest while I get ready for the school kids to arrive home."

Juliet looked over at the playground where some of the children were whispering and pointing at her. "Sounds great. Although I think I may be needed for some playtime soon."

I'm going to get my kid-fix here, that's for sure.

Heart full, she kissed the baby's head and followed Madison back into the building.

* * *

Juliet sat up in a strange bed, disoriented and exhausted. What day of the week was it? Friday? Probably. She had changed into shorts and a T-shirt, then laid down for a ten-minute power nap. She checked her watch. Make that four hours.

So much for playtime. She was a lousy guest. Time to go and see what was happening. Her stomach rumbled. Maybe some food.

Other than a gentle hum of conversation, all was quiet and a glance at the window told her it was dark outside. Had she missed the children? They probably went to bed early to give the grown-ups a break.

She rolled off the bed and padded over to the tiny sink in the corner of her room, where she splashed cold water over her face. Better. She found a towel hanging next to the sink and patted her skin dry. Her reflection in the mirror made her grimace. She pulled her hair free of her braid and ran her fingers through it. Slight improvement. Smoothing her hands over her crumpled clothes, she looked down at her bare feet.

Flip-flops. Madison had given her instructions to wear something on her feet at all times in the home due to scorpions. *Scorpions*? She didn't need telling twice. She slipped into her flip-flops with a shudder and went in search of her hosts.

Juliet stopped at the edge of the living area and found Madison and Luke on the sofa talking with Carla. "Hey, guys. I'm so sorry. I must have fallen asleep."

"No worries, it's a long journey and the heat kind of hits you right away." Madison walked over and gave her a hug. She was always good at sensing when others needed some extra loving care. Juliet was in that category, for sure. "Why don't you sit down, and I'll grab you some food."

"Please don't go to any trouble. If you point me in the right direction, I can make myself something."

"Nonsense. I saved you dinner so it's no bother.

Tomorrow, you can roll up your sleeves and fend for yourself with us at mealtimes. Today, you let me fuss over you." Madison bustled around the open kitchen adjoining the living room.

"If you insist." Juliet fell into an armchair in the corner and curled her legs underneath her.

"I'm going to say goodnight." Carla leaned down and gave her a hug. "I have a date with a novel in my room. My nice, quiet room." She cupped her ear with one hand. "Do you hear that? It's the sound of children sleeping. Bliss."

Luke chuckled. "Don't believe a word of it. Carla is the first one up in the morning. I'm convinced she goes into the kids' rooms and pinches them so they wake up to see her."

"Whatever." Carla giggled as she disappeared down the corridor.

Juliet's mouth twitched. "It's eerily quiet. Are they all asleep?"

"All except this one." The tiny housekeeper, Maria, sauntered in bouncing Angel in her arms. "He doesn't want to miss out on anything."

"I'll take him." Luke relieved Maria of her load. "You go on home, Maria. Thanks so much, and we'll see you on Monday."

"Yes, Señor Luke. Have a good weekend. Nice meeting you, Miss Juliet."

Juliet stood and bent over to give the dear lady a hug on her way out. "Thanks, Maria. It was a pleasure to meet you."

"Here you go—take a seat and you can eat on your lap." Madison came around the kitchen island and presented Juliet with a tray laden with a plate of enchiladas and a glass of mango juice.

"Thanks, this smells divine. I hadn't realized how hungry I was."

"Courtesy of Maria. She's an absolute gem. We all love her to bits." Madison sat on the couch and stretched her arms above her head.

Juliet bit into her enchilada and the flavors exploded in her mouth. "Amazing." She wiped her lips with a paper napkin. "Your staff here seem fantastic."

"They are." Luke bobbed up and down with the baby. "Maria joined us several months ago and now I don't know how we survived without her. Carla has been here for maybe four years. Then we have a local couple who live in the village and work here as needed from Monday to Friday. They don't have kids of their own, but they know some of the families of our children here. They've been invaluable as mediators and advisors. Madison and I do whatever else is needed, from teaching English to fundraising. On top of being house parents, of course."

"Sounds busy. You have around a dozen kids at the moment?" She asked between bites of the best food she'd ever tasted.

"Thirteen including Angel. It fluctuates." Luke kissed the baby's head. "Some kids are true orphans but some are from families who are unable to care for them or don't want them."

Juliet lowered her fork. "That's awful." Her soft heart broke open as she watched Luke with Angel. "At least they have you and Madison. You're doing good work here, and seeing you with the children in real life beats chatting with you guys over the phone for updates."

"The phone." He winced. "I meant to tell you before, you had a call while you were asleep."

"I did?" In her exhaustion from the travelling, she'd forgotten to call Max. She had promised and he would be concerned. Or he may have news on the Red case…

"I took his number and wrote it on that piece of yellow paper on the fridge." He nodded toward the kitchen.

"Don't worry, I have Max's number." She just needed to remember where she put her phone.

"No, it wasn't Max." Luke tilted his head. "I think his name was Richard."

Juliet's mouth fell open. "What?" Her pulse quickened. Should she feel creeped out or flattered? "How on earth did he track me down?"

Chapter Twenty

Max inhaled the ocean air as he stood outside The Lighthouse and knocked on the front door. The jeep was parked in the driveway. *Adam must be in.* He worked his architect business from home most days—who could blame him? With an ocean view for inspiration and zero commute, it made perfect sense.

"We're around the back." Adam's shout came from the side of their house.

Excellent. Bella was home, too.

She would be more helpful with regards to his question.

Max dug his hands into his jacket pockets and went in search of his friends. "Hey, guys. Sorry to intrude on your Saturday morning."

"No problem." Bella leaned her broom against the wall on the patio and walked up to him with a warm hug. "Always nice to see you."

"I thought you might be at The Book Nook."

"I'm heading in after lunch, but I think you have given us a perfect excuse for a break. Right, honey?"

Adam chuckled as he set down a half-full garbage bag of leaves and debris. "A break sounds good to me. Got time for a coffee, bud?"

Max surveyed the backyard overlooking the beach. They had a decent-sized lawn beyond the patio with two trees which had shed most of their golden leaves already. "I don't want to interrupt this major cleanup operation." He didn't envy their full-on homeowner responsibilities.

Bella let out a laugh. "Are you kidding? It's blowing a gale out here. We're trying to tidy up from the last windstorm, but I think there's another one coming in." She lifted a shoulder. "Seems like a useless endeavor to me. I'll make coffee."

Adam pecked her cheek as she passed by. "If you insist."

"Seriously, I can't stay long." Max checked his watch. "I stopped by to run something past you guys."

"Let's at least get out of this wind and talk. Perils of living on a clifftop. Come on inside."

Max followed Adam through the back door into the spacious kitchen. "It smells amazing in here."

Bella turned from the coffeepot and grinned. "Adam made cinnamon buns this morning before the yard work. Sometimes I have to pinch myself to make sure I'm not dreaming this man up."

"No, they smell real enough to me." Max eyed the plate of sugary goodness on the granite counter top.

"Help yourself." Adam punched his shoulder. "You know you can't resist."

He was running on fumes this week with all the extra workload from the Red case. He needed all the sustenance he could get. "Don't mind if I do." Max grabbed a bun and a small plate and settled himself on a bar stool. He bit into the cinnamon bun and closed his eyes for a moment. Soft, sweet, and comforting. Perfection. The aroma of freshly brewed coffee wafted over to him and the winter sun shone through the wall of windows.

This is what I want, Lord. An easy Saturday morning with the love of my life in a home full of joy and good food...

"What's on your mind?" Adam washed his hands at the sink.

Max finished his mouthful and swallowed. "I want your opinion." He glanced over at Bella. "Both of you."

"Okay." She twirled her hair and leaned against the counter. "Shoot."

"I've done something and I don't know if it's romantic or ridiculous." He gave a half-smile. "I booked a plane ticket to go and see Juliet in Mexico." And paid a handsome price for the most direct last-minute flights he could find.

Bella's mouth dropped open.

"Whoa." Adam's eyebrows shot up. "Bold move."

"Too bold?" Max squirmed. "That's my question. Do you think I've overstepped or stepped up?"

His friends would be honest with him. He just wasn't sure he wanted to hear the truth. All he knew was God had told him to go. Not audibly but he knew it in his heart. He had been praying ever since the sad goodbye to Juliet on Wednesday evening and the answer resounded over and over: Go.

"I don't think it's too bold. I'm excited about it." Bella's nose crinkled. "But what about the case? What's the latest?"

"Yeah, can you even leave now that you're in the middle of it?" Adam dried his hands.

"I believe so. Red hasn't made any moves since Tuesday. He's either slowing down, completed his mission, or maybe moved on to an alternative district, which means we'll have to wait for our contacts to report a similar crime. We're still pursuing the lead I was following on Sunday but the guy seems to have curbed his attack pattern."

"I, for one, sure hope this whole thing is over." Bella shuddered. "It was making me nervous and I'm not a nurse or a redhead."

Max nodded. "I hope so, too. The hospital staff are still on high alert and until we arrest someone the case is still considered active, but I persuaded my superior that I would be of more use as a bodyguard for Juliet. He knows we have a history and also that I haven't had time off in forever. After pulling these late nights and early mornings at the office, I feel like I could sleep for a week."

"On a beach in Mexico?" Adam smirked. "I see how it is. Well, you certainly deserve some time off. You've been run ragged this week. I presume they'll keep you notified of any progress while you're away."

"For sure. They have strict instructions to keep me in the loop, and I can fly back straight away if necessary. I'm more concerned about Juliet. Have you heard from her yet? All I received was a one-liner text late last night saying she arrived and was safe."

"I had something similar." Bella's brow furrowed. "But she has Madison there to talk to and she's a wise woman. Juliet needs space to process things at the moment. It's been a traumatic month caring for her mom, watching her die, this maniac on the loose, and, to be frank, you showing up again after breaking her heart." She shrugged.

Max gazed through the patio doors at the remaining mess the windstorm had caused. It needed intentional work to get it cleaned up. Not unlike the windstorm he had caused with Juliet…

"You know about our conversations, I guess?" Max's cheeks burned.

"Yes." She glanced at Adam. "I'm sorry about everything and I know there are issues you both need to address. She's angry now, but I'm hoping a change of scenery will be good for her, and I'm praying that above all she'll turn to God for comfort and answers. Her faith was always such a big part of her life before Pippa's cancer came back. She's having some major trust issues, and it's heartbreaking to watch."

Can't argue with that.

"But do you think arriving in Mexico will be a good surprise? I don't want to make her feel suffocated but it kills me to think of her there all alone."

"She's not alone." Adam folded his arms. "She has Madison and Luke with her. Let's be honest—this is more about you *pursuing* her than protecting her. I know you're worried about her making a rash decision about the two of you, aren't you?"

Hit the nail on the head. He had already made a devastating rash decision in leaving her earlier this year. He didn't want her to do the same. "Yeah, I'm worried she won't give us a second chance. I want to protect her and know she's safe but that's not all. If she's going to be doing some serious thinking while there, I'm scared stiff she'll react from her memories of me being a jerk when I left last spring."

He wiped his mouth with a paper napkin and let out a sigh. "I've done a lot of praying this week, and I believe I have to give us one last shot. I have to tell her I love her and show her how much. I'm willing to move back to Florence, if that's what she wants. Heck, I'll go to the ends of the earth for her. Call me crazy, but I figured flying down to Mexico was a step in the right direction."

"Crazy in love." Adam snickered. "You've got it bad, buddy. I agree, you have to at least try or else live the rest of your life wondering what might have happened."

Max's mouth twitched. "That's what I'm thinking."

Bella beamed. "This is so romantic. When do you leave?"

"Tonight."

* * *

Now this is a perfect way to start a Saturday morning.

Juliet leaned back into the hammock and exhaled. After a dreamless night's sleep for the first time in weeks, she awoke early to the sound of children's feet scampering in their rooms and down the corridors. It was a joyful sound, and made her heart ache for children of her own—but she would not be morose. She was in a beautiful place with friends to support her, sweet children to love on, and a hammock on the beach with her name on it.

"Knock yourself out." Luke had laughed when she asked permission to start her day lazing on the beach. "Don't forget sunblock."

Hello, I am a nurse and a redhead.

The thought made her shudder. She had almost forgotten about the nurse-killer back home. Almost. Now she had a full hour to relax before her cuddling duties began with baby Angel and the kids.

"Juliet? Phone call for you." Madison's voice carried across the expanse of beach from the orphanage.

"Doesn't everyone know I'm super busy?" Juliet grinned as she swung her legs over the side and plodded across the sand until she reached Madison. "Thanks. Do you know who it is?"

"A guy. I'm guessing it's the mysterious Richard." She raised an eyebrow as if reminding Juliet they needed to chat, and then hurried back inside.

Juliet winced. She should have called him back late last night. Now her procrastinating had interrupted her hammock time. What did he want anyway? Was the handsome man interested in her? Only one way to find out.

She followed Madison into the kitchen, where the phone was off the hook waiting for her. She picked it up. "Hello?"

"Juliet. It's Richard. From the plane. I hope I haven't called too early." His confident voice was warm and soothing. She couldn't help smiling.

"Oh, hi. How are you?" She caught Madison's suspicious glare across the kitchen island and turned away to look through the window.

"I'm great, thanks. Have you recovered from the journey?" He was so considerate. Juliet hopped onto a bar stool and heard Madison walk out of the room.

"Almost. It was a long one. Sorry I didn't call back last night. How did you find me here?"

"There aren't many orphanages in Sonaja. I hope you don't mind." He remembered from their conversation. Interesting.

There was a growing hubbub coming from the bedrooms and Juliet anticipated bedlam in the kitchen any second. "No, not at all." It was flattering to be pursued after being rejected months ago by Max. "But to warn you, it's about to get noisy on my end."

He laughed. "I can imagine. Listen, this isn't my style, but I felt comfortable talking with you on the plane and I'd sure appreciate a friend while I'm here. Is there any chance we might meet up when you have time? If you want to, that is."

Juliet froze. A date? Should she? What about Max? They weren't a couple again. Although they had shared some unforgettable kisses…

"To be honest with you, I'd love to chat about the orphanage where you're staying. I like to support several causes and would be honored to make some kind of donation."

Maybe it wasn't a *date* date, after all. Her shoulders relaxed.

"Really? You want to donate to the orphanage? I'd be happy to tell you what I know. I'm sure my friends have some brochures I can bring along. Unless you want to come here and check it out for yourself? I can arrange that, too."

"No, no need. I don't want to intrude. They must be busy with the children, but yes, please bring any information along. Are you free this evening by any chance?"

Juliet bit her thumbnail and tasted bitter sunscreen. No, she had a date with a palm tree and some manuscript ashes tonight. That was the main reason she was here, after all. "I'm afraid I have plans…"

"Tomorrow then? For dinner?"

Wow, this guy was persistent. Was that a compliment or a red flag? She was overthinking things. What did she have to lose? It was dinner with a new friend and besides, it was for a good cause. "Sure. Let's make it after six. That way I can help with the evening meal here first. Do you have anywhere in mind?"

"I sure do." She could tell he was grinning. "I heard about a perfect place where the food and the view are spectacular. Plan to arrive at six-fifteen and you'll be right on time for the best sunset you'll ever see. You're going to love it. It's called La Catedral. Want me to send a taxi for you?"

Sounded romantic for a platonic meal. She stalled. Perhaps she should stay here with Madison instead. Call Max.

"Juliet? If you don't like my choice…" Now she had hurt his feelings.

She gave her head a shake. "I'm sorry, no. La Catedral sounds great. I'll remember that name. Six-fifteen. I can grab a cab and meet you there." In case she needed to make a swift exit.

"Sounds great. Enjoy your day, and I'll see you tomorrow."

"Bye, Richard." She ended the call and stared at the phone. Had she done the right thing? When had making decisions become such an ordeal for her? She was exhausted.

"Everything okay?" Madison's voice made her jump. "With your flying companion?" She popped a grape in her mouth.

"I didn't hear you come back in. Yeah." Juliet knew her face was glowing red after arranging a non-date date. "He's taking me to dinner tomorrow." She studied Madison's face for her reaction.

"Is he?" She bounced baby Angel on one hip and cocked her head to one side. "Are you comfortable with that?"

Juliet lifted her chin. "What do you mean?"

Madison squinted. "I'm watching out for you, that's all. You don't know much about the guy and you're in a strange country. Want me to come along with you?"

"No." Juliet studied the countertop.

"Sure?"

She looked up to see Madison grinning.

"Oh, you were joking."

"I was, but I'd love a dinner out on the town and would come along with you in a heartbeat if you're feeling uneasy about it. Is he picking you up?"

"No, he said he would send a cab but I told him I'd take my own."

Madison perched on the stool next to her and scowled. "Weird he wouldn't pick you up. Or at least come in the cab to get you if he's not driving."

I hadn't thought of that. He had been pushy with all the details. Was he trying to impress her with his talk of donations and a posh restaurant?

Juliet stroked Angel's chubby cheek. It was like the smoothest velvet. "He was asking about the orphanage though. I think he'll make a donation if I take some information with me."

"Hmm. Maybe he's not such a bad sort..."

"I think you can relax. He's a kind guy."

Madison handed Angel over to Juliet. She slid behind the large island and started pulling plastic cups from a cupboard. "I'm sorry. I guess I feel responsible for your safety while you're here even though I realize you're more than capable of taking care of yourself. Where are you meeting him anyway?"

"Someplace called La Catedral. Do you know it?"

Madison whistled. "Swanky. It has a fabulous view over the ocean." She frowned. "It's romantic, too."

Juliet bit her lower lip. "That's what I thought."

"But are things really over with you and Max? I hate to ask. I understand you're going through a lot but I thought he was the one for you."

Juliet hugged the baby close. He smelled of coconut oil. "I don't know. I told you we have things to work through." She lowered her voice. "Mostly about why he dumped me six months ago when he found out he can't have kids biologically and decided I wouldn't be good with it. It seems it was his decision to make." She gritted her teeth. It caused her blood to boil every time she thought about it. Deep breaths.

Madison's face fell. "That's why you broke up? I'm sorry. It's awful all around." She pulled up a stool. "I sometimes wonder how I would feel if for some reason we couldn't get pregnant when the time comes."

"How *would* you feel?"

"Sad, for sure." At that moment, a line of excited children filed into the dining area with Luke and Carla, and they all sat around the huge wooden table. Madison lowered her voice. "Yet I have to trust God knows me better than I know myself, and that He provides what I need." She beamed. "Sometimes more than I need."

"I'm having difficulty trusting God at the moment." Juliet grimaced.

"Because of losing your mom?"

She lifted one shoulder. "Mostly. He didn't come through for me when I asked Him to heal her. Now I'm alone."

"I understand, I do." Madison nodded toward the table full of kids. "Let's feed these little darlings and then have a chat outside while they have play time. It's been ages since we had a proper catch-up."

"Sounds good to me. Come on, Angel, let's get you something to eat."

Juliet watched from one end of the table with wide eyes as breakfast happened. A flurry of cereal, sippy-cups, mangoes, and toast appeared and was consumed in record time. Only Angel and two-year-old Sophia were left in highchairs once the others left to get cleaned up and ready for play.

"Wow. Breakfast was quite something." She collected plates and wiped down the table. "They all eat well… and fast."

Luke packed away the cereal boxes in the upper cupboards. "Wait until Sunday breakfast. That's a whole other level. It's an experience eating here. Most of the kids have hearty appetites, so that helps them get used to the rest of our rules with playtime and swimming and everything."

"You and Madison are amazing with them."

"Thanks. I've been here a few years, and it's second nature to me. Madison has taken to it so naturally and I'm so proud. I knew right away she'd make a fabulous mom. Even with chosen children." He blushed.

"Chosen children?" Could this guy be any sweeter?

"Yeah. It's what we decided to call our non-biological children. The kids we get to care for here at the orphanage. We've been chosen by God to be their parents for a season at least, and they've been chosen to fill our hearts." His mouth curved into a smile. "We're blessed."

Juliet's eyes filled as she gazed at Angel. Why couldn't Max see it that way, too? If she could have chosen children, there was no one she'd rather raise them with than Max.

"Thank you for telling me. *Chosen children*—I think that is the most beautiful thing I've ever heard."

Chapter Twenty-One

"THIS COFFEE IS AMAZING." JULIET TOOK another sip and set her mug back on the sand next to the deck chair. They had dragged two chairs onto the beach in front of the orphanage and settled under a palm tree with an unobstructed view of the ocean.

"Thanks." Madison passed her a coconut yogurt and sat on a matching seat next to her. "Here. You might as well embrace the tropical experience and eat this outside."

Juliet grinned. "Wonderful. It's perfect here in this shady spot. I'll get enough sun later when we take the kids in the ocean. I have to say it's good to feel the warmth of sunshine on my shoulders again. The Oregon Coast is deep in winter mode. Damp and chilly. I'm making the most of this while I can."

"I know what you mean. I can hardly believe I'm living here now. It's a far cry from Seattle. Speaking of which, do you want to vent about Max yet? The kids are all occupied with playtime and Luke offered to watch them and give us chance to chat."

Juliet swirled the yogurt with her spoon. "That's where you first met Max, wasn't it? Seattle." *Back before Mom got sick again. When life was simpler.* "Oh, I don't know what to think. My heart still yearns for a future with him, and yet forgiving him and trusting him again seems like an insurmountable mountain for me to climb."

"Forgiving him for what? Leaving you?" Madison pushed her sunglasses on top of her head and knit her brows together.

"It still hurts that he left me in an instant with no reason or closure. I was a mess. What really stings is that he thought he had the right to make the decision for me. He decided I wouldn't be able to handle a life with him and not have biological kids. He took that decision from me and left me with nothing." *Besides, I don't know if I can trust him not to do it again.*

Juliet scanned the desolate beach. Exactly how she felt. Empty. Lacking. Waiting for something—or someone to bring her back to life.

"I'm sorry. About all of it. You still love him?"

Of course. I can't imagine not loving him. "Yes." It came as a whisper. Is that why she felt empty sitting here now? Not only from missing her mom but because she yearned for Max? Maybe there was a way for them to work this out. Maybe…

Madison reached over and squeezed Juliet's hand. "I don't want to sound like a counsellor here, I want to be your friend, but I've felt the hurt and abandonment and grief you are experiencing. Remember when you first met me?"

Juliet cringed as she recalled Madison's tearful outbursts and lack of sleep. "Yes. You've been through a lot."

"Grief made me angry, exhausted, and sad—it came in waves." She nodded at the ocean. "Then when I finally thought I was surviving, something would set me off and I'd be inconsolable. Getting out of bed every morning felt like mission impossible."

"I'm acquainted with that particular feeling, but you did it. You got through it all." Juliet turned to her.

"You were so strong." If only she could get through all this, too.

"Not me. It was because I found God. He was my strength when I had none. I can't begin to imagine what would have become of me if I hadn't turned to Him. It still took baby steps. One day at a time. I did the next thing in front of me, no matter how small."

"Yet look at you now." Juliet swivelled back to take in the orphanage where squeals of delight drifted on the air.

Madison laughed. "I didn't see this coming. God did." She was silent for a few moments. "You know He hasn't abandoned you, don't you?"

Feels like it. She turned back to face the ocean.

"My head knows, but my heart is not so sure." Juliet ate a spoonful of yogurt while she processed her thoughts. "When Mom's cancer came back last spring, I was certain God would heal her. He'd done it twice before. So, I prayed and pleaded and waited—and then watched her get sicker and weaker for months. She was always so positive, but ultimately, we knew the end was coming."

"I'm so sorry. It must have been excruciating for you."

Juliet brushed a tear from her warm cheek. "It was. At least Mom was at peace with God in those final months." Yes, her prayers for her mom's salvation had been answered, but it had been bittersweet to watch her mom grow closer to God as she grew weaker in body.

"Wait. She was at peace with God?" Madison sat up in her chair. "Juliet, that's amazing. I know you'd been praying for your mom to become a Christian for years."

"Only to lose her." Juliet scowled.

It's not fair, God. It's not fair.

"It hurts so much today and you can't understand God's plan for her—but, don't you see, you'll get to be with her forever?"

"It's not much consolation to me right now. Or when I get married one day." An image of Max in a tux flashed in her mind. "Or when I have kids—her grandchildren." Another pang of regret pulled at her heart for the loss. "She'll miss it all." Juliet choked back a sob. "I miss her so much."

Madison took the yogurt from Juliet's hand and wrapped her in a hug. "I know what you mean. It's the hardest thing in the world to release control of our lives, what we see as our future—but when we do, when we allow God to lead us and comfort us along the way, each day gets a little easier. I'll pray for you. If there's anything I can do, you name it."

Juliet pulled back and tucked a strand of wayward hair into her ponytail. "There is something. I was hoping to take some time this evening right after dinner and scatter Mom's manuscript ashes under one of the palm trees here on the beach. Is that okay? I don't know if that works with your schedule."

"For sure. I love having you here and the kids adore you already, but you came to Mexico for this very reason. You should have the evening to yourself and then try to sleep in tomorrow. Think of it as healing and self-care. This is important. Take all the time you want."

Juliet sniffled as she surveyed the beach. Her mom would have loved it here. "Thanks. By the way, did I tell you the title of Mom's manuscript?"

"No, I don't think you did."

"It's *The Orphan Beach*. How perfect is that?"

"Seriously?" Madison's hands flew to her face. "I

can't believe it. The locals call this stretch of sand Orphanage Beach for obvious reasons—I guess it's been this way for years."

"I suppose it's possible that this could be the actual beach Mom had visited years ago. I like that. Scattering the ashes here will mean even more to me now."

"God must have known."

Hmm. Maybe, but she couldn't think about that yet. One thing at a time.

"Anyway, thanks for understanding why I can't help with the kids tonight. I know it's hectic getting them fed and ready for bed." She squirmed. "I'm afraid I'll also need time away tomorrow night right after dinner."

"Right. Your date. About this guy—"

Juliet held up her hand. "I understand you don't approve of the fact that I'm going to dinner at a romantic spot with someone I met on a plane but he said he wants to donate funds to the orphanage. I'm doing this for you guys. You're welcome."

"Purely for the orphanage. I'm sure." Madison smirked as she pulled her hair into a topknot. "So, if I don't get to even meet our mystery man since he's not picking you up, tell me about him."

"Not much to tell so far. I chatted with him on the flight from Oregon to L.A. and got a quick glimpse of him on the next flight to Colima. I was at the front of the plane and he was way at the back."

"Uncanny that he was on the same flights." Madison raised an eyebrow.

"Right? But I didn't speak with him again once we landed in L.A., so I presumed it was a one-off conversation and that was that."

"I guess you thought wrong."

"Seems like it. Anyway, he's tall, dark, and handsome. Stubbly beard. Thirties. He's in sales. A great listener." Juliet paused. "And he also knows loss."

"Oh dear. How so?" Madison set her elbows on her knees and leaned forward.

"The poor man has been through so much." Yet he still reached out to help her. Tears filled her eyes. "He lost his wife in a car crash and his young daughter to cancer."

Madison shook her head. "That's awful. I'm sorry. I know you've seen so many sick kids with your work. It must have hit home for you."

"I have." Juliet craned her neck to peek back through the open gate as the two little sisters squealed and ran circles around the plastic playhouse. "We lost a sweet patient right before I left, and it broke my heart. I can't imagine what he's been through to lose his own daughter." She remembered their handshake in the plane. The tattoo on his wrist. It must be to remember both his girls. A constant reminder of all he had lost.

"How do you think he's doing? Did he say how long ago he lost both of them?"

"I'm not sure when his daughter died. I think he said it was six years for his wife." Juliet moved her chair back a little to stay in the shade of the palm trees. "We didn't get into details on the plane. He has this tattoo on the inside of his wrist though. Two hearts. I guess one for each of them. I feel for the guy. Maybe I'll ask him about it tomorrow night."

Madison's eyes widened. "Sounds like you could be in danger of falling for him if you're not careful. Back to Max—is the situation irreparable between the two of you? I know he made a mistake but isn't your relationship worth fighting for? You guys seemed so perfect for each other."

We were perfect for each other, and could be again if we could only get past the issue of children. "He has some stuff to figure out. About his future, fatherhood, family. He can't spend much time thinking about all this when he's neck-deep in the nurse-killer case."

"Didn't you mention he was on the case because he cares about you? Isn't that why he's back in Florence?"

"I suppose so, but it's his job, too. We know how invested he is in his career."

"Plus, he's excellent at it."

"Yeah." She pictured him in his police uniform. Man, he looked good in it. "It's his vocation. Protect and serve." It was in his blood. Hadn't he been trying to protect her heart from broken dreams when he left?

"How about *your* vocation? What are you feeling about nursing at the moment?"

"Heavy. It's feeling heavy in this season." She slumped back into her chair as if experiencing the sudden weight of it all. "Nursing has always brought me to life, and I've never wanted to do anything else—but now I'm not sure. I took a chunk of time off to care for Mom, and the thought of going back to nursing scares me, which sounds ridiculous."

"Because of how painful it was for you?"

"I don't know. There's so much to think about. Watching Mom fade away and die before my eyes was the hardest thing I've ever experienced. My heart feels trampled, and I'm not sure how much I have to give anymore. Is that selfish of me?"

"Not one bit. You've been through a stressful experience and you need some time to grieve and heal and get your life together." Madison checked over her shoulder. "And you're not freaked out about this crazy nurse-attacker? That's a whole other layer. My imagination's on overdrive and I wouldn't blame you if you were scared."

Juliet rubbed her temples. "It was getting to me back at home, but I won't let him ruin my time here. It seems like he's lost the taste for it, anyway. I haven't heard anything new so maybe he's done with it and moved on."

"Or lying in wait for the right time." Madison shuddered.

Juliet snorted. "You're a great comfort." She scanned the beach. They were alone.

"Sorry, but I've experienced stalkers and I know they rarely give up."

* * *

It was time. Juliet washed her face in the tiny sink, hoping to revive herself after a full day. Her muscles ached from playing with the children and carrying little Angel around on her hip. She smiled at the memory. They had all splashed in the shallows of the ocean until nap time and then Madison and Luke did activities with the older kids while she had helped Carla make dinner. A constant hive of activity.

I love it. It was refreshing to be around life and joy and sunshine. There had been little time to fret and worry. Now she needed to focus on her final farewell to her mom.

Her stomach churned as she dried her face and ran fingers through her wavy hair. The beach awaited. Sunset was so symbolic in putting her mother's story to rest. She straightened the creases from her cotton white sundress she had changed into after dinner and picked up the mahogany box from the bedside table. Max's box. She bit her lip.

This is harder than I imagined.

Luke was reading on the sofa when she passed through the living room.

He looked up from his book. "Lovely box you have there."

"Thanks. Max gave it to me." Her heart squeezed at the thought of his tenderness. Of his comfort. Of his kiss. "I should get outside before I miss the sunset."

"Are you sure you want to be alone?" He set his book on his lap. "We can come along, or Madison can keep you company. She's helping Carla get the kids showered and ready for bed but she won't be long."

Juliet hesitated. "Do you think it's dangerous to be on the beach at this time of the evening?" She hadn't thought of that. Madison had made her a little nervous earlier and soon it would be dusk.

"No, I think you'll be fine. It's not your safety so much as having someone to keep you company. It's a sweet remembrance of your mom, but I can't imagine how painful it must be for you."

She squared her shoulders. "I have to get used to being on my own from now on."

"What if Madison and I sat in the yard and drank our lemonade? Then you could enjoy your privacy but if you are uncomfortable at any moment, you could give us a shout and we'll hear you."

Not alone. Nice compromise. "Sounds good. Thanks. I appreciate it."

Luke followed her outside and sat on a lounger while she continued to the end of the yard with bare feet and opened the gate to reach the silky sand beyond.

The evening breeze smelled sweet as it lifted her

long hair. She pulled it to one side and headed for a palm tree she had chosen earlier. This one leaned toward the ocean, longing to be free. It was in a clump of three trees, their skinny trunks raising fronds as if in praise. Not too far from the orphanage. Close enough to watch the children play on the beach, like her mom had watched the orphans play so many years ago. A tear meandered down her face and she let it fall. There would be many more.

As her toes sank into warm softness, Juliet considered her next steps in life. What would she do after this trip was over?

God, I miss talking to You. I'm still mad, but I miss You.

There, she said it. Admitted the truth.

Is that why I'm not getting any clarity with Max? Because I'm not praying about it?

Not so long ago, all her decisions were run through the filter of what God would have her do. She prayed about everyone and everything. He had been her anchor. She was His daughter, as He had reminded her not so long ago—and He was her loving Heavenly Father.

My father. She shuddered as dark thoughts of her biological dad crowded her mind, and she pushed them to one side. One day, she would need to deal with them. Work through them. Not today though. He would not mar this moment honoring her mother's memory.

Focus. She ran her fingers over the smooth wooden lid of the box. It was kind of Max to think of this special keepsake. She would treasure it after she had deposited the ashes.

I have no idea what I'll put in it, but it'll be a sweet reminder of Mom's story.

How would her own story unfold? It could go in so many different directions—this moment in time seemed pivotal somehow. She could start fresh in a new city. Maybe work here at the orphanage for a while if she got a visa. She could give up nursing and try something different. Be brave. Be like Pippa Farr.

At the leaning palm tree, she sank down onto the sand at its base and faced the ocean. A seagull squawked overhead and Juliet watched it dive and soar across the water. Free. Her mother's words came back to her, how she had been jealous of the bird's freedom and known at that moment on a beach in Mexico that she needed to flee her own captivity.

You did it, Mom.

She lifted the lid and stared at the ashes, the remnants of her mother's story—her own beginning. A sob caught in her throat.

"Mom, you know how much I miss you. I'm not doing great without you, am I? So much for being brave and strong like you." She sniffled. "So, here I am. I found a perfect beach for you, right by an orphanage where kids come and play and are truly loved and cared for. I'm going to leave your story here. I'm grateful I got to read it and understand more about you, and about us."

A slight movement in her peripheral vision caused Juliet to spin around. No one was there. In fact, the entire stretch of beach was empty. Clumps of shrubbery dotted the area and the occasional palm tree sprouted from the sand, but it was just her.

Man, she was jumpy. Madison's comments hadn't helped. Understandable back at home, but here? She needed to relax. Madison and Luke were close by—she could hear the murmur of their voices on the evening breeze—and would come in a flash if she needed them. Still, the hairs on the back of her neck prickled as she checked one more time before focusing again on her special task.

With one hand she dug in the sand and made a deep trough and then turned the ashes into it. She patted the bottom of the box to make sure it was empty.

"I don't need to carry the story with me, Mom. Not when I'm carrying you around in my heart." With slow strokes, she covered the ashes with soft sand until they were concealed. They were safe. Exactly where her mom had dreamed her story would end—and where Juliet's story was beginning…

As she went to close the lid, Juliet noticed a tiny folded piece of paper at the bottom of the box. Must have been Max since he was the one who filled the box up back on the beach in Florence. Curious, she picked at the corner and the paper fell to the sand. With trembling fingers, she unfolded the note and blinked back tears in order to read his familiar handwriting in the fading light.

"I know what I'm doing. I have it all planned out—plans to take care of you, not abandon you, plans to give you the future you hope for." Jeremiah 29:11

The exact words her heart needed to hear.

Thank you, Max.

Yes, God knew what He was doing. He would never abandon her. She need never again feel abandoned. She was His. Hadn't she been adopted into His family? Chosen. A chosen child, like the kids at the orphanage. Her eyes leaked but this time the tears held an element of joy. A stream of acceptance.

Juliet clutched the verse to her chest and looked up in time to see the most breathtaking sunset. It hadn't been there seconds before. It was as if the Master Artist had seen her tears and chosen to gift her with a miracle finger-painted across the sky in deepest violets and softest pinks.

"It's beautiful." Tears blurred her vision and she swiped them away, not wanting to miss a second of it.

"Heavenly Father, I'm not ready to be full-on with You yet. I'm still mad, but I guess I don't need to tell You that." She licked her lips. "But thank You for this moment. My own miracle in the sky. Please, would You give Mom a hug for me and hold her in Your loving arms until we can be together again?" Madison was right. Eternal perspective.

Juliet pulled herself to her feet and leaned against the gnarly trunk of the palm tree and stared out over the ocean. She inhaled the exhilarating freshness, appreciating each glorious moment as the great ball of fire descended below the horizon.

Goodnight, Mom.

As she plodded back toward the orphanage, she rested a hand on her heart. Was something breaking— or was Someone breaking through?

Chapter Twenty-Two

"WELCOME TO SUNDAY MORNING CHAOS AT Esperanza." Madison grinned from the kitchen, a huge frying pan in her hand.

Juliet laughed. "Wow. Luke did warn me. What just happened?"

The dining area looked as if a hurricane had swept through leaving wreckage in its wake.

"Breakfast."

She winced. "Sorry I wasn't around to help. I didn't bother setting my alarm and ended up having the best sleep."

"No problem, I told you to sleep in. You must have needed the rest. Besides, Carla is a morning lark and always pitches in when Maria's not around."

Juliet inhaled. "Do I smell pancakes? Is that even a Mexican thing?" She began collecting the dishes smeared with syrup from the table. The least she could do was clear up.

"It's a tradition I started when I arrived here, and the kids love it. Every Sunday morning, I make pancakes for a yummy early breakfast and then they get ready for church in a timely manner like good children. Getting to Sunday School on time is a small miracle but this seems to work."

"I love it. You brought a piece of home with you."

"Literally." She held up two bottles of syrup. "I saved you a couple of pancakes if you can find a clean spot to sit down."

"Thanks so much, but let me help clear up here first. In fact, why don't you go and get ready for church and I'll finish this while you're gone." There was a growing commotion coming from the children's rooms. "Sounds like Luke and Carla could use some help."

Madison tilted her head. "You're not coming with us?"

"Not today." Juliet loaded sippy-cups into the sink. How could she explain her relationship with God?

Madison's face fell. "We'll miss you. I think you might like it—the people are so warm and welcoming, even if you can't understand the message in Spanish."

"I'm sure. I promise I'll come next week if I'm still here. Today, I want to spend some time being still with God in the fresh, ocean air."

"That's great. I mean, it sounds like perhaps you're opening up to Him again."

Juliet's hands stiffened in the sink and she blinked back tears. "Something's stirring in my heart. I can't deny it, but I need time."

"You got it." Madison gave her a hug as she passed by. "Are you sure you don't mind clearing up after Hurricane Esperanza?"

"Not at all, but make sure the kids come and say goodbye to me before you leave."

***

Peace and quiet.

The entire household was at church, and Juliet had the place to herself.

Back home, Juliet had detested the absence of noise. Probably why she enjoyed the hubbub at the hospital. The past couple of weeks had been the loneliest of her life and the silence had been deafening. It forced her to hear her own thoughts and they had been ugly. She had blocked out the comfort of friends and the peace God offered and instead allowed fear and fury to reign in her heart. She didn't want to be a bitter woman. That was not who she was, even if she'd had a rough season.

Enough. This morning was different and she chose to embrace the quiet.

Juliet collapsed onto the armchair in the living room, the kitchen clean as a pin and her stomach full. From here she could see palm tree fronds waving to her from the sand beyond the yard. Beckoning. Yes, she would go for a swim. Maybe even talk to God while she basked in the beauty of His creation. Allow Him to come back in and give her soul rest. Not that He had been away. No, it was her own doing. He had been with her all along.

The beach was too tempting. She hurried back to her room to change into a swimsuit, slathered her body with sunblock, grabbed a towel, a sunhat, and a book, and she was set. As she went to open the backdoor, she had a moment's hesitation. She was safe, right? Perhaps a quick peek to see who else was on the beach.

She pulled her straw hat onto her head, padded down the pathway in the yard and opened the gate to the sand.

I could get used to this. A home backing onto the beach. A tropical version of Bella and Adam's lighthouse.

A swift breeze almost claimed her hat. She made the decision to leave it behind in the yard and set her novel on top of it to keep it from blowing away.

Wow, I'm living on the edge. No sunhat.

Surveying the expanse of beach, she nodded. It felt more than safe with several private homes along this stretch. Three young families were dotted along the shore to the right and an elderly lady dressed in her church finery was resting beneath a palm tree near the public beach access.

Perfect. She closed the gate behind her and ambled toward the glistening water, her toes sinking into the warm sand. It was as if her body was being healed from within, her muscles were relaxed and her mind sharp and observant. The azure sky was so vibrant she was grateful she wore shades, and was it her imagination or did the air smell of sweet coconuts?

Thank You, Lord. For this reminder of good things. For being with me always. For being patient with me.

Juliet dropped her towel at the shoreline and stepped into the white shallows as frothy as a little girl's Sunday dress. She closed her eyes and stood still. The slight chill was welcome and soon melted into a soothing balm.

With each step farther into the ocean, she prayed. Gave thanks. Reached deep to rediscover gratitude. By the time her freckled shoulders were submerged, she lifted her feet and was buoyed by more than her swirling hands. Was it possible she had found joy again?

***

After the most glorious hour imaginable, Juliet dried her prune-like skin with the fluffy sun-warmed towel and sighed.

Now this is what I call a Sabbath.

She turned toward the beach and watched siblings building sand castles and mothers cradling babies in the shade. What would her family look like if she had one?

The image of Max's face came to mind, his blond, spiky hair and sparkling blue eyes. How often had she imagined the appearance of their children back when they were dating? A lump formed in her throat at their loss.

I guess I'll leave it with God for now.

She licked her salty lips as she sauntered back to the orphanage. Thirsty. Yes, she needed to hydrate and reapply sunblock. Then maybe read under a palm tree until the others came home from church. She didn't notice the gate was open until she reached it.

Weird. I'm positive I closed it when I left.

Juliet scanned the yard but no one was back here. Maybe Madison and Luke were home already. She had lost track of time a while ago. Wouldn't she hear the kids?

"Hello?" She closed the gate behind her, wrapped the towel around her waist, and tiptoed down the path toward the back door. "Anyone home?"

She brushed the sand from her toes and stepped inside the cool living area. "Madison?"

Silence.

She glanced at the giant clock on the wall. Almost midday. They would be back any minute. It was too quiet inside after being on the beach amidst lapping waves and children's squeals. Juliet spun around and hurried back outside. Better. Yet something felt off.

Hating herself for being too chicken to go to her room for the sunblock, she decided to stay in the yard in the protective shade of one of the huge palm trees. Yes, she would relax and read until she heard the others arrive, and then she could help make them lunch. Everything would be fine.

She retrieved her book and pulled her hat atop her damp hair. Before she settled herself in a lounger, she double-checked the latch of the gate. Maybe a gust of wind had blown it open before. It was possible.

Relax, girl.

Dry, warm, and weary all of a sudden, Juliet stretched out on the lounger and reached for her novel. She had read late into last night and now needed to finish her suspense story.

I should start reading less intense books, especially after Madison's comments about stalkers. They aren't helping my nerves. Maybe a romantic comedy next, but for now...

She flicked through the pages to find the place she had bookmarked last night.

"Strange."

Her bookmark was gone. The one her mom gave her on her last birthday with the kitty identical to Ebony on it. She bit her lip and tears pricked her eyes. It had to be there. She turned the book upside-down and shook it. Something else dropped to the ground. "What on earth?"

She picked it up and gasped. It was no bookmark. It was a red paper heart.

* * *

"Are you sure none of the kids went in my room?"

Juliet bit her thumbnail as she paced the kitchen, now showered and clothed in fresh shorts and a T-shirt.

"I asked them all. I'm sorry, I don't know what to say." Madison sliced mangoes and bananas on the countertop. "There's no way they had time to go into your room before we left for church this morning. We've tried to teach them about boundaries and personal space."

"Sorry. I'm not usually this neurotic." Juliet came to Madison's side and placed a hand on her arm. "Please don't think I'm accusing anyone of anything—goodness, it was a paper heart, not a death threat. In fact, if it was one of the kids, I would be relieved."

Madison squinted. "You're sure you closed the gate when you went swimming?"

"Yes. Do you have any idea how paranoid I am at the moment?" Juliet grimaced.

"I can imagine." She gave a shudder.

Luke strode into the kitchen with Angel in his arms. "Nothing seems amiss in any of the rooms. I don't think anyone's been inside here. There are plenty of things they could have swiped."

"You're right, and nothing was out place in my room when I showered." Juliet peered through the large windows at the kids playing in the yard with Carla, letting off steam after being confined to an hour at church. "I want everyone to be safe, that's all. I hate to think I might have brought trouble to your door."

"Juliet." Luke plonked Angel into her arms. "Cuddle a baby. Relax in the sunshine. Heal. Eat. Try to stop stressing. I can't explain the paper heart in your book. We'll keep an eye out for your actual bookmark, but I think you're going to have to let it go for now."

She nuzzled Angel's soft, fluffy hair. "I'm sorry. Maybe I'm going insane."

Madison leaned against her husband. "You don't suppose Max might have slipped the heart inside your book at some point, do you?"

She shook her head. "I can't think when he could

have done it. How did I miss it when I was reading last night? I'll check with him next time we speak, but that still doesn't explain where the bookmark from my mom went."

"In the meantime, Luke's right. Why don't you get some fresh air and help supervise the munchkins outside while we make lunch. It'll take your mind off the bookmark mystery."

"Sure."

Juliet slipped outside with Angel and stared at the gate.

I know someone was here.

Lola came and grabbed Juliet's hand and dragged her toward the slide.

Heavenly Father, please just keep these sweet darlings safe.

Chapter Twenty-Three

"Max?" Madison's eyes nearly popped right out of her head. "Oh, my word—this is such a lovely surprise."

Max blushed as he hovered by the front door of the orphanage.

I hope it's a lovely surprise for Juliet.

This was going to take some explaining. The journey had been long in the cramped seats and stressful when he almost missed his connection in L.A. Now he was desperate to see a certain nurse. He'd been rehearsing what he wanted to say to her all morning. Perhaps they could go for a Sunday evening stroll on the beach and he could share his heart with her.

"Hey, Madison. I'm sorry to burst into your Sunday evening unannounced. It's out of the blue, but I decided at the last minute to surprise Juliet." His mouth twitched. "She'll either kill me or kiss me."

"I'm sure your life isn't in any imminent danger." Madison smirked. "Come on in." She stood to one side, and a tiny human peeked from behind her legs.

"Don't mind Sophia. She's shy with everyone." Madison bent down and kissed the tiny girl's forehead. "Can you say Hi to Mr. Max, sweetheart?"

The dark-haired beauty shook her head and batted her enormous eyes at Max.

He crouched down. Poor thing must be terrified of a giant blond hulk.

"Hola, Sophia. Hi." He held out his large hand.

Sophia tentatively placed her tiny hand in his. Adorable. His face broke into a grin.

"That's a first." Madison shook her head. "It usually takes forever for her to warm up to someone new. She's still wary around Juliet."

Talking of Juliet...

"Is she here?"

Where else would she be?

"Come on in." Madison eyed his rolling suitcase and led the way further into the building. The cool air was a welcome relief. "Umm, no. Juliet is… out at the moment." She sounded hesitant. Max's radar went up.

Out? "On her own?" His protective nature kicked in.

She kept walking. "No, she's not alone. Hey Luke, guess who just arrived?"

Luke's head appeared around a doorway. "Max? Welcome here. It's been a while." He enveloped him in a bearhug. "I don't think we've seen you since Bella's wedding."

"I guess that was the last time. How are you guys doing?" He scanned the whitewashed stone walls and neatly stacked toys. It was calm and peaceful with the murmur of subdued voices echoing down the hallway. "It's quieter than I imagined for an orphanage."

Madison picked up Sophia. "We start the day super early here so we try to have them in bed by six-thirty. The older ones read for awhile but it's our winding down phase." She checked her watch and grinned. "Looks like we're fifteen minutes ahead of schedule tonight as it's been a long day. Speaking of which, I should get this one tucked in. Luke, why don't you make Max something to drink, and I'll be back as soon as I can."

Max winced. "I'm sorry. I don't want to interrupt your bedtime routine. Please carry on with whatever you both need to do."

"It's no problem. I was coming to make some drinks anyway." Luke's eyes gravitated toward Max's case. "Why don't you set your stuff down in the hallway for now and I'll grab us something cool to drink."

"Thanks, man. Sounds awesome." He would sort out accommodations once he knew what kind of reception Juliet would give him.

But where was she?

Max slid his case out of the way and entered the large open living area. Luke picked a blanket from the floor on his way to the kitchen. "Mango juice? Water? Or would you rather some tea or coffee?"

"Juice would be awesome. Thanks." Max rested on a bar stool and leaned on the counter separating the kitchen from the living room. "I'm sorry to spring a visit on you like this. I guess I wasn't thinking straight. I should have at least called to warn you." He peered at his case in the hall. "I'm sure I can grab a local hotel if space is an issue."

Luke set two glasses on the counter. "We love visitors, and you're always welcome. You may have to sleep on the couch in here until I figure out other sleeping arrangements, though."

"Thanks. I can sleep on the floor if necessary. I thought I should see how the land lies before making reservations anywhere else."

"Let me guess—how the land lies with Juliet?"

"Yes." Max pulled at the collar of his T-shirt. "Things have been... awkward, to say the least."

"I gathered as much." Luke emptied a bag of nacho chips into a huge china bowl. "You might want to pick

Madison's brains on the details but I can tell Juliet's going through a lot at the moment."

"Her mom's death hit her hard. They were close. Then I came back on the scene..."

Luke pushed the bowl in front of Max, along with a small dish of salsa. "Was that because of this Red case? She hasn't said too much about it, other than he's targeting red-headed nurses and she was anxious to get away." He stroked his chin. "Can't say I blame her. That's one specific profile."

"Right?" Max pulled out his phone. "Which reminds me that I need to touch base with the station. I haven't heard anything all day which I'm hoping means there have been no further attacks."

"How long since the last one?" Luke popped a chip in his mouth.

"Five days, which is promising, given his recent pattern. Let's pray this guy has come to his senses or is getting help." He moved the phone to his other ear and stood. "Excuse me. Won't be long."

"Go ahead. We have a guest room at the end of the hall on the right. You won't be disturbed down there." Luke followed him to the hall. "I'll help Madison wrap things up for the night with the kids and see you back here when you're done."

Max gave him the thumbs up as he walked toward the guest room.

"Max? Is that you? The connection's not great."

He ducked into the small room and put a hand over his free ear so he could hear his colleague. "Yeah. Hey, Rob. I'm in Sonaja. Anything to report?"

"Yes, you could say that." The young detective cleared his throat.

Max sank onto a bed in the middle of the room and stared at the whitewashed wall. "Tell me everything."

"It's good news. At least I think so. There hasn't been another assault, so you can exhale."

Max did as he was told, not realizing he had been holding his breath.

Thank You, God.

"So, have we found him?"

"Yes and no."

This was painful. "Spit it out, Rob."

"Sorry. Well, we have a positive ID. Just haven't been able to track him down yet."

"Seriously?"

"Yes. It's a David Fitzpatrick. From California. His sister came forward after piecing together a whole bunch of clues."

Max rested his elbows on his knees. "Have you spoken with her in person?"

"Sure have. She came in late last night and has been super cooperative. She's distraught, but there's no doubt it's him. Psychopathic tendencies, most likely set off after his daughter died eighteen months ago. He's been missing for several weeks which lines up with the escalation of attacks. Gone AWOL."

"But what makes you so sure? We have to cover all the bases with this one. I need you to go through all the recent video footage from the Florence hospital now we have an ID. Have any of the victims seen a photo of this David Fitzpatrick guy?"

Not that anyone saw his face...

"I've been in touch with three of them today. He fits the height and body type but that's all they could verify."

"Okay. Send me a headshot as soon as you can. Need I ask about the one distinguishing feature Red has that we know about?"

"The sister has confirmed and we have photographic evidence."

Max heart rate sped up. "Tell me."

"David Fitzpatrick has a tattoo of two hearts on his right wrist."

* * *

Juliet gasped as the taxi driver pulled up at the massive arched entrance of La Catedral. *Swanky. Madison had that right.*

"This is it, señorita." He gestured at the restaurant with pride. It was by far the most prestigious building in the area.

"Gracias." She leaned forward and placed the cash in his upturned hand. Before she even had chance to exit the stuffy vehicle, Richard appeared and opened her door.

"Hi. Sorry I'm a bit late. Believe it or not, we got stuck behind a donkey." Juliet gazed up at him and her stomach flipped. Why did he make her feel like she was a hormonal teenager?

"Hi, Juliet. No problem. Glad you found it." He reached for her hand and helped her out. "You look gorgeous, by the way."

"Thanks." Her face was now a pitiful shade of scarlet, for sure. She hadn't felt like this since she started dating Max. She smoothed the silky, navy fabric of the one fancy dress she brought with her, grateful she had decided to throw it in her case at the last minute. "You don't look so bad yourself."

Understatement. He was dashing in charcoal dress pants and a white collared shirt which enhanced his fresh tan. "I see you've been in the sun already."

He grinned. "I've been so busy with work the past few months, lying in the sun seemed like the perfect recovery plan."

"I hear you. If I knew I wouldn't burn to a crisp, I'd be there, too." She glanced down at her shoulders. They were pink already.

"I'm betting your nurse head tells you not to spend too long in those rays of harmful sun. Am I right?" His arm brushed hers. It wasn't horrible. Not at all.

"You might be onto something." Goodness, flirting was fun. It had been a while.

Juliet walked beside him deeper into the restaurant's foyer area, where he waved at the hostess. "They already have our table set for us."

He must have been waiting for some time, thanks to that stubborn mule in the road. "Great. Something smells delicious."

They walked past the bar in the direction of intensifying aromas, rich with spice and zest.

"We're out on the patio in the corner." Richard pointed to a small table for two but all Juliet could see was the spectacular view.

"Wow." The panoramic vista stretched as far as the eye could see—the sky ablaze in a dramatic abundance of color. "The sunsets here are stunning. I've never seen such a red sky." The crimson setting sun sat on the horizon like jelly in the center of a golden doughnut atop a midnight sea. Bronze fingers splayed across an expanse of lavender deepening into sapphire hues.

She exhaled. "It's a masterpiece."

"I arranged it especially for tonight." Richard's prideful tone caused her to bristle and look him in the eye. He gave her a wink and guided her past diners at the surrounding elegant tables in the direction of theirs.

Juliet's heart deflated.

Max would have pointed to the Creator for all the sunset glory.

Why was she thinking about Max tonight? She turned to focus on Richard. Paying attention to a handsome man shouldn't be this hard.

What did Richard believe? They hadn't touched on faith or God or anything in their brief conversations so far.

Perhaps it doesn't matter to me so much anymore.

No. God always caught her attention in the beauty of creation...

"Do you believe in God?"

Wow, did I actually just ask that?

Richard held out her chair and scowled. "I'm sorry, what did you say?"

"I was curious. When I see something like this"— she gestured to the enormous sky as if she were a hostess on a game show— "it makes me wonder how people can think this is all an accident. You know, a big bang and here we all are. Accidental breathtaking sunsets. The miracle of childbirth. All the good stuff."

I'm rambling. He looks horrified.

Richard lowered himself into the chair opposite and attempted a smile. Maybe more of a grimace. "I shared sunsets with my now-dead wife and watched the miracle of my now-dead child's birth. God is not on my radar."

Ouch. She knew how he felt. Up until yesterday she was of the same opinion. The old, faith-filled Juliet would have said, "You're on God's radar."

Juliet bit her tongue. She had offended him. Why had she delved into this poor man's private world before they even had chance to peruse the menu? At least she knew where he stood, but she could have been subtler about it. Had she ruined the evening already?

Smooth, Juliet.

One of the servers approached their table but Richard waved her away. He was not happy.

"I'm sorry." What more could she say? She noticed their water glasses were already full, and took a sip from hers.

"No, *I'm* sorry." He stretched his arm across the table and held out his hand. "That was rude of me. Forgive me?"

His eyes glistened with unshed tears and Juliet's heart stirred. "There's nothing to forgive. It was my bad."

She set the glass down and rested her pale hand in his. The hearts on his wrist tattoo rippled as he squeezed her fingers. She sat up straight in her wicker chair. Was this weird? A little much for the first five minutes of a first date? She should pull away yet she couldn't tear her eyes from the tattoo and all it represented. So much loss.

"You are entitled to your own faith. I'm sure it's been a help with the loss of your mother."

Juliet looked up into his eyes. They were heavy with the weight of grief.

"I guess so." Who was she kidding?

She had ignored the comfort of her Heavenly Father and replaced it with stubborn resentment. Until her time on the beach last night.

"I mean, yes. I know God is going to help me through all this sorrow and loss, and I'm sure I'll come out the other side stronger in my faith and ready to see what He has planned for me next." After this morning, she was on the right track. "But I'll admit I'm struggling at the moment." She raised a shoulder. "It still hurts."

Richard let go of her hand. "Right?" His raised voice caused the server who was hovering beside them again to retreat to the bar.

"People don't get it. They carry on like everything's fine, but it's not. Health care is a joke and they pour so much money into these trials they can't even offer desperate patients." His face darkened.

Whoa. Where did that outburst come from?

"Is that what happened?" Juliet's voice was a whisper.

"What?" His eyes were slits and his teeth clenched. Why was he so mad with her all of a sudden?

"To your daughter? Was she unable to receive treatment for some reason?" She had to know. It might help her try to soothe him.

"What do you care?" The words spewed from his lips before he stood and stomped off past the bar in the direction of the foyer.

Juliet's mouth hung open. She didn't know this man at all. She would give him chance to calm down. Let him know she *did* care about his loss.

I'm a nurse. Caring is what I do.

Chapter Twenty-Four

MAX STOOD AND SLID THE PHONE into the back pocket of his jeans. Good news. This was good news. They had a solid lead, and he trusted his guys would hunt this Fitzpatrick down with the extra manpower they had been allocated. He rubbed the stubble on his chin.

Half of me itches to be back there.

No, he had to speak with Juliet. That was his first mission.

He rolled his shoulders as he finally gazed around the room. Juliet's room. Yes, this was where she was sleeping alright—the giant bottle of sunblock on top of the small stack of books on the nightstand was a giveaway. He picked up her light blue cardigan from the bed and buried his face in the familiar softness. Lavender. Definitely Juliet. Since her mom died she had taken up the mantle of her mom's signature scent. It suited her.

Madison's laughter drifted from the living room. Max returned the cardigan and hurried back down the hallway. "Hey guys, sorry about the call."

"No problem. Come on in and make yourself comfortable." Madison sat on the love seat next to Luke, a pink-cheeked baby on her lap. "This is Angel. He's teething and needed love and attention, so this husband of mine is pulling some interesting faces to keep him amused."

Luke draped an arm around Madison's shoulders and tickled the baby.

Max grinned. "You two are naturals at the parenting thing. I know you've been here a few years, Luke, but Madison—it suits you, too." He sank into an armchair.

"I'm so proud of her." Luke kissed her cheek. "It's been a learning curve, to say the least."

"But I love it here. Of course, we couldn't do it alone—we have Carla full-time, she's taking a shower right now but I know she'll want to meet you. You'll see the rest of the team in action tomorrow. They all help things run smoothly and then I fill in where needed." She beamed. "I think I've found my vocation—kids. Whether they're mine biologically or not." Her head jerked up. "Oh, I didn't mean to say that." She grimaced. "Sorry Max. I think I'm digging myself deeper into trouble here."

Obviously, Juliet had explained his problem. Great. He grimaced and shook his head. "No need to be sorry. I knew Juliet would share everything with you— she needs her friends around her. I think I've done a stellar job confusing her while trying to deal with the issue myself. No wonder she doesn't know what to think. How has she been?"

Madison chewed on her lip. "I'm not going to lie, I've been worried about her. When she arrived on Friday, she seemed to be carrying a lot on those shoulders of hers. She'd lost her sparkle, which is understandable given what she's been through. I know she's having a bit of a faith crisis as well, which is going to weigh heavy on her heart. She's always had such a strong relationship with God."

"It's hard to watch, isn't it? Selfishly, I want her to come back to me, but I know she needs to come back to God most."

"He isn't going anywhere." Luke shrugged. "She's His child and He loves her." He looked down at Angel. "He's a good Father."

Max swallowed a lump of emotion.

Madison snuggled the sleepy baby in close. "I think she's making progress already judging by our conversations. Let's keep praying."

Lord, help me to trust Juliet into Your loving care.

He checked his watch. Six twenty-five. It felt much later after a day travelling. "You mentioned she was out tonight—can you tell me where?"

Luke got up and retrieved the chips and salsa from the kitchen island and set them on the coffee table within grabbing reach. "Can I get you a refill on the juice?"

He was stalling, no doubt about it. "Thanks, that would be great." He turned to Madison and raised both eyebrows. "What aren't you telling me?"

She focused on the baby. "This is super awkward. The thing is, she met this guy on the plane..."

Max's heart sank like a rock. "Wait, what?" He gripped the arms of the chair. "She's on a date with a guy she just met?"

Didn't see that coming.

"Please don't jump to conclusions." Madison's voice remained calm. "Like I said, she's not her old self and even though I was concerned about this man from the plane, in the end it was kind of encouraging to see she even wanted to go out at all. It's nothing serious. I think perhaps she's doing us a favor."

Luke handed the glass to Max and sat back down. "She is?"

"Yes." Madison glared at Luke.

Max stifled a chuckle. If he wasn't feeling so devastated and blindsided, this could be amusing to watch them bicker a little.

Madison turned her attention back to Max. "He was interested in offering some financial support for the orphanage. They got to talking on the flight and he called yesterday to see if they could get together."

"I guess she's over the grieving then." He pictured her beautiful, tear-streaked face at the beach when he had comforted her—and then the kiss…

"Max." Madison tilted her head. "Don't be hard on her. She sprinkled her mom's ashes last night. It's a lot for her to deal with."

"I'm sorry, that was childish of me." He took a sip of juice. "I expected to find her here still broken and on a path toward some healing. I didn't expect the dating thing… but I have no right to judge her." He leaned back his head. "I've messed up big time when it comes to matters of the heart."

"Don't give up, man." Luke winked. "When she sees you've flown all the way here to surprise her, she'll see you're serious. Actions speak louder than words." He narrowed his eyes. "You *are* serious, aren't you?"

You have no idea.

"The thought of losing her forever was my wake-up call. I've been miserable since I moved back to Seattle. I thought I was doing the best thing for her, giving her the chance to have a whole, healthy, child-filled future with someone else. Now I realize I shouldn't have made the decision for her."

"That's good." Madison grinned. "Because I happen to think you two have a future together. She may be frustrated and angry now, but she still loves you. I'm sure of it."

Max's heart swelled. "I know it, too. We need to

sit down and talk it all through. Discuss our possibilities." His gaze shifted to little Angel, his huge brown eyes drowsy on love. "I don't think we're here at an orphanage by accident."

Luke pointed upward. "God does work in mysterious ways."

Madison looked at her husband with adoring eyes. "We can attest to that."

"You're right." Max set his glass on the table and reached for a handful of chips. "So, what do you know about this guy she's with tonight?"

Madison's nose crinkled. "I'm guessing he has money as they're at La Catedral for dinner, which is the nicest restaurant I know of in the area. Juliet took an information sheet with her because of his interest in the orphanage."

Better be all he's interested in.

"Did she mention a name?"

"Yeah, he's Richard something-or-other."

Richard. Max bristled. Perhaps he was a lonely old dude wanting some company. Juliet was a sucker for a sob story and super patient with the elderly.

"So, like an older guy then?"

Madison tried to hide a smirk—and failed. "Sorry to burst your bubble but, no. He's a young widower. From what Juliet said, he's been through the wringer."

"What do you mean?"

She scooted to the edge of the couch with the now-sleeping Angel. "It's heartbreaking. His daughter died not long ago, I believe. Cancer. That hit a chord with Juliet, as you would expect. After losing her mom and then being a pediatric nurse and all..."

A widower. Lost a child. Like the suspect Rob had described on the phone. Max's blood ran cold. "Madison, are you sure his name is Richard?"

She stood with the baby and swayed. "Positive. I even spoke on the phone with him. Why?"

Max rose and walked over to her. "This is going to sound ridiculous but please humor me. Did Juliet describe him at all?"

She squinted. "I feel like he was the tall, dark, and handsome type. Not much else though."

"But did he pick her up from here? Didn't you get to meet him?" He needed that description from Rob as soon as possible.

She leaned a hip against the side of the sofa. "No. That was one thing that didn't impress me. Juliet said he didn't offer to pick her up or even come in a taxi to take her. She had to make her own way to the restaurant in a cab. It's only a fifteen-minute ride but I don't think it was very chivalrous."

"So maybe it *is* more of a business meeting after all." Luke leaned forward. "You may be worried over nothing, Max."

His gut told him otherwise. "Did Juliet mention anything to either of you about this Richard having a tattoo by any chance? Please think hard." His words were measured as his skin prickled.

Madison gasped and handed the baby to Luke. "Yes." The color drained from her face. "This is strange, but, yes. She said he had this tattoo and I remember it because it was so sad. It was on his wrist—two hearts, one for his wife and one for his daughter." She gulped. "How did you know?"

NO.

Max's mouth was bone dry. He struggled to choke out the words.

"Juliet is with Red. This *Richard* is the nurse-killer."

Chapter Twenty-Five

THEY ALL FROZE IN PLACE FOR a beat. *Think.* Max had to remove his heart from the dire situation before him and allow his head to take the lead. Detective mode.

"Are you sure?" Luke was the first to manage words.

Max's shoulders slumped. *How can this be happening?*

"Positive. The assailant is using an alias and he's right here in Mexico. I need to report back to the team in Florence and have them check flight details and possible hotel reservations in the area." How had the madman pulled his plan together?

Luke looked from Max to Madison.

"Honey, you've gone pale." He led her back to the love seat.

"I can't just sit here." Her face crumbled. "Not when Juliet is in danger. Oh, my goodness, this is awful." She clutched Luke's hand. "That business this morning with the bookmark. You don't suppose it was connected, do you? Could it have been Richard somehow?"

"We know he had her address because he called her here..."

Max held up both hands and frowned. "Slow down. I need to know everything. Any details could be crucial. What are you talking about?"

Madison tucked her hair behind her ears. "It was bizarre. A silly thing. Juliet was convinced her bookmark had been taken from the novel she was reading and had been replaced by a paper heart. She found it when she came back from swimming in the ocean this morning." She looked up at Max with liquid brown eyes. "I thought maybe you had planted it in her book."

Max gulped. "Me? I have no clue. Tell me about this heart."

"It was paper. Cut into the shape of a heart. Basic. Red. Juliet said her bookmark was missing and then when she turned the book over and shook it, this heart fell out from between the pages. She was adamant she'd never seen it before."

"And when did she last read the book?"

"Last night. None of the kids had been in her room or anything, and there's no sign of her original bookmark. It was from her mom, too."

Max blanched at the thought of her losing a treasured gift from Pippa.

Madison grabbed a tissue from a box on the coffee table. "I had a bad feeling but I thought it was me being overprotective after all she's been through. I should never have let her go out this evening. I could tell she was still shaken from earlier."

"You mustn't blame yourself." Max folded his arms across his chest. "We all know Juliet is a sweetheart but she's also as stubborn as it gets, and if she decides to do something, nobody can stop her."

I'm supposed to be her protector. Now he had to hand it all over to God. Unless they could work together to keep her safe…

"I don't understand how he followed her here all the way from Oregon." Luke rocked the baby in his arms. "She made such a last-minute decision about coming. How could he have even known?"

"He's been watching her." Max's fists clenched. "It was my worst fear. We knew this guy had access to hospital staff files but who knows how he hacked into her phone or computer. He could have bugged her apartment." The mere thought made his blood boil. He would have to get the team to check that out.

I failed her.

Wasn't this the whole point of him returning to Florence in the first place? To protect Juliet from this deranged madman? Now he had let her down.

I should never have let her come here alone in the first place.

Like she would have listened to him anyway. He had relinquished all say in her life when he told her they couldn't be a family. Now she had no family whatsoever...

"Max? What are we going to do?" Panic sounded in Madison's voice. He winced. This was going to be hard on her—she had survived her own experience of being kidnapped less than two years ago in Jamaica. The memories were still fresh.

But now it was time to rescue the woman he loved. *Let's do this.*

"How long has Juliet been gone?"

Madison checked her watch. "She left here at six. I think the reservation was for six-fifteen. You only just missed her."

Max pulled his phone from his pocket. "I have to text her right away."

"Why not call her?" Madison wiped her eyes. "We need to hear her voice. Make sure she's okay."

"Trust me on this. If she sees me calling, her she may choose not to pick up."

She's on a date after all...

"Then let me call her?" Madison wrung her hands.

"No, we can't chance it. She may see your name and decide she can catch up with you later. She could think you're just checking in."

"True. So, you'll text her?"

"I think that's best." He found her details on speed dial. "If she sees I've texted her, she might be ticked but she'll be curious. I'm sure of it."

Luke paced the living room with Angel still in his arms. "Makes sense."

"I think so. I'm going to tell her there's an emergency at the orphanage and she needs to call *me* immediately." His fingers tapped out the message as he spoke. "That way if she suspects anything at all or is uncomfortable with this guy, it gives her an excuse to step away. Then we can speak and get her out of there."

Lord, please let this work.

He hit send.

"But what if she has her phone turned off?" Luke's eyes squinted. "She's on vacation, after all."

"I know Juliet." Max checked his phone. "Force of habit. She always keeps it on in case of an emergency. She hates to be out of the loop." Although she had turned it off when she was reading Pippa's manuscript and he needed to contact her. His stomach sank. *Father, I'm giving this over to You.*

"Sounds like it could work." Luke set his jaw. "I can take you to where she is."

"You can?"

"Sure. I know La Catedral restaurant. It's fifteen minutes by the coastal road but I know a shortcut that can shave off five minutes at this time of day." He passed the baby back to Madison. "Honey, you're going to have to hold down the fort here."

He hurried over to the kitchen counter and grabbed his keys. "Fill Carla in as soon as she's out of the shower. She won't mind helping out. We'll call and let you know what's happening."

Madison nodded as tears streamed down her cheeks. "Please bring Juliet home."

"We will." *Or I'll die trying.*

Max clutched his phone, desperate for Juliet to respond to his text. "Let's go. Luke, can I use your phone to call the station back home? I want to know the latest on Red but I need to keep my phone clear in case Juliet calls back."

"Here." Luke handed him his phone and kissed the top of Madison's head. "Love you."

"What can I do?" She stood and followed the men to the front door. "Shall I call the local police?"

"I'll get my guy at the station back home to do it. They can then send through all the info they have on Red." Max turned to Madison as he reached the van. "But you can pray. Please pray."

"I will." She cradled the baby to her chest and watched them leave. "Be careful."

They jumped in the vehicle and Max slammed his door and buckled up as Luke reversed the van down the driveway with gritted teeth. Max recalled Juliet telling him about the way Luke had rescued Madison from her captors. He was level-headed and determined. *Thanks, Lord.* This wasn't his first rodeo.

"Rob." Max held one phone to his ear while he watched for a response from Juliet on the other. "Listen carefully. Red is here in Sonaja. David Fitzpatrick. He's calling himself Richard, and he made contact with Juliet on the plane and is with her at this moment."

Two seconds of silence. "No way. I'm sorry, Max.

I guess it was meant to be that you're on the ground there. What can we do from here?"

Max proceeded to give him instructions for contacting the Sonaja police with the restaurant details and then the airline to see if he had travelled as David or Richard or some other alias. Why had he gone to such effort to follow Juliet specifically? There were other nurses to choose from. He never said a word to any of the others. Yes, her apartment would need to be scanned. Red must have bugged it somehow. *Some guidance here, please, God?*

"Got it, boss. Keep us informed?"

"Will do." Max ended the call and set Luke's phone on the center console and stared at his own.

Come on, Juliet. Please don't choose this moment to be stubborn and not answer me.

"You okay?" Luke kept his eyes on the winding road as they past clusters of small homes.

Max wiped a hand down his face. "Yeah."

I will be once Juliet's safe.

"I have to admit I'm blindsided by this. I didn't expect Red to be this bold. His M.O. up until now has been discreet." What am I missing here? *Lord, I need Your wisdom.*

"You mean with the other nurses?"

"Right. He caught every one of them by surprise. Never even revealed his face."

"He got bold." Luke's voice held an edge.

"Too bold." Max gripped his phone, his knuckles white. "And in a restaurant? He must be intending to take her elsewhere afterwards."

"That could buy us some time. She's a smart girl." Luke swerved around a corner with as much precision as possible in a minivan. "What's the plan when we get there?"

Max chewed on his lip. "I'm hoping she'll respond to my text and we can get her out of the dining area, presuming it's where they are now, to somewhere Red can't hear her speak. Then I'll get her to come with us. How long until we arrive?"

Luke checked his watch. "Five or six minutes."

"I'm not going to put you in danger here, Luke. I appreciate your help but you must stay in the van."

Luke grunted. "Let's see what's going on first. You don't have a gun or anything. What if he does?"

Luke's phone chimed and Max grabbed it. "It's a photo of Red. Or Richard or David or whatever we're supposed to be calling him."

There he was in all his glory. It was a cropped image of a family man with a good sense of style and an easy smile. A smile he would like to put a fist into about now. At least he knew who to look for beside the beautiful redhead at the restaurant.

"Let's see."

Max turned the screen to face Luke and he took a split-second peek at it. "Seems like a regular guy."

"Psychopaths often do. He's been in and out of hospitals mingling with staff and nurses, and none of them had a hot clue who he was. He looks like a respectable dude. Nothing alarming about him whatsoever." His throat clogged. "Juliet's discerning when it comes to people, but she wouldn't have detected anything suspicious with this individual. I'll bet he was charming." Max flared his nostrils. "In a psychopathic way."

Luke's phone chimed again.

"Good. The local police have been informed and should be on their way. Let's hope they take this seriously."

"Maybe you should wait until they arrive. You need back-up if he's as dangerous as you say."

Max shook his head. "I'm going in. I have to." He willed the other phone in his hand to respond.

Come on, Juliet. He was going to have to send another text.

"The woman I want to spend the rest of my life with is in there with a maniac." He glanced at Luke. He would understand after experiencing the same thing in Jamaica with Madison. "I will do everything in my power to save her."

Chapter Twenty-Six

JULIET STARED AT THE MENU ON the table through watery eyes.

Don't cry.

What was all that about? Granted, she didn't know much about Richard other than his loss and his travelling but she hadn't expected the Jekyll and Hyde treatment tonight. Her head ached.

The server returned with a glass water jug. Her hand shook as she lifted Juliet's glass and refilled it—she must feel awkward after witnessing this strange American guy's outburst. The girl opened her mouth as if to speak but clamped it shut and turned on her heel without a word.

What do I do now?

Juliet's appetite had disappeared as rapidly as Richard, and now she was going solo in a romantic restaurant with an exquisite view. She should pray. After all, she was back on talking terms with God now.

Father, I'm not sure what to do here. I'm feeling kind of vulnerable in this strange country on my own, and I don't know what to do about Richard. He's hurting. I get that. Does he need my help? Should I get to know him better?

Max.

The name flooded her mind like a tidal wave. She was trying not to think about him tonight. Trying to concentrate on Richard—he was buying her dinner, after all. She could think about Max tomorrow. Or later tonight when she was back at the orphanage among friends.

Her phone chirped from her purse on the floor. She bent down to check in case the message was important and when she sat up with the purse in her hand, Richard was back in his chair.

"Whoa. Where did you come from?" Juliet tried not to sound annoyed but this date was not going as she had imagined. She was a whisker away from calling it quits and hailing a cab.

"I'm sorry."

Juliet set her purse on the table and tilted her head, waiting for him to explain.

"Really, really sorry." He buried his face in his hands. Juliet gave him time to compose himself.

"Are you okay?" She studied the top of his head and noticed a couple of gray hairs. Her heart sank. This guy had been through so much. The least she could do was cut him some slack, be a listening ear. Nothing more.

"Yes." He lifted his chin and peeked at her through his fingers. "That was not cool. I'm so ashamed of myself." He set his hands on the table and surveyed the surrounding diners. They had resumed their meals now that the spectacle had died down. "I didn't mean to cause a scene."

Juliet put one elbow on the table and rested her chin on her hand. This whole ordeal was taking its toll and weariness set in. *Let's get this wrapped up and maybe I can get back to the orphanage.* "Want to talk about it? I'm a good listener. Maybe not as good as you were on the plane." She shrugged. "But it seems to me like you could do with someone to shoulder a little of the burden you're carrying."

"You're volunteering?"

"I want to help."

A shadow fell over his face. "I think I'm past help. Thanks anyway." He opened the large menu in front of him. "What do you fancy for dinner?"

Juliet did a double-take. This guy was hard to keep up with—the way he changed subjects and moods so quickly.

"Do you like seafood?" Richard grinned over the top of his menu, his grief-stricken self a distant memory.

Perhaps he's learned to compartmentalize in order to cope.

"Umm, sure. I live on the Oregon Coast. Seafood is a staple."

"Oh, yes." He winked. "I don't think they'll be able to match your Florence clam chowder here. I think I'm going to go for lobster."

Juliet studied her own menu. Weird. Had she mentioned that she lived in Florence? An uneasy sense of dread washed over her from head to toe. The thought of any food in her stomach made her nauseous. The desire to flee was strong. Something was wrong.

"Juliet?"

"Sorry, what were you saying?" She took a big swig of water.

"Your hair. It's stunning. The exact shade of the sunset at this very minute." He stared out over the ocean.

What was it with guys and the fixation on red hair? He was spot on. The ever-changing skies were now aglow with what looked like strands of her locks.

God, do you see me here?

Max.

His name was front and center. Again, her phone chirped. This was too much of a coincidence. Was God telling her something?

"Excuse me, I should check that."

"No." Richard placed a hand over her purse. "I don't think you need to."

Indignant, Juliet snatched her purse from under his hand. "I beg your pardon?"

"I think it can wait, don't you?" He leaned back in his chair and a charming smile crept over his lips. "This evening is about you and me."

Juliet's stomach tightened. Something was not right with this sick man. Perhaps he had unresolved issues and had become a tad unhinged. Why hadn't she seen it at the beginning? Perhaps grief had clouded her judgment.

She focused on her purse, which was now on her lap. "I really do need to check this. I hate to think anyone's in trouble. It's the nurse in me."

He clenched and unclenched his fist on the table as she whipped the phone out.

Two text messages.

Both from Max. Her heart skipped a beat.

JULIET. PLEASE PHONE ME NOW. EMERGENCY AT ORPHANAGE.

The messages were identical. Her pulse raced. The orphanage? Why would he be texting her about the orphanage?

"Everything okay?" Richard drummed his fingers on the closed menu. "We should order. Would you like wine?"

"No, thank you. There's a problem at the orphanage." She tapped a question mark in reply to the message.

"Can't they do without you for one evening?" He scowled.

What was with the jealousy? She needed to think quick and get out of here. "Listen, I know Madison wouldn't ask me to go back to the orphanage if it weren't important. She knows I was looking forward to coming out tonight."

"You were?" The softness returned to his eyes.

Juliet nodded. Soothe his soul a little. "Yes, I was, but I can't make out why a... mutual friend... in Oregon is telling me to go to the orphanage. It doesn't make sense."

Her phone sounded. Max again.

CAN YOU PHONE ME IMMEDIATELY?

She squinted. "Now it's my turn to apologize but you need to give me a second. I have to make a super quick call. In fact, I'll make the call up in the foyer."

Richard opened his mouth.

"Then I'll join you with the lobster." She stood with her purse. The subject was closed. "I'll be two minutes." She took a moment as her head spun. Why was she woozy?

Must have overdone it on the beach.

"Are you feeling all right? Perhaps you should sit back down." Richard smirked.

She gripped the edge of the table and took a deep breath. "I'm fine. Thank you." Her anger simmered, but she rounded it off with the sweetest smile she could muster.

Before he had chance to make a fuss, Juliet turned and wove her way around several tables and found the ladies' room to one side of the foyer. Her heart pounded and her palms were clammy as she ducked in and pressed Max's number on speed dial. Whatever could be so important?

"Juliet?"

"Max? What's wrong? Is it Madison?"

"Juliet, you need to listen to me." Detective mode voice. He was serious.

"I will, but you're scaring me."

"This man you're with tonight—tell me about his tattoo."

Had Madison told him she was on a date? "What? How do you know—"

"Juliet, please, sweetheart. Tell me."

She leaned against the marble countertop and pinched the bridge of her nose. "The tattoo? It's two hearts kind of overlapping. Why?"

"Where is it located?"

"On his wrist. The inside part." She closed her eyes to visualize it. "His right wrist."

"As we thought. Juliet, I know you like to be aware of all the details but just this once you have to trust me. Can you do that?"

She stared at her reflection in the mirror above the sinks. Her eyes were glazed.

"Juliet? Are you still there?"

Her vision blurred as she tried to concentrate on Max's words. "Max. I'm not feeling great."

"Where are you? Are you still inside La Catedral?"

Ringing. Soft ringing was coming from somewhere. In both ears. "I'm so tired."

"Juliet." Max yelled into the phone and she jumped.

"Yes. I'm here. I'm in the women's bathroom. Why do you want to know?" Was he jealous of Richard? Perhaps he had phoned Madison and was mad she was out with a guy. Yes. No. Her thoughts were jumbled. She braced herself against the counter. "Max, I think I may have been drugged. I only had water to drink. I shouldn't be feeling like this."

With her free hand, she turned on a faucet and splashed her face.

"Stay in there, please. Stay in the bathroom. I'm on my way."

On his way? She must be losing consciousness. It sounded like Max was coming for her. That was ridiculous. He was back in Florence. It would take a full day for him to get here. She was not waiting in the bathroom for a full day. Besides, her head was beginning to throb and she needed fresh air. Now.

Juliet hung up and somehow stuffed the phone back into her purse and stumbled to the bathroom door. Nothing made sense. She tugged it open and tried to stay vertical when every bone in her body longed to lie down on the shiny, tiled floor. It looked so enticing.

No. One step in front of another. Focus. She needed to get away. Through the door.

Why? Where was everyone? Max. Madison. Mom. *Oh, Mom, how I miss you...*

"Hello, Juliet. I missed you."

Her head jerked up.

"Richard?"

Chapter Twenty-Seven

"Wait, where are we going?" Juliet's head swam as she struggled to think through the fog. "What about the lobster?"

Richard's grip was tight around the top of her arm as he half-dragged her past the distracted hostess and through the foyer toward the entrance.

"Ouch. You're hurting me."

"Quiet." He squeezed tighter.

"Car." He handed a slip of paper to a valet and deposited Juliet onto a stone bench. "Make it quick."

Confused. So confused.

A cool breeze lifted her hair from her bare shoulders and Richard took a handful of it. He brought it to his face and inhaled deeply.

Juliet flinched.

"Your hair is extraordinary." His voice was low. Menacing.

She pulled away from him. "What's going on?" Her limbs were like lead. "Did you drug me?" Even her words were slow.

He put an arm around her shoulders and pulled her close. "You're different. Special. I wanted to spend more time with you. I believe you are the one."

"The one?"

Max. *I need to phone Max.*

Juliet attempted to open her purse.

"You won't be needing that." Richard tore the purse from her hands and hurled it behind them into a bush.

She let out a yelp.

"Here's our ride."

A red car pulled up. Some kind of sports model. The fast kind. Richard opened the passenger door and folded her into the front seat before she even knew it happened. The smell of leather was overpowering. She turned to the entrance of the restaurant. Nobody was there. What about the valet?

"Help." Juliet yelled as loud as she could and willed her fumbling hands to open the car door. It was locked. She heard Richard laughing behind the vehicle.

He gave the valet a wad of cash and patted him on the back. What was happening?

Richard jumped into the driver's seat and re-locked the doors. "He thinks the lady has had way too much to drink this evening. Shame on you."

He reached into his shirt pocket and pulled something out with a flourish.

Juliet squinted to bring it into focus.

Her bookmark. The missing one her mom had given her. He dropped it in her lap and sneered.

She stared at the kitty image, relieved to have her treasure back. It took a moment for her to comprehend. He had stalked her. What was going on?

"No. It was you? You came to the orphanage this morning?"

He laughed and slammed his foot onto the accelerator and they sped away from the safety of the restaurant. She slid the bookmark into the side-pocket of her dress and, somehow, had the presence of mind to secure her seat belt.

He was driving way too fast. Trees blurred in her peripheral vision. Bright lights from stores still busy. Seconds of open ocean view. It took every ounce of energy to keep her eyelids open.

"Why did you put the paper heart in my book? What were you even doing there?"

"I was watching you swim. It was intoxicating."

She whimpered.

I knew it. I knew someone had been there.

"What's going on, Richard?" She hated how frightened she sounded. "Where are you taking me?"

His jaw tightened as he squinted through the windshield.

"What are you going to do with me?"

"You still don't get it?" He tutted. "Come on, Nurse Juliet. Drugged or not, you must have figured it out by now." He reached across with one hand and picked up a ribbon of her hair. "Yours is the most beautiful red hair of all."

Juliet gasped. *No.* It couldn't be. She turned her head toward him in horror.

He nodded. "That's right."

Red. He was Red? How could this be? Nausea swirled in the pit of her stomach as she turned away from him. A trickle of sweat meandered down her back. No more words came. What could she say? She was half-drugged with a murderer in a foreign country all by herself. Her chin wobbled.

I will not give him the satisfaction of seeing me cry.

She bit the inside of her cheek until she tasted blood.

God, I know You see me. You always see me. I'm Yours. I don't know what's going on or why, but I need You to give me some clarity of mind here. What do I do?

Juliet closed her eyes. Conserve energy. She would fight the monster with everything she had. She bit back a sob. Max. Yes, he had phoned her and knew she was at the restaurant—but how would he know where she was going now? She didn't even know.

Breathe. Juliet took in a slow gulp of air and held it for several beats before exhaling. Her heart was racing like a rabid greyhound and she needed to keep her cool. Her head already felt lighter and less groggy. Perhaps the drugs were wearing off or maybe the extra water she gulped had diluted the potency. Would that even matter if he was going to kill her?

She snuck a side glance and tried to guess how strong he might be. He wasn't super muscular but he was no weakling. The bruises on her arms would prove that.

The silence in the car was chilling. Richard—or Red—seemed to be in complete control. Gone was the raging insecure guy she witnessed minutes ago. Here was a measured man on a mission.

He's going to kill me.

A lone tear snaked down Juliet's cheek at the stark realization. She let it fall. Half of her was tempted to give in to the exhaustion that pressed in like a straight-jacket. Emotionally, she was spent. Physically, she was suffering the effects of narcotics. Spiritually—where was she? Hadn't she already cried out to God, knowing He was her hope? Her only hope.

Father, forgive me. I see now You are all that matters in my life. Even if it's going to end tonight. You've had my back all along. You grieved with me. You went through Mom's pain alongside her. You know what Max is going through in a grief of his own.

The orphanage lights shone up ahead.

If I don't see him again, would you show Max that children come in all sorts of packages? That he can be a blessing to kids in a myriad of different ways? With chosen children.

Like Madison and Luke...

Wait. The orphanage? Juliet sat bolt upright in her seat and grabbed the dashboard. So much for staying calm.

"What are you doing?" Her voice was shrill.

His face was expressionless. "I told you I had an interest in the orphanage, didn't I?"

* * *

The van screeched to a halt in front of the entrance to La Catedral. Luke unbuckled his seat belt and Max grabbed his arm.

"I was serious, Luke. You have to stay here. Watch your phone in case my guys at the station call back—they have your number now." He gulped. "And if there's trouble, I'll text you."

"You have my number?"

"I already added it."

Luke frowned and checked behind them. "Empty road. No police yet."

"They'll be here soon. I can't risk waiting. Not when I know she's in there somewhere. Will you hang tough here and pray?"

"It's a given. Be safe, buddy."

Max nodded. Juliet had phoned him from the restaurant bathroom and it sure sounded as if she had been drugged or something. She even suspected as much.

Please be there, sweetheart. Don't try anything brave and crazy.

His heart hammered in his chest as he jumped from the van and passed an empty valet's stand.

Cool. I have to stay cool.

He breezed past the lobby desk and flashed a smile

at the young lady manning the phone. First stop had to be the women's bathroom, which would be awkward. He checked his cell one more time. Nothing since her call five minutes ago.

Five minutes. She had to still be here.

He caught sight of male and female bathroom signs pointing to the right of the foyer.

Better make sure they aren't sitting back at a table.

He scanned the dining area which spilled out onto a beautiful patio and the vast ocean beyond. At least he knew what Red looked like now and on first glance, nobody fitted the description. He would recognize Juliet's glorious red hair in an instant.

No. Nothing. On to the bathroom.

Max formulated an impromptu plan en route. He would barrel into the ladies' room and feign ignorance and embarrassment if necessary. Fortunately, the two washroom doors were side-by-side. An honest mistake any man could make.

Please be there.

He took one last scan of the corridor before pushing the heavy wooden door and entering the women's washroom. Empty.

"Juliet?" He ran to the stalls and pushed each door wide to make sure she hadn't collapsed or was hiding. "Juliet?"

No reply.

The soft strains of romantic Latino music drifted in from the dining room.

Max slammed his hand down on the marble countertop. "No."

The bathroom door opened and Max was face-to-face with an elderly woman with a walking stick. She gasped.

"Sorry." He put down his head and stomped past the confused lady in the direction of the hostess.

"Hello." She beamed as he approached. He must appear American enough for her to practice her English.

"Hi. I wonder if you could help me, Miss. This is an emergency."

Her eyes widened. "Sí."

Max tapped his phone and showed her a photograph of Juliet. She would be more recognizable than Red. "Have you seen this woman tonight? She was here minutes ago."

"Sí. She was here." The girl stroked her own long black hair. "The beautiful hair."

Max's heart leaped. "Great. Do you know where she is now? Is she still here?" He peered around. She had to be. He tapped her number into his phone and held it to his ear.

The girl shook her head and a frown caused two lines to deepen between her dark eyebrows. "She is gone."

No.

"With a man?"

"Sí. They left here, señor. She did not seem good. Maybe too much to drink?" She raised one slim shoulder.

No. Juliet rarely drank alcohol and when she did, it was just one glass. She was right about being drugged. His stomach dropped. "Where did they go? Did they say anything at all?"

Stay calm, man.

"Oh." The girl looked down below her desk. "Sir, are you calling the woman's phone by any chance?"

Max nodded and his eyes widened when she produced Juliet's clutch bag. The silver one he bought for her birthday last year.

"Where did you get this?"

"It was found at the entrance, sir."

"When?"

"Moments ago."

The clutch bag was ringing. Max grabbed it and opened the clasp. Her phone lit up like a Christmas tree and he pulled it out while pocketing his own. Nothing. No new messages. No clues—that would have been too much to hope for. He dove back into the clutch and retrieved a lipstick and the information leaflet from the orphanage. At the bottom he pulled out a few crumpled bank notes along with her passport. Good. At least they wouldn't get far.

Another young girl appeared at the desk, a server dressed in black and white. She spoke rapid-fire with the hostess and they both turned to look at him, their expressions shocked.

"What is it?"

The hostess spoke. "This server saw your man put something in the water glass of your lady. Some powder."

The young girl bowed her head. "I am sorry." She turned and hurried back to the restaurant.

"She wanted to say something to the lady but did not know what to do. She has many regrets now. We all do."

Max nodded. "Gracias. That confirms she was drugged."

Think. The car. "What can you tell me about the car they left in?"

"I don't know. Wait. We will ask Joe." She beckoned to a smartly dressed young guy who rounded the corner from the parking lot.

"Hello." He nodded and clasped his hands behind his back.

Yes, another English speaker.

"Hi. I need to find this woman and a man. It's an emergency." He flashed his phone. "They left a few minutes ago."

The boy nodded. "Emergency? Yes. I brought the car around. Is there a problem?"

You could say that.

"Please think. What was the color and model of the car, son?"

He squinted. "I'm not sure of the model. Red sports car. The roof was up. It was new. Smelled of leather."

"Good." Max saw flashing lights in his peripheral vision. The cavalry was here. "Do you have any idea where they were going?"

As he shook his head, glossy dark curls bounced on his forehead. "He was fast. Super-fast. The lady, she looked sick."

"Sick?"

"Like maybe too much alcohol? She was sad."

Definitely drugged, more like. Oh Juliet. Where are you?

"Listen, the police are going to want to know all the details so please repeat it all to them." Max looked at the hostess. "Including the drugged water, the man's reservation details, and anything else you can think of. I have to go."

He tucked the clutch under his arm, left the two bewildered members of staff, and sprinted to the van, where Luke was mercifully speaking Spanish to two police officers.

"They left. It must have been minutes ago." Max nodded to the police. "Could you tell them we need to chase down a fancy red sports car?"

Luke relayed the information and Max watched as one officer got on his radio and spoke in clipped measures while the other one strode into the restaurant. Luke jumped behind the wheel of the van and nodded at the clutch on Max's lap. "Juliet's purse?"

"Yeah. They left it here. Let's go."

"I haven't heard anything more from Oregon. The police here are sending more back-up, and one of them put out an alert for the red sports car with a man and woman. He is heading into town first so I suggest we take the regular road back along the coast. If this guy's not a local, chances are he doesn't know the route we just used. I'm guessing we have no clue as to where they are heading?"

Max buckled up and wiped perspiration from his forehead as Luke started the ignition. "No idea. He's trying something new. The staff here seemed to think Juliet was drunk, but it's not true. The server just came forward saying she saw Red put a powder in her glass."

"And she told you she felt like she may have been drugged. Let's hope she's hanging in there and we're on the right track following the ocean road."

God, I'm begging You. Please don't let him hurt Juliet. Don't let us be too late.

Chapter Twenty-Eight

MAX GRIPPED THE EDGE OF HIS seat as they rounded a corner on the coastal road, thankful traffic was sparse on this Sunday evening. "I guess we'll stick with this route for now." He scanned the area as they sped past a few open stores, desperate for any sign of a red sports car.

This feels hopeless.

"I texted Oregon and told them they could use my regular phone now that we know Juliet isn't going to call." He shuddered at the thought of her not being able to communicate with anyone from here on in. "The local police have our numbers, right?"

"Yes. I gave them both our phone numbers. I've met the one officer before and he's a good guy. Goes to our church."

"Okay." Max placed the clutch bag on the floor while he checked the phones again. "I'm sorry. I don't do so well when I'm not in charge."

"This is hard. I get it."

Max jumped when Luke's phone burst into some upbeat Caribbean tune.

"It's Madison. Can you pick it up? I want to keep both hands on the wheel here."

"Sure."

The speed you're going, I want you to keep both hands on the wheel, too.

Max picked up the phone.

"Luke?" Madison whispered into the phone.

"It's both of us. I've got you on speakerphone. Luke's driving. What's up?" Why was she whispering?

"You guys, you're not going to believe this, but I think Juliet is here."

"What?" Luke and Max responded in unison.

"Honey, what do you mean?" Luke glanced at Max. "And why are you talking so softly? I can hardly hear you."

"I was getting some milk for Angel in the kitchen and I looked out across the beach. I saw some shadows and didn't think much of it. You know the locals sometimes walk here in the evenings."

"Right." Luke's voice was tight.

"I heard a scream, so I opened the back door to our yard but there was nothing. I couldn't see anyone at all. Then Carla called to me from her room. There was a strange car parked in our driveway."

Please, no.

Max ran a hand through his hair. "What's the car like, Madison?"

"Like nothing any of us drive. It's a red sports car."

* * *

"Why have we come here?" Juliet rubbed the side of her face and kept her voice to a frantic whisper. Her initial cry as she tripped over a tree root in the sand had earned her a swift slap. She wouldn't let that happen again.

Why had Richard parked outside the orphanage? It was like he wanted her missionary friends to know he was there. She had noticed Luke's van was gone. Was he out for the evening? Maybe Carla had used it. Was Madison alone with the kids? Her skin prickled. What was he going to do with her? With them? What if

270

Madison heard her and came wandering onto the beach? She couldn't endanger Madison and the kids. She had to stay quiet. Stay calm.

God, help me—and please protect those children.

"I had to think on my feet. Change of plan." Richard dragged her along the beach. His grip was tight on her upper arm and she felt more deep bruising where his fingers dug in hard. Madison must have heard them pull up in the sports car with its ridiculous engine. Maybe she would call the police and not venture outside.

"Why this beach?" Talk. She had to keep him talking. Wasn't that what they did in the movies and in her suspense novels?

"I do my best thinking on the beach."

"Me, too."

"Plus, the orphanage is here." He curled his lip.

Her stomach dropped. This madman had a plan. Must make it personal. Appeal to his heart.

Wait, this guy is a murderer.

But he had seemed so nice, so normal on the plane. When he talked about his daughter, Juliet's heart had split wide open. Yes, the daughter...

"What was her name?" She tried to drag her feet as he pulled her closer to the palm trees. She needed time. Give Madison chance to spot the car in her driveway and alert the authorities.

"What?" He scrunched up his face.

"Your daughter. What was her name?" Juliet held her breath.

He stopped and turned her around. "You don't get to talk about my baby girl. You all deserted her when she needed you most. You killed her."

"No, you can't blame me for that. I don't know any

details about your little girl and I never treated her as a patient. You're from California, right?"

"Yes. We had a perfect life once upon a time, but you all refused to give me the one thing I wanted."

"Treatment for her?"

"You all gave up on her like she didn't matter. You wouldn't even try the experimental medicines I researched." His nostrils flared. "My whole career I sold pharmaceuticals to help save people, and when it was my turn..."

Juliet's heart hammered in her chest. "I'm sorry. I don't know the details but they must have had good reason to—"

He pulled a Swiss army knife from his pocket. "Stop talking."

Juliet gasped.

Please, Lord, not like this.

With the flick of his wrist, a menacing blade glistened silver in the moonlight. She tried to pull free from his grasp and for a split second he lost contact with her arm. Shocked, she fell backward and caught herself before collapsing to the sand.

Run.

She took two steps away in the direction of the orphanage but he was fast. Too fast.

Juliet felt her hair being yanked at the roots and bit back a cry of pain.

"No, Juliet. You're not leaving me. I've been left too many times. You're mine now." He twirled her to face him, their noses inches apart.

Trapped in his embrace, she rubbed her head. "Why me?" Her voice was a whisper as tears welled in her eyes.

"You are the perfect choice. I had to consider others but then I researched and found you."

"Why? Why am I the perfect choice?"

His contorted face relaxed along with his voice. "You have the heart of a nurse. Like my late wife. The identical hair of my daughter."

His hands behind her head, she sensed him lift a section of her hair and then she felt a swift tug underneath. Had he cut some off?

"Isn't it captivating?" He held a long tress of her hair between his fingers while the other hand grabbed around her waist.

This can't be happening.

"The color is perfect. Copper in the moonlight. Exquisite."

She watched as he stuffed it into the breast pocket of his shirt. This was beyond sick. Would her cut her throat next?

"Our future daughters will have glorious hair like yours."

Future daughters? He's serious.

A sob rose in Juliet's throat.

He turned her in front of him and they stumbled toward the patch of palm trees where Juliet had sprinkled her mother's manuscript's ashes the previous evening. Had he been watching her then?

"I saw you."

What? She jerked her head up. Those hazel eyes she had trusted with her story on the plane. They appeared vacant now up close. Hollow. Cruel.

"You watched me last night? Here?" She grimaced as he clutched one of her arms in his strong grip. How dare he spy on her most intimate moment? Her sacred time with her mother's memory.

He pulled her down to her knees on the sand and stood over her from behind, the flicked knife in her peripheral vision was open and poised to take a swipe. "We have so much in common. I have to make you see. I knew I'd find my soul mate again."

Juliet's entire body trembled. Soul mate? This man was sick. A grieving husband and father. Violent. A killer. Had that poor nurse fought back before she died? Did she have the same shade of hair as Juliet? She shuddered. He wanted her as his soul mate?

"I've researched you. You're all alone. No family. No husband. No kids. Like me." She glanced back at him and his leer made her skin crawl.

Max, where are you? I need you.

The mere thought of him gave her courage to keep the maniac talking. The effect of the drugs was dulling and she hung onto hope. Max. "You want more kids? A family?"

Richard took two steps around her body and stood before her, shoulders slumped. "Yes. It's all I ever wanted."

The knife pointed at her face. Even if she wanted to escape and run to the orphanage, he was now standing in her path. Fleeing in the opposite direction would eventually take her to a dead end. She tucked strands of hair behind one ear. He watched, enraptured. Keep the conversation going. "You don't have any family members who might be missing you back home?"

He glowered. "A sister. She's busy with her own kids."

"I see." Juliet studied her hands, now in her lap. Could she grab the knife from him? Go against everything that came naturally to her nurse-self and stab the man in front of her?

I can't do it. I just can't do it...

"You do want kids, don't you?" His voice held an edge.

Play along. Tell him what he needs to hear to buy some time.

"Yes. I love children."

He nodded and his face split into a grin. "I knew it."

Her mind went to Max. Hadn't he asked her the same question back when they first started dating? She had been so adamant that, yes, she wanted a truckload of kids—and he had joined her in the dream. They even talked about names. Their first would be Lucy or Joshua. No wonder he was so devastated when he discovered he couldn't have any babies of his own.

God, would You heal his heart? The place where he longs to be a daddy. I may not be around to comfort him and tell him he's okay.

"It's going to take a while." Richard clutched Juliet's hair with his free hand and looked out over the dark ocean.

What is he talking about? And what's he doing with my hair?

She dared not ask. She would find out soon enough.

"How many kids in the orphanage?"

Juliet started to answer and then clamped her mouth shut. She wouldn't endanger any of those precious children. They had been through enough in their short lives already.

He dropped down in front of her, leaned on one knee and put the blade to her throat. She gasped. The tip bit into her skin.

"Are you going to kill me, too? I thought you

wanted a family with me." Her voice was a pitch higher than usual. Breathe. Don't move an inch. This guy was a loose cannon.

"Then answer me. How many kids are there? Don't even think of lying. Nurses have lied to me before, and other nurses have paid the price for those lies. It doesn't end well. Trust me."

His breath was hot on her neck where he had pulled her long hair to one side. She shivered and the blade caught like a bee sting. Still. Stay still.

"I think they have about a dozen there."

"Any babies?"

She licked her lips. She could lie. She could try to protect them, but what if he burst in there and discovered sweet Angel or Sophia, the toddler? Who knew what sick way he would pour out his wrath on her or the children.

"One baby. He's less than a year old. Why?" Her mouth went dry. "I thought you wanted babies with me?" Bile rose up her throat. "Babies with red hair?"

He loosened his grip and she no longer felt the pressure of the blade on her skin. A trickle of something warm meandered down her neck but at least she could take a deep breath.

"Yes. That *is* what I want. You're right, but these things take time." He ran the dull side of the blade down the length of her arm. "We need to start our family now. With the baby."

No.

He couldn't be serious, could he? He wanted them to take Angel and run away to who-knows-where and start a bizarre life together? Was that why the car was parked out front—for their great escape? He was deranged. How was he planning on taking her away without identification? Yes, they needed to go back to the restaurant for her purse. Buy some time.

"My passport," she stammered. "It's in my purse. We should go back to the restaurant…"

His laugh was menacing. "How stupid do you think I am? We won't be needing your passport. You can forget about your old life. I have a new one ready for you. For our future together."

Juliet closed her eyes. Everything within her wanted to scream and run, but perhaps she should play along for now. Perhaps Max was on the case and would rescue her from the clutches of the most evil being she had ever encountered.

Please God, let this be true. He said he was coming for me. Please let it be soon...

Chapter Twenty-Nine

"How much longer until we get to the orphanage?" Max checked his watch.

"Two minutes, tops." Luke focused on the winding road. "Madison, are the kids all in bed?"

"Yes." She exhaled into the phone. "Except Angel. I still have him with me."

Max heard the baby babbling something incoherent. He had to think. Why would Red be at the orphanage? It couldn't be good. He might use the kids as hostages to get Juliet to do whatever his twisted mind wanted her to do. First things first. Keep the children safe.

Luke's fists tightened around the steering wheel. "We have to keep the kids out of harm's way."

"Agreed." Max cleared his throat. "Madison, I need you to tell Carla what's going on. Get her to go down the hallway to where the kids are. How many bedrooms are they in altogether?"

"Four large rooms. Two for the girls and two for the boys."

Max ran his fingers through his hair. Mustn't freak her out. "Carla needs to get the kids all in one room. It's a big ask, but you have to trust me on this."

"Honey," Luke spoke into the phone. "Tell her to put them all in the older boys' room. It's bigger. She can make it a game if the kids ask questions. They won't all be sleeping yet anyway."

Brilliant. "Yes. Do that, Madison. Try to keep the kids calm."

"I'll tell Carla. Then what do you want me to do, Max?"

"I need you to go around and lock all the doors and windows. Pull all the blinds and curtains."

"But Juliet's out there somewhere..." Madison's voice broke.

"I know but we have to think about the kids' safety." Max wiped a sweaty palm on his jeans. "We'll be there soon. We'll park at the end of the drive and I'll send Luke into the orphanage to be with you. You understand?"

Luke nodded.

Madison sniffled. "Yes. You have your front door key, Luke?"

"I do, so don't panic when I come in. I'll find you in the boys' room. Make sure you lock the bedroom door and don't open it until I get there. I'll knock three times so you know it's me."

She let out a shuddering breath. "Please be careful, both of you."

"Always. Hang in there and I'll be with you in a few minutes. I love you." Luke bit his lip as the line went dead. "I'll update the local police as soon as I'm inside."

"Thanks." Max exhaled. "I'm sorry to put you guys in this position, and the kids..."

"Hey, man, it's not your fault. I'm scared for Juliet and worried about why he's at the orphanage in the first place. What are your thoughts?"

Max checked his phone. Rob was sending email after email as more information was coming in. He had to read it but needed to come up with a plan. Fast. He scanned the messages as he spoke.

"Let's see. We know Red has changed everything with this case compared to the previous attacks." He cringed. How could he call the woman he loved a *case*? Although he needed to stay clearheaded every step of the way here. "No other surviving victim has seen his face or even heard him speak. He seems to have targeted Juliet—perhaps he sees this as his last attack."

"You think he's suicidal?"

Max scrolled through the messages on his phone. "He has a history of mental illness according to his medical records and his sister. We know he lost his wife in an accident, and then more recently, their only child. A daughter. Cancer."

Luke groaned. "I can't even imagine."

"The records point to him being a psychopath. Which makes him impossible to predict." Max stared through the windshield. They whizzed past sporadic coconut trees and a smattering of tiny homes. Homes where life was going on as usual. A regular Sunday evening for them.

God, this is risky. I need You to tell me what I need to do here. Juliet's life is at stake. Not to mention an orphanage full of kids.

"So, why the red-headed nurses? There has to be a reason."

Max had already read up on that part. "He was devastated when they couldn't save his daughter. He was in pharmaceutical sales—which gave him access to hospitals—and he went crazy trying to get her on a bunch of trial drugs. The medical team did all they could but were unable to offer her any further treatment. He took it out on the nurses. Raged and lost it with them. It's all in a report."

Luke nodded. "And I'm guessing one of the nurses had red hair?"

Max winced. "No. It was his daughter who had long, red hair. She lost it all with chemo." He messaged Rob as he spoke. It was imperative that they all stay updated.

"Wow. This is so messed up. We're almost at the end of our road. What are you going to do?"

"Pull up somewhere inconspicuous. I need you to run straight into the orphanage like we told Madison. Be as quick and quiet as possible. I'm relying on my hunch that Red and Juliet are on the beach somewhere and won't be able to see you."

"What makes you think they're still on the beach?"

"Madison said she heard a scream and it'll be pretty dark there. Also, it says in this last report David Fitzpatrick lives next to the beach in California. I'm going with my gut. It's the place where he's comfortable and he can think. As clearly as possible for a psychopath."

Please let my gut be right, Lord.

Luke parked behind an enormous dense bush dotted with white tropical flowers. Night was pulling in fast but the moon was full and the star-studded sky was still a light inky color.

At least I'm going to be able to have decent visibility.

Max lowered his voice. "This is where we part ways." He hopped out of the van and Luke did likewise, both of them closing their doors with minimal noise. Max hurried around to the driver's side and clamped a strong hand on his friend's shoulder.

"Be careful. Stay down, close to the trees along the driveway until you reach the orphanage. Wait a couple of seconds until you run for the front door. I'll watch you from behind."

Man, I wish I had my gun.

"You're going to the beach alone to find them?" Luke's eyes were wide.

"Yeah. That's the plan. Keep them away from you guys, at least. Who knows why he brought Juliet here? I'll text you if I can but don't come out until I give you the all clear."

"Then I suggest you stay to the right of the orphanage where the foliage is thicker." Luke pointed down the driveway. "At least until you figure out where they are. I'll fill in the police."

"Sounds good. I already texted my people in Florence to contact your police and tell them what we know, so they should already be up to speed." He wiped sweat from his forehead. "I'm worried Red might do something rash if he hears them arrive with sirens and lights, so they know to arrive without fanfare."

"You don't want to wait for back-up?"

"Can't wait, Luke. I have to find Juliet."

Luke nodded. "I understand. Really, I do. God bless you."

With that, Luke took off at a swift pace in the direction of his family.

* * *

It took every modicum of restraint for Juliet not to run. Richard had the knife and he was not afraid to use it. She thought of his other victims and cringed. He was a murderer. Yet he seemed to have a soft spot for her— even though it meant holding her and an orphan baby as a captive family somewhere far from home. No. He wouldn't get away with this. Max would see to it. He wouldn't let them disappear.

She shifted her gaze to the orphanage up ahead of her. She couldn't see the windows from here but she could picture the children sleeping, oblivious to the dangers outside. So much love was contained in that building by the beach. So many children given hope.

I can't let him get to the kids. Especially Angel.

"We should go and get the baby." Richard was sweating profusely. His face shimmered as he turned to Juliet and jerked his head toward the orphanage. "I'm going to give you a choice."

Juliet gulped. This could be a way out if she could somehow get him to let down his guard believing he had won—she may have a chance to escape his clutches and the life he was scheming to share with her and Angel.

"Okay." She kept her voice slow and steady. "What are my choices?"

He pointed the knife at her. "You could go in and take the baby. Your friends know you and they can trust you will care for the kid. You're a pediatric nurse. It's perfect."

As long as they forget the part where you are the psychopathic killer.

"What if they refuse to let him go? They love the baby so much."

"Then I go in and kill anyone who gets in my way." His eyes flashed.

Juliet believed him. Nausea roiled in her stomach at the thought of those children experiencing more violence in their young lives. "I think they'll trust me." Not to mention they would get a message to Max. "You're right. The baby knows me, and he'll be more comfortable if *I* take him and pick up his diapers and bottles without any trouble, don't you think?"

"Yes. I hate seeing kids upset." Pain flickered across his face. "Kids should be happy. Happy and healthy."

Was that a slight softening? Juliet tilted her head. Maybe Richard wasn't too far gone. He was racked with grief and missed his family. She could appeal to his paternal heart, if it was still buried somewhere inside his twisted being. She had to give it a shot.

"Richard, do you think we should leave the baby instead? Imagine how much he would miss his house-parents and all the brothers and sisters he has here. We have to think of him—he *is* happy and healthy at the orphanage. We could just leave together. You and me." Her skin crawled at the thought—but at least the kids would be safe.

With a growl, Richard grabbed a fistful of her hair and pulled Juliet to her feet. "Nobody's taking my family away from me again." He shouted the words and shoved her in the direction of the orphanage. "Go."

A cry escaped Juliet's lips as she rubbed her sore head. She considered running until she felt the knife tip press between her shoulder blades.

"Keep walking. We have a baby to collect."

Just for a moment, Juliet saw something move in the shadows. Was it her imagination? She slowed her steps.

I have to think of a plan. I can't put Madison and Luke and all those children in danger.

A sudden pain sliced across her back and she cried out as she fell forward onto the sand.

"Juliet. RUN."

Max?

Chapter Thirty

MAX WINCED AS HE LANDED HARD on his shoulder. His plan had been to jump Red from behind and keep Juliet safe from harm—not for the knife to cut across her back in the process.

She spat sand from her mouth and turned, her eyes wild.

"Please? *Run.*" Max shouted through gritted teeth as he wrestled with Red on the ground. The two men were well matched in strength but Red still gripped the knife.

Must. Get. Knife.

Max was surprised at the strength of this guy—he was wiry but fit, and he had a death grip on the weapon.

"Max?"

He managed to turn his head long enough to see Juliet had frozen in place, tears streaming down her face as she hunched over on the beach ahead of them.

If this went sideways, he didn't want her to witness his demise. "Go."

"Max, I love you."

Red looked from Max to Juliet and let out an almighty roar. A surge of energy seemed to come over him and he flipped Max onto his back.

Where did that come from?

The next second, white hot pain shot through Max's leg as Red dug the knife deep into his thigh muscle. Max convulsed beneath the madman, aware that Juliet was now screaming. Why wasn't she running to safety?

* * *

God, where are you?

Juliet couldn't move. Her back stung but pure fear froze her body in a crouched position on the sand. She should run. Flee to the orphanage and lock all the doors.

She heard herself scream, but it sounded foreign to her ears.

How could she leave Max in the savage hands of this maniac? It was her fault. She should never have run from her life. From Max. Now... she gasped as Richard dug the blade into Max's leg.

"No."

She sprang into action. Without time to think it through, she leaped back into the fray as Richard lay over Max's body, both men squirming and punching. She grabbed handfuls of Richard's hair and snapped his head back, catching him by surprise.

In a split second, Max seized the opportunity to elbow Richard in the face. A crack. He collapsed in a heap at Juliet's feet. He was out cold, the bloodied knife dropped in the sand.

"Max." Juliet leaned over and kissed his forehead while she put pressure on his wound with one hand.

"I'm okay." He was writhing in pain. "Red?"

She glanced over her shoulder. "Unconscious. You broke his nose."

"Grab the knife?"

She reached back and clutched the small weapon, her other hand still tight on Max's injury. "He's not going anywhere. Police. Do you have your phone? I should call for the police."

"Already on their way." Max grimaced. He was in more pain than he was letting on. "Are you all right?"

"I am now." Her hands were trembling. "It was so awful..."

A sudden movement from the side. Max's eyes widened as Juliet felt her hair being yanked back. Her breath caught in her throat as strong fingers gripped her neck and squeezed.

No. Max couldn't watch her die like this. No way. She needed air.

The knife. She still clutched it in one hand. As if in slow motion, she thrust the knife back, connecting with Richard's body. A howl in her ear. He let go of her and she fell to one side, gasping for breath and watched him stagger backwards, the blade stuck in his flesh.

Max rolled over and somehow leaped up and charged at Richard, knocking him to the ground with a sickening thud. Juliet rose to her knees as breathing came easier and stared horrified as Max flipped Richard over onto his stomach like meat on a grill, the knife sinking deeper in his belly.

Richard gave an animalistic groan.

The nurse in her longed to tend to the wound—the wound she had inflicted—but no, this man could attempt to hurt her again. Kill her or Max.

She turned her attention instead to Max. His muscles rippled beneath his white T-shirt as he straddled Richard and held him down. Blood oozed from the wound in Max's thigh and he was in danger of bleeding out. She had to help him. Richard wasn't going anywhere. In fact, he had stopped struggling altogether.

Juliet's limbs were like lead as she pulled herself to her feet. Muffled sounds swooshed in her ears.

What do I do now?

Shock settled over her as she concentrated on breathing. She couldn't drag her gaze away from Max, as if he might collapse if her eyes left him. Around her, a flurry of activity descended upon the horrific beach scene. Uniformed police officers swarmed the area, an ambulance had arrived, and lights flooded the beach with brightness. How had all this happened in seconds?

"Juliet."

She turned to see Luke running toward her from the orphanage, followed by Madison. They were safe. She blinked and pivoted back toward Max.

He stared at her, his eyes wide and glassy. She could see he was surviving on the last of his adrenaline. He was pulled up from Richard's prostrate body by a police officer, who promptly cuffed her attacker's unmoving wrists. They were taking no chances with a murderer.

Still, she hadn't moved a muscle.

Max stumbled toward her. "We're going to be fine, sweetheart. We've got him."

She managed to hold out her arms to him before collapsing.

Strange.

Juliet sensed her own body being supported and then realized Madison and Luke were there with them, holding them both up and walking them toward the ambulance.

"I don't even know what to say..." Madison sobbed. "I'm so relieved you're both safe. They'll soon have you patched up. We'll come to the hospital with you."

"But the children?" Max's bruised face was etched with concern.

Juliet's heart squeezed. He longed to protect those precious young lives.

"They're all fine." Luke nodded. "Carla has them tucked up in bed and Maria is on call if she needs her. Now we have to take care of you two." Another ambulance arrived. "Thank goodness." Juliet didn't relish the thought of being in the same one as Richard. Or Red. Oh, how close she had come to being his next victim. Max, too.

"Do you think he'll make it?" Luke craned his neck to the area where Richard had fallen.

"I don't know." Juliet's voice was a whisper. "I hope so. I hope he gets to survive and take the punishment he deserves. Justice for his victims. Maybe he'll even get some help for his mental state. He's so messed up."

Max kissed her cheek. "You're one brave woman."

They reached the ambulance and leaned against it. An ambulance was something familiar for Juliet. It felt safe and secure.

Luke clasped Max's shoulder. "We'll take the van and meet you there. You may need some help with the language." He spoke with the paramedics while they assessed injuries.

Madison took off her cardigan and put it around Juliet's shoulders. "Make sure they take care of that cut on your back. It looks like it could be deep."

She had forgotten about her own wound in all the pandemonium but now it burned like fire. "Thanks, I will. It's fine. I'm more concerned about Max."

He now lay on the gurney inside the ambulance as one of the medical team cut the leg of his jeans. He'd lost a great deal of blood already.

"I'm good." His voice came from inside. "I may need someone to hold my hand, though..."

Juliet's heart soared. It felt wonderful. "I should go sit with the patient. We'll see you there."

She plodded into the ambulance feeling a hundred years old. She sat next to Max and held his hand while a medic tended to his wound. The ambulance doors slammed shut and it rolled into motion.

"I have no clue how this all panned out and I'm pinching myself that you're here in Mexico. You're my hero. I can't even imagine what would have happened..."

He shifted on the gurney to look into her eyes. "Hey, we are both safe and Red is going away for a long time."

"If he makes it." She pressed her lips together.

"It's out of our hands now. We did what we had to do in order to stay alive."

She nodded. The ambulance jostled her around over uneven ground. Her back was beginning to throb now. She might need a few stitches. Max's leg definitely would, but they would heal in time. In every way.

She licked her lips. They were dry and salty.

"Come here." Max reached up and pulled her head down close. "Take my mind off whatever this dude is doing to my leg?"

They kissed with an urgency that took her breath away.

"I like your bedside manner, Nurse Juliet." His blue eyes sparkled.

Hers filled with tears. "Thank you. For coming all the way to Mexico to rescue me. For catching the bad guy like I asked you to."

"Of course I came." He spotted the cut on her neck and winced. "I just wish I'd arrived sooner. It's about more than rescuing you from Red."

"It is?"

He traced the tears on her face with his fingertips. "I came for you, Juliet. I don't want to do life without you. I love you. We *can* be a family. You and me. Then if God wants to bless us with children somehow, I'm willing to explore whatever it takes. I had to come and tell you..."

That deserved another kiss.

Thank you, Father. I know Max is the one. He's always been the one. If You want us to have our own chosen children, You'll make a way.

"Why more tears?" He furrowed his brow.

"It's all good. They're tears of relief. You know, I was scared I had lost my identity. Lost my sense of home. With Mom gone, Bella married, and no more *us*, I felt so abandoned and alone. I didn't even know if I wanted to be a nurse anymore."

Her entire body shuddered and someone placed a blanket around her shoulders.

"But then God reminded me I am His child. Always... and now I know home is wherever you are." She stroked his cheek as they pulled up outside the hospital.

"*You* are my home, Max."

Epilogue

"WHO GIVES THIS WOMAN AWAY?"

Juliet grinned at Bella and Madison on either side of her. This was happening, for real.

"We—her best friends—do." Madison spoke for them both and took Juliet's bouquet from her quivering hands. The emotion in the humid air was palpable at the May wedding in Mexico.

"In memory of her dear mother." Bella kissed her cheek.

She had the best friends a girl could ask for. They both stepped back and Juliet turned to face Max. Her heart skipped a beat at the sight of him in his tux. His skin was tanned against the white dress shirt and his blond hair had been lightened by the sun. There were no signs of stress and his features were relaxed other than the huge grin he wore...

Yes, Mexico was a healing balm for them both. Juliet could never have anticipated the path her life had taken her on these past six months. Her heart fluttered at the mere thought. Their undeniable love was sealed with an immediate engagement as soon as they arrived back in Florence after the attack by Richard. Or Red. Or David... Whatever his name, his death was something they had brought before God, and their journey of grace and mercy bound them ever tighter as a couple.

But today she was looking forward. Forging ahead as a married woman.

She breathed in the heady scent from the floral crown she wore atop her loose, flowing hair and exhaled.

If only Mom could see me now.

She was a bride gazing up at her groom.

"We are gathered here today..."

As Luke opened the ceremony, Juliet's mind wandered, as it was prone to do these days. This place would always hold a little piece of her heart. She made a habit now of counting her blessings, looking for the everyday miracles in this wonderful, unpredictable life. The ocean glistened sapphires before them and rustling palm fronds were their background music. She shivered at the beauty of it all. How had this happened so fast?

"Juliet."

She turned her head to Luke.

"Do you take this man to be your husband to live together in holy matrimony? To love, honor, and cherish him, to keep him in sickness and in health, for as long as you both shall live?"

She stared back into the dreamy blue eyes before her. Eyes so full of love and devotion. "I do."

Her heart was full as she listened to Max commit the rest of his life to her.

Hard to believe it was on this very beach just six months ago, she thought her life was coming to an end at the hands of a murderer—but she and Max decided this place would not be defined by one hideous memory.

It was also where her mother's manuscript ashes were scattered. It was special.

She flitted her eyes to the palm tree and sighed. Her heart still ached with the void left by her mom's absence. Today especially.

You would have loved everything about today, Mom.

Under the same palm tree, God had whispered truth into Juliet's life and given her hope. She knew in her heart that she was not an orphan—she was a true, reunited daughter of the King, and on this expanse of sand she had come to the realization that Max was the love of her life. He was her home and her hero. Now he was about to become her husband.

They exchanged rings—simple gold bands of love. The service was short and sweet, as they had requested, and then as a couple, they turned to face the audience. Their people.

Bella and Adam, Max's sweet mom, and Angie from the hospital had all flown out for the wedding. Luke, Madison, and the staff and kids from the orphanage were here to witness the start of their new adventure.

Max planted a kiss on her lips and swung her around in a circle. She was grateful their knife wounds had healed and now they were about to start this momentous journey together as man and wife. Flawed and forgiven, a fresh start for them both.

Max set Juliet down with care and walked over to Madison. "May I?"

An ebony-haired baby boy with the longest eyelashes reached out pudgy arms. He giggled in delight as Max took him and swung him around in a circle, too.

"Come to Mommy, Angel." Juliet embraced her new family, tears in her eyes.

As Bella joined them, her whole face lit up. "Congratulations. We can't wait to have all you guys over for dinner at The Lighthouse when you get home."

Adam tousled Angel's hair. "And we need to get in some serious baby practice."

"What?" Max slapped Adam's back. "Are you for real?"

Bella winced. "Honey, we were supposed to keep it quiet until after today."

Juliet kissed Bella's blushing cheek. "No way. Today we all celebrate. Also, I know it's the nurse in me, but I totally called it when I heard you were sick last week and at the rehearsal dinner. This is the best news. Congratulations, both of you."

Ah, yes. She was genuinely thrilled for her friends. Adopting Angel had given her a fresh perspective on motherhood and a deeper love of all children.

Madison joined in the group hug. "I called it, too, when you skipped on the champagne at breakfast. This is so exciting."

Juliet winked at Madison. "Hey, maybe you guys will be next."

She laughed and pointed over at Luke, who was playing tag with the older kids. "Somehow, I think we have our hands full at the moment. Although we will be missing one child here after your honeymoon."

Juliet squeezed her friend's hand. "This has all happened in such a whirlwind but I'm going with it. I get a husband and a child all in one glorious package. I'm so blessed. You know you'll always be a part of Angel's life."

Madison's eyes brimmed. "I couldn't be more grateful knowing Angel is going to be loved so well. A detective to protect him and a nurse to care for him. God knew what He was doing all along."

"He did, didn't He? I never imagined giving up work but now it feels so right. Caring for my Angel-boy and whomever else comes along." Juliet glimpsed the orphanage in her peripheral vision. "I'm excited for what's in store."

"Me, too, but today is your wedding day, so why

don't you and your husband have a walk along the beach alone while we get things ready for the reception. Trust me, you'll want to take time for the two of you whenever you can."

Max tugged her to his side. "I like the sound of that."

Madison took Angel and wandered over to chat with Angie and Max's mother. The sweet woman was enamored by her new grandson. Today held so much joy for everyone.

Juliet grabbed her husband's strong hand. "Walk with me?"

He looked down and cupped her cheek in his palm. "I'll walk with you anywhere."

She reached up and kissed his lips. "You have no idea how happy that makes me."

They strolled toward the ocean, the waves lapping the shore in happy slaps. Further down the beach, several families were enjoying a perfect day out, oblivious to her bliss.

"I never thought I'd get married in bare feet."

He chuckled. "Me neither."

Juliet observed their toes as they sank into the soft, white sand. "It feels right though, doesn't it?"

He nodded. "I love how you wanted to start our marriage barefoot like this. Ready to go wherever God wants us. Ready to explore life together. Ready to play with our child. Ready to run into the ocean..."

"Wait. What?" Juliet squealed as Max lifted her into his arms and took giant strides straight into the water. She grabbed fistfuls of her cream tulle dress as the cool droplets splashed her feet and legs.

"What are you doing?" She threw back her head in laughter, her long hair almost touching the water.

Max stood knee deep, his pant legs soaked and his brand-new wife in his arms. "I wanted to get you alone so I could tell you how much I love you."

Juliet squeezed her arms around his neck as fresh, ocean air assaulted her senses. "Then tell me."

"I love you more than you will ever know. This has been the wildest ride of my life but I'm so proud of you."

"You are?"

"You bet. I know we've both learned a lot about ourselves this past year but you've come through it with a strength and softness that's blown me away."

"Strong and soft?"

"Tough and tender, babe."

"Oh, I'm liking this. Carry on, husband." The last word gave her butterflies. He was her husband.

"Well, let's be real—we both have challenges ahead but I want you to know I am always here for you. Always."

He spun her around to face the shore.

"And I'll bring you back to this special beach whenever you need to come. This is family. This is part of Angel's history and part of your history is buried here, too. We'll help Madison and Luke in whatever ways we can and we'll visit as often as possible."

She lay her head against his shoulder. "We will?"

"I promise."

"Thank you. You have no idea how much it means to me." She kissed his cheek and then observed her loved ones on the long expanse of sand. Her precious Orphan Beach. As they all waved at the newlyweds, Juliet memorized each face. Her family. Her future.

Thank You, God. I have done nothing to deserve this. That's just like You—giver of grace.

She leaned her head against Max's broad chest and knew joy in its fullest measure.

Finally, her eyes travelled to one particular palm tree and the treasure buried beneath.

Mom, you were right about everything.

Her mouth curved into a smile.

Of course, you were.

Her heart swelled. It was healed now. Whole.

And Juliet was ready.

Ready for all the chosen children God desired for her and Max to love, and ready to write her very own chapter in *The Orphan Beach* story...

"I know what I'm doing.
I have it all planned out—
plans to take care of you,
not abandon you,
plans to give you the future
you hope for."
Jeremiah 29:11 (MSG)